Shadeskin

Shadeskin

Jason Craft   B. L. White

Amanda White

Supremacy PRESS

Acknowledgements

The three of us would like to thank Beth for clearing up our grammar, our demo readers: Markus, Will, Jonnette, and Laura for providing valuable feedback on our work, and Robin Ludwig for adding the amazing bling on the cover.

Jason

Thanks so much to Amanda and Brian who latched on to my crazy idea and made it a reality. Thanks to my sister, Beth, for supporting my dreams and believing in me. And thanks to Zoe Winters for inspiring me to trod the indie path. All of you were instrumental in the start of my writing career.

Brian

I would like to give a heart felt thanks to God for the gifts he's given me, a playful thanks to all the zombie video games for the inspiration, and a gracious thanks to my part time dry-cleaning job for all the money.

Amanda

I would like to express my heartfelt thanks to my husband, Lance. If it were not for your continual encouragement and willingness to take over my duties of cooking and other chores, I would not have been able to immerse myself so fully in this fun world. Thank you to Dad, Mom, and Susan. The three of you have always inspired me to keep writing and never look back. Beth, you are an awesome editor and an even better friend. I look forward to subjecting you to more of my work. Brian and Jason, this would not have even happened if it were not for you both. You guys have helped me to grow as a person and a writer and I look forward to many more years of debating the intricate details of genre fiction. Lastly, thank you to God for making my paths smooth and straight so that I can find it again when I lose my way.

Table of Contents

Walk the Crimson Path

by
Jason Craft

The axehead scraped along the concrete, leaving behind a trail of warm blood. Blackened viscera clung to its sharp edges. Awash in red, a thin hand wrapped tightly around its handle and pulled it along with a stammering jerk. Escaping the carnage behind them, pale feet stumbled before the crimson path.

The rising sun kissed the face of the young woman dragging the axe. Shadows crept around her, hiding from the growing rays of light. Her long, black hair, matted with blood, lay flat against her back. She staggered along until finally reaching the street curb.

"So, this is destiny," she whispered, a forced smile curving her lips.

Several bystanders gathered around her. Proud to be a spectacle, she smiled and drank in their fear and confusion. One man summoned the courage to follow the bloody trail into the nightclub. He didn't last long before running back outside and vomiting over the pavement.

She admired his tenacity. On any normal day, he or anyone else in the crowd might have been able to alert the authorities, but she knew the force permeating their minds weighed them down. Their eyes were glazed over.

In the still air, the young woman's hair began to sway at the approach of a powerful entity. A cloud of unnatural darkness materialized behind the bystanders, drawing their gaze. A man stepped regally from the cloud and walked toward her. The crowd parted to make way for his purposeful stride. Renewed fear sparked inside everyone, save for her.

"Where does your destiny take you?" he asked.

"To you," she replied, feeling her ties to the physical realm loosening. It felt like she was awakening from a dream.

"Now," he said, his voice cutting the air with finality, "You are mine. Hold on to this."

He brought her in for an intimate kiss. The moment their lips connected, a peaceful wave rolled through her. Quivering under his power, she let go of the axe and wrapped her arms around his strong neck. The axe handle slapped the concrete, flinging droplets of blood. A surge of warmth resounded within her heart, healing all the torment she had so recently endured.

The sun's light faded, withdrawing its warm touch from her face. She held on to him for stability as the pavement dissolved. A multitude of sensations charged through her. Opening her eyes, she was alone in darkness. Then, she began falling.

Clara's furious eyes bore through her mother's gentle stare. Her father had quickly bowed out of the argument to steel himself in the living room.

"How many times do I need to make my point?" Clara

asked through clenched teeth. "You manufacture conspiracies from the tiniest actions of any company that works with the government, especially when it comes to things you don't even understand, like internet security. Mandrake Solutions is your latest target only because I have a chance to work for them!"

"Conspiracies?" her mother replied. "This is about you turning your back on your father and me to prove a point. Just by taking this interview, you are opening yourself up to a world of corruption. You should know to stay true to your values and not involve yourself with malicious people. We taught you better than that."

"Oh yes, fearing everything was a great lesson." Sarcasm dripped through Clara's words, "In school, I was the weird kid that couldn't eat the cafeteria food because of its 'poisonous content' implanted by the government. It took me forever to convince you that cell phones were safe from wandering ears. I am still shocked you relented on that one."

"Clara, I know working for a top security firm may seem like a valuable societal contribution, but can't you see the danger? You will be connected to sensitive areas of our government that will make you a high-profile target. I am just trying to shield you now like I did when you were young. You paint me as an over-zealous mother during your childhood, but, just like then, you are still too young to see the oncoming storms."

"Mom, this isn't the Cold War. There aren't covert agents living among us, planning assassinations for everyone. We live in an information age where our digital lives need protection. I *will* shield you, even if you don't appreciate or understand it."

"Please, rethink this. You have enough talent to work for anyone you choose. Take an interview with any other company, just not Mandrake, not with government contracts. I just-" she paused, her face wincing with thought. "Believe me, you will understand one day when you-"

"When I grow up?" Clara interrupted. "I *am* grown up. You can keep your conspiracies while I escape this prison and enter the real, rational world."

Her mother clutched at the side of her burnt-orange skirt with nervous fingers. A tear formed in the corner of her eye, but she escaped Clara's room before it fell.

Clara instantly regretted driving her mother to tears again. She heard her father trying to calm her down in the living room. Clara stood fuming in the middle of her room, waiting for the inevitable. After a few minutes, her father appeared in the doorway. Tall and slender, he was the pole that kept their rocking gondola stable.

"I try not to fight with her, Dad," Clara offered.

He just smiled and hugged her. "She knows that, but you two are so stubborn and entrenched in your own ideals that neither of you will yield. Not even for peace's sake."

"True," she laughed, looking up into his dark, comforting eyes. A cloud of stubble shadowed his face.

"Remember, Clara, this world is yours to conquer, but at least pay some attention to what we say. We aren't as crazy as you might think."

"Just eccentric," she playfully responded, her anger subsiding.

"The time will come when your perspective will

change." He put his hand on top of her head. "You'll always be my little girl, no matter how tall you get or how far you travel."

"Nathan, we need to go," her mother called from the kitchen.

Clara looked in her mother's direction. "Tell her I'm sorry."

"Make a little time tonight to stop by the club and tell her yourself." Nathan leaned in and kissed her on the forehead. He gently squeezed her shoulder before rushing off.

Clara sighed and fell backward onto her bed, cushioned by a mountain of pillows. Her ceiling fan rotated, laughing at her with its periodic squeaking. She lifted a round pillow over her head and punched it a few times before laying it on her stomach. She could almost feel the 'negative energy' swirling around the room. Her mother certainly had an odd way of seeing the world.

From the moment she was born, Clara was set up for failure. Her parents thought the world of their only child, but they never grounded her in reality. Instead, they spoiled her into thinking she was special with bedtime stories about how she would someday save the world. While harmless for a young child, the stories didn't stop as she grew older and instead transformed into prophecy.

As a budding teen, Clara's talent for re-telling her destiny just seemed weird. The captivated audience she was used to began rolling their eyes and trying to switch the subject to music and boys. Clara, the fated savior of the world, watched her social life go up in flames.

The 'special' food she carried to school each day tasted

more like ash the longer she was alone. No one believed her anymore about how her food kept her safe from dangerous toxins. The fact she had never seen a real doctor created rumors she couldn't escape. At first she hated the kids at school for their cruelty, but by high school, she realized her parents had done this to her with their crazy beliefs.

The constant supply of rumors branded her an outcast. Ostracized, she accepted her true fate as the weird kid. She hated her parents every lonely minute of high school. However, they were still her parents and for all their numerous flaws, at least they nurtured her academic side. By the time she graduated, she had outpaced her classmates in every scholastic measure.

Thankfully, college evened things out, allowing her a taste of normal life with actual friends. She started life anew with a clean slate. No longer would she allow anyone to know her as the 'false destiny chick.' The sooner she moved away from her parents, the sooner her childhood scars would heal.

The muffled sounds of closing doors announced Clara was alone in the house. Friday nights initiated the nightclub cycle, and her parents offered the best, non-conformist experience down at the Hookah Palooka. They hated it when Clara referred to it as a 'hippie bar,' even if it was true.

She sat up on the edge of her bed and looked in her vanity mirror. Frizzled auburn hair fell just past her shoulders. Murky rings cupped her brown eyes, reminders of her argument with her mother. Still, she remained fixed on her goal of shining in her interview with Mandrake.

A pop song burst through the silent air, signaling an

incoming call. Clara reached for her phone, her face lighting up after seeing the caller ID.

"Hey," she answered.

"Hey you," Drake replied. "Have any plans tonight?"

"Just avoiding my mother. We clashed pretty fantastically today." Her voice shook more than she realized.

"Yeah, you sound out of it. More speeches about how you're wasting your life?"

"Of course. She wants to shelter me from everything, and I am beginning to realize that nothing I ever say will change her mind." The memory of that earlier conversation burned inside her head.

"Mothers," Drake said sarcastically, "They think you owe them your life because they made a decision to bring you into this world."

"Ha. I like to pretend it doesn't bother me, but I only lie to myself."

"Well, keep reaching for your dreams and take her advice where you can. It's not like she wants you to fail. She still loves you."

"I know," Clara admitted. "It's just lately, I have been really stressed about this interview."

"I don't think any of the other interview candidates can even hold a candle to you."

"You mean the ones coming from Ivy League?"

"Hey, optimism always wins out, and when it comes to intellect, you have it all," Drake said firmly.

"I wish I had your cheery disposition."

"Do you want some of it tonight?"

Clara looked at her computer desk where stacks of

books surrounded her cherry-red laptop. "I have a few more things to look over."

"You need to unwind sometime in the near future." He seemed a bit pleading.

"I will, just as soon as this interview is over."

"I will definitely take you up on that."

"I was hoping you would," she said, bringing the conversation to a close. Hopefully he wasn't as dejected as he sounded.

"Ok. I love you."

She hung up before realizing she had not reciprocated. She started to call him back, but the doorbell rang. She rose from her bed with a sigh and headed to the front door.

A haze of sunlight filtered into the living room through vertical blinds covering a pair of French doors. Past the doors lay a well-kept back yard. A couch and a pair of easy chairs sat around a glass coffee table in the center of the room. Her mother's tea grew cold in a yellow mug near the table's edge.

The doorbell rang a few more times before Clara made it to the door, inciting her to fling it open in frustration. Louisiana's humid summer air greeted her with its wet kiss. She stepped outside and looked around the bend of the house to find no one. Studying for this interview must be more draining than she thought.

She moved back to her room. Opportunity wafted from the stack of books surrounding her computer as she sat at her desk. She cracked open the book on mathematical graph theory she had been reading before her mother's earlier interruption. Pages of handwritten notes sat wedged throughout, representing the milestones of her college course.

Most students never understand the close relationship math shares with computer science, but when it comes to digital security, the two are inseparable.

Her mind floated into the pages of her studies. Information flooded back to her while she read, reminders of a simpler time. Only now did she see the real-world application of what she had learned, and Mandrake would be most interested in the interview candidate who clearly demonstrated such insights. Competition was fierce, but so was she. Well, at least Drake believed in her.

The doorbell rang again, breaking her concentration. Annoyed, she threw her book onto her bed and went back to open the door. A cloud passed overhead, toning down the cheery light in the living room. She opened the door and again saw no one. She let out a frustrated sigh.

Instantly, a loud banging noise snapped her attention to the French doors. A human shadow cast on the blinds wildly slammed its fists into the glass. Clara froze in place, paralyzed with fear.

"Help me!" the shadow screamed desperately before collapsing onto the ground.

Clara's limbs awakened at once and she rushed to the French doors, quickly sliding the blinds aside. Instead of lying on the ground, the figure leaned upright against the glass, startling her. She fell backward onto the hardwood floor in surprise. A thin young woman with long, dark hair looked down at her through a pair of black over-sized sunglasses.

A chill tingled Clara's spine, sucking her breath away. She screamed inwardly, commanding herself to move, but she remained pinned to the floor. Fear sliced into her heart like a knife.

The woman swung an axe into the French doors. Harsh lines of cracked glass grew outward from the center of the door. With a twisted smile, she thrust the axe straight into the door, blowing tiny shards of glass into the house.

Clara felt a dark presence reach in and touch her soul. She rolled onto her hands and knees, clawing at the floor in a frantic dash to the front door. The woman laughed softly behind her.

Clara grabbed the edge of the coffee table and pulled herself up. The woman buried the axe deep into her lower back. Clara slammed onto the coffee table, spilling her mother's tea. She screamed through the pain, trying to crawl across the table.

Bare feet landed on either side of her. The axe tore into her side, cracking through bone. Clara curled around it, trying to hold it in place. With a quick jerk, the axe swept out again, taking with it a chunk of flesh. Clara lurched onto her back and screamed until blood poured from her mouth, choking her voice.

Feeling the cold metal of the axehead press against her neck, she looked up in terror at her assailant. The woman bent down, placing her lips next to Clara's ear.

The woman spoke in a gentle, impassive voice, "Your vision is too narrow, but only through this pain will you expand it. Tear your heart in half and bury your soul."

The woman jumped off the table and exited through the front door, leaving it open. Clara looked outside, feeling throbbing pain numb her body. Carefree birds sang her eulogy. She reached for them, wishing they would save her. Blood seeped between her fingers over the glass of the coffee table. Daylight faded away, leaving her in darkness.

In the early morning hours, the Hookah Palooka quietly recovered from the crowds that had so recently filled it with life. Tie-dyed shirts covered its walls and were as much a merchandise promotion as decoration. Brightly colored ribbons arched across the ceiling, highlighting the out-of-place disco ball. Several distinct niches of couches and coffee tables filled its main room. Hookahs of various sizes and colors sat on almost every table. Sweet, fruity aromas mixed with the smoke in the room, attesting to the popularity of the club's namesake.

Over at the bar, Clara's father sat with a stack of financial papers while her mother drank a cup of tea across from him.

"We both knew we couldn't escape the consequences of our choices, Jailyn," Nathan said to his wife without looking up from his papers. His sharp face remained intent on hiding his emotions.

Jailyn glanced over the main room, trying to find something to fix so she wouldn't have to respond. Her yellow blouse blended with the decorum, but not with how she felt. She tugged at her hair, threading her fingers through it.

"How long do we have left?" She cringed while asking.

"How long does any human have left?" Nathan

continued, stoically poring over the financial statements.

"Are we wrong? We can't protect her if she gives herself over to Him. What do we do if-" her voice trailed off.

Nathan looked into Jailyn's eyes while reaching over to curl his thin fingers around her hands.

"Never. We will never let Him get to her," he said with certainty. "I love you and her too much to let anything happen to break us apart."

"Maybe it's not Him. I worry about Clara trying so hard to get away from us."

Nathan kept a wise gaze fixated on her. "You two are destined to be at odds, but in the end she still loves you. I had fully expected her to show up tonight, but don't let th-"

A knock at the back door interrupted their conversation.

"Don't people know when we close and how to use the front door?" Nathan asked lightly. Jailyn smiled as he got up to answer it.

The moment he turned down the back hallway, he paused, sensing a presence he had not felt in years. A street lamp cast a thin silhouette over the back door. The hairs on the back of his neck bristled as he went to open the door.

A pair of sunglasses reflected the surprise in his face before an axehead slammed into his throat, knocking him onto his back. He coughed while trying to catch his breath and shuffle away from the woman walking through the open door. The woman swung the axe at his chest, but he quickly rolled to his side and exploded upward, knocking her back with his elbow.

"You will not take her!" he yelled and launched at her with his fists.

She deflected his attacks with the shaft of her axe before dropping to her knees and slicing his shin with the axe blade. He recoiled, giving her enough room to swing the axe over her head and bring it back down on him. He reached out with his hand and the axe stopped mid-swing. A viscous cloud seeped from his skin.

"Your insatiable lusts brought this upon you. Are you really surprised?" she asked quietly.

"Programmed poetry is not becoming of you, Zyne," he quipped back, speaking directly to the one who controlled the woman before him.

The lighting in the hallway dimmed. A pair of murky hands materialized just above the floor and latched onto Nathan's ankles. The hallway tilted away from him and he slammed down on his back. The hands grew into a large cloud that pinned him to the ground. He tried to warn Jailyn, but no sound escaped his throat. The woman stood over him, leaning against her axe with a hollow smile.

The hurried sounds of footsteps brought the woman's attention to the front of the hallway where Jailyn now stood, horror-stricken. Nathan arched his back, trying to see her one last time. Black veins sprouted across his skin, sending waves of pain crashing through him. Jailyn moved toward him, but an unseen force held her back.

She looked on helplessly as Nathan twisted in silent pain. His veins pulsated with energy before a black cloud completely enveloped him. She caught brief glimpses of his body decaying into a blackened skeleton before the cloud dissipated, leaving only a small pile of ash.

Her strength left her and she dropped to her knees.

Tears poured from her eyes onto the floor. At the end of the hallway, the woman picked up her axe and walked through the ash, kicking it around. Jailyn blindly reached out into the cinder-filled air, willing herself to move.

The woman stopped directly in front of Jailyn. She struck the floor with the axehead, bringing Jailyn's furious gaze up to her. The woman bent down to eye-level.

"We would like a word, if you please," she said, gesturing toward the main room. She stood back up and moved past Jailyn, dragging the bloody axe behind her.

Jailyn looked at the remnants of her husband. She slammed her fists against the tiled floor. The tiles cracked under her assault. She continued pounding them until they were ground to dust and full of her tears. She cried out in anguish to the empty hallway.

The whine of feedback sounded from the main room. A feminine voice came through the stage speakers, drawing her name out in a childish manner, "Jaaailyyyynnn!"

Jailyn breathed deeply before standing and returning to the main room. The woman sat on the stage, holding a microphone to her lips—the axe lay at her feet. Jailyn looked for the real threat and saw him sitting in the opposite corner.

He stared her down with his penetrating black eyes. Long spikes of dark hair jutted out of his skull while a short beard wrapped around his jaw. Any pedestrian would have mistaken him for a man in his late twenties; oh, how little men know of the ancient beings living alongside them.

A half-smile and slight nod signaled her to take the seat across from him. She obliged, knowing she really had no choice. The soft contour of the couch felt like a sinking pit from which she would never escape. She felt her blue eyes grow large in such proximity to a dark presence.

"You're going to kill me anyway, aren't you, Zyne?" she queried.

"Yes," he immediately replied.

Clara's eyes shot open, a rush of memory spinning through her head. She instinctively cradled her side, but found no wound. A cold pool of blood congealed around her face and across the coffee table. She pushed herself onto her knees. A mixture of blood and sweat slipped down her cheeks. She felt her entire body for injuries, finding none.

A sudden rustling sound from behind sent her jumping off the table and tripping over the edge of the couch. She twisted around and saw a few birds pecking at the shattered glass littering the floor. A weak cry escaped her mouth. Heat from the noon sun bathed her entire body in sweat. How long had she lain here?

Several minutes passed before she worked up the courage to head toward the bathroom. She turned on the shower and sat down in the tub, letting the cold water shock her senses. A haze of memory clouded her mind with doubt, but the blood soaking through her clothes told her the attack was very real.

The water eventually warmed and rained down a light feeling of assurance over her. She stared at the white tiles lining the wall, her mind trying desperately to process the horrific event. She had never before felt such an unnatural terror overtake her. It left her cowering in the tub when she should be calling 911.

The crunching noise of footsteps on glass sent her heart racing. Fear once again paralyzed her. The footsteps moved quickly until they were running down the hallway toward her. She shut her eyes, willing them to be silent. They scrambled toward her and stopped just before the bathtub. She screamed as a pair of wide hands engulfed her.

"Clara," a concerned voice called to her.

The scent of familiar cologne grounded her back in reality. She opened her eyes to the welcome sight of a round face with curly brown hair.

"Oh, Drake," she said, reaching over to embrace his pudgy frame. "Tell me I am not insane."

"You're not insane," he said, tightening his grip. "I've got you."

She latched onto him with water raining down on both of them until she was strong enough to let go. Looking into his eyes, she offered a smile before turning the shower off.

"I rushed over here as soon as I found out, but I never thought you would try to take your own life."

"What?" she asked before noticing the scars out of the corner of her eye.

She looked down and saw deep gashes running along the insides of her forearms. The cuts were fresh, but they weren't bleeding at all.

"It's amazing you're still alive," he said, speaking her thoughts verbatim.

She looked up at him, frowning in confusion.

"Let's get you bandaged up," he asserted.

An hour later, Drake sat across from her at the kitchen table with a wide-eyed stare after she told him what had really happened.

"Are you sure it was a thin, dark-haired woman?" he asked.

"Yes," she replied, scratching at the gauze stretching around her forearms.

He sat back in his chair, grabbing his chin with his hand. He was holding something back.

"What did you come here to tell me?" she asked.

He took her hands in his and swallowed a deep breath before speaking, "Listen. I don't know about this anymore than you-"

"Just tell me," she demanded.

"I got a call from one of my buddies in the police department. There was an incident reported a few hours ago down at the Hookah Palooka." He paused for a moment. "A woman exactly as you described, sunglasses and all, fled the scene. Both your parents have been murdered."

An image flashed in her mind of her parents looking into the cold reflection of the woman's sunglasses. She blinked the image away, tears welling in her eyes. Drake walked around the table and slid a chair next to hers, gently pulling her as close as he could.

"I assumed they tried to call here first, but obviously they didn't get through."

She sobbed against him, hoping to wake from this nightmare. Pain ached in her side at the renewed memory of the woman's axe.

"I didn't even tell her I'm sorry," Clara yelled, slamming her fist into the table. She wished she could lie cradled in Drake's arms forever. They were her only comfort against the miserable end her parents met at the woman's axe. Why was she spared?

Jailyn looked into Zyne's lifeless eyes, searching out his motive. A black soul stared back at her, hinting at immense, raw power. He wanted something; it was the only reason she still drew breath.

She reached into her pocket and took out a large coin with an engraved image of a pair of angelic wings wreathed in fire. She rolled the coin through her fingers a few times before setting it on the table with a metallic rap.

"Still keep the Faith?" Zyne said, looking down at the coin.

"It is all I have of my past life," she replied.

"Hmm." He looked up at her. "You never were one to run away."

"Look, we just wanted to be left alone and raise our daughter in peace. We broke no laws, nor treaties. We never even left this volatile city. Could you not honor our simple request?"

"I refuse to honor any request made through deceit." A smirk crept onto his face, "Especially when one of the deceitful parties was my closest friend. I have always hated you for taking Nathan away from me, and I blame you personally for misguiding him."

She glanced back to the coin and wondered how much power she had left. If she could just wield the Faith like she used to, she could easily cast out Zyne and rescue her husband. The thought of her husband's fate gnawed at her mind.

"Where did you take Nathan?" she demanded.

He smiled widely. "I have him contained within the Shifting Plains. As you saw, I rid him of his mortal form. A few decades of reconditioning will restore him to his former glory. We Shades look out for one another."

"And still you have not learned love from the humans," she retorted, feeling the blue in her eyes spread into her pupils.

"My, what big blue eyes you have." He mockingly covered his heart. "Are you simply reacting to me, or has this 'love' you speak of taken over your senses? I have learned to love without being blind to everything around me."

She knew Zyne's version of love: making slaves out of women and warping them into his own little pets. The one sitting patiently on the stage across the room attested to this. She would not let Clara suffer that fate.

"Return my husband and leave my daughter alone, or suffer a woman's scorn and a mother's wrath." She spoke firmly, staring into Zyne's eyes.

"Now we get to the main issue: Clara." Zyne leaned back into the couch. "Does she even know what she really is? Or even what her mother is?"

Jailyn's heart beat furiously with concern for her daughter. Speechless, she just watched him.

Zyne narrowed his eyes. "All this time and the two of

you never explained to her the supernatural beings living in this town? She actually believes she is human?"

Finding her voice again, Jailyn said, "I implore you to leave her alone. She must find her own path without involvement in our world."

"We all share the same world, Jailyn. She will become entangled within it eventually," he replied, stretching a full smile across his face, "Especially if both her parents are taken from her."

Jailyn's eyes deepened their hue.

Zyne continued through her angry silence, "Besides, can you really stop me? I doubt you have any spark left. Even Nathan, my old friend, who at one point had more power than me, was taken down by my associate here." He motioned to his pet, who smiled at the sudden adulation from her master.

He continued, "So, did you leave the Illumin, or did they cast you out? As the immortal guardians of humanity, I wouldn't think they approved of your union with a Shade."

Jailyn realized he wasn't looking for anything from her. He just wanted to savor her fear before ripping into her flesh.

"I will not let you take her," she uttered with restraint, holding back the rage that wanted to strike out across the table

Closing her eyes, she centered herself and thought of her coin. She had not wielded the Faith in a long time, but its familiar waves coursed through her heart again. The room grew quiet, and the coin began to glow with a soft, white light. She was still Illumin, no matter what the others thought of the title.

"Clara, do not let go of who you are," she whispered, opening her eyes. Zyne's smirk vanished as Jailyn reconnected to the Faith.

"The funeral is tomorrow, Clara. Take time to mourn your loss," Drake implored. He and Clara sat in his car just outside Mandrake Tower.

She continued staring out of the window at the immense structure that beckoned to her. Defying convention, it was turned 90 degrees so that its flattened corners pointed into the middle of the bordering sidewalks. Though not the tallest building in downtown Shreveport, sunlight bounced off its silver walls as a declaration of the power of the corporation that owned it.

"I have nothing left except this interview." She turned back to him, seeing the concern in his eyes. "Thank you for your support. Without you, I wouldn't have even made it here."

She reached over to hold his hand. They looked at each other in silence. The horrors of yesterday had flown swiftly by. Drake had remained at her side the whole time keeping her calm. She didn't know what she would have done without him.

"You can't go from losing both your parents one day to an interview the next."

"Mandrake Solutions, Inc., is a Fortune 500 company fully diversified through several tech-related industries. Everyone wants to work here. If I walk away from this opportunity, thousands of other applicants will file in and take it from me." She gently squeezed his hand.

"Then let them. Why should you trade your sanity and well-being for the possibility of a career?" he asked.

"I can't even think straight right now. I have to do the only thing I can and nail this interview. Tragedy won't ruin my life. My parents are gone forever, and I will mourn them tomorrow. As for now, all I can do is walk into that building and enter into the career I have worked toward my entire life."

A few minutes of silence passed between them before Drake checked his watch.

"Don't be late," he said, forcing a smile.

She leaned over and kissed him.

"I will definitely come back to you, Drake," she replied. "Someone has to keep me in check."

Clara stepped out of the car, prepared to face the ensuing gauntlet alone. Mandrake Tower seemed even larger now that she faced it without any glass shielding her from its dominance. She craned her head, wondering if anyone in the top levels looked down with contempt at her ambition.

"They all started out here on the concrete," she reassured herself before gathering enough courage to enter.

The cold handle of the door halted her for a moment. In an instant, all the conversations with her mother about Mandrake rumbled around her head. The unfounded terror in her mother's eyes flashed across her mind's eye.

At the time, it had seemed ridiculous, but here, standing on the company's threshold, it felt strangely real. Like a faint buzzing in the distance, a slow warning built inside her, telling her that this place was dangerous. She quickly reminded herself it was nothing but her mother's superstition.

Shrugging off the memories, Clara was grateful Drake had handled everything with the police and her parents, but why hadn't she been contacted? Surely there must have been some official report she needed to sign? For that matter, what was she doing here instead of filing her own report for the woman who assaulted her?

"Excuse me," a man said behind her.

She whipped around, realizing she was blocking the door.

"I'm sorry," she mumbled, stepping to the side and holding the door open for him to enter.

Embarrassed, she turned and waved to Drake one final time before rushing inside. While she loved her mother, she couldn't let her crazy ideas sway her own life decisions.

Brilliant, blue light beamed from Jailyn's eyes, casting the room in a haze. She felt her connection to the Faith restoring. Peace calmed her choppy heart and time slowed down.

For Clara, she thought.

The Faith began flowing through her like a quiet stream. She stepped into its waters, smiling in retaliation to Zyne. She darted her hand over the coin, and they both watched it shoot into the air, trailed by a white stream of light.

The Faith propelled Jailyn upward, following the coin. Her entire body glowed with a near-blinding light. Zyne squinted at her and saw the faint outline of wings stretching from her back. Nearly brushing the roof, she grabbed the coin and felt it transform into a long, silver dagger.

"With this light, I dispel the darkness before me!" she cried before lunging down at him, the dagger aimed at his chest.

Zyne jumped against the wall an instant too late. The dagger slashed across his chest, tearing through his shirt into his skin. The blade stabbed into the couch where he had just been seated. Jailyn turned around as he floated upward and kicked off the wall back toward the middle of the room. As he landed smoothly atop a coffee table, his pet quickly moved to his side.

"No, this is my fight," he said, pushing her back. He kicked a hookah off the table to give himself more space.

Jailyn's wings fluttered, holding her in the air. She watched Zyne's pet step away from their battlefield, noticing the reluctance in her action. Jailyn flew down toward Zyne for another strike.

Black tendrils emerged from his extended arms and snaked around her torso and arms. As she closed in, his tendrils pulled her hands outward. She backpedaled with her wings, but he jumped and landed a kick squarely in her jaw. He groaned with exertion, her intense light burning his skin.

Smoke drifted from his body. He retracted his tendrils, watching her fall away and crash into a couch, toppling it over. She rushed to her feet, quickly regaining her fighting stance.

Jailyn swung her dagger in front of her, channeling more of the Faith into it. It glowed brighter and morphed into a sword, her ancient weapon of choosing, used countless times to vanquish many of Zyne's ilk. It was much heavier than she remembered.

"Shade of the earth, I command you to look into the light!" Her voice filled the room. She floated into the air with the Faith swelling around her heart. Zyne reluctantly looked into her eyes. "You threaten to enslave my family, but I deny you. Leave now and return my husband before I bring divine vengeance upon your brow!"

"Vengeance?" A smirk found its way back onto Zyne's face, even though he was still unable to break her gaze. "Is this personal? I thought your kind were supposed to be the servants of humanity. Have you lived among humans so long you have forgotten this?"

She gripped the hilt of her sword even more tightly. "I vanquish you, demon," she whispered.

She flew down at him swinging her sword. He leapt forward, sliding below her blade. His fingers tapped the floor and guided the rest of his body into a roll that set him back on his feet behind her. She twisted around with her wings, quickly slashing down at him. He reached up to block with his forearm.

The edge of her weapon sliced into the meat of his forearm. Her arms trembled while keeping him at bay. Drops of black liquid fell to the floor. He pushed her blade away and swung his alternate fist at her face. Jerking backward, she dodged his swing.

She thrust her sword at his exposed torso, piercing air as he twisted to the side. His foot kicked against her shin, the knifing pain pushing her off balance. A flurry of attacks from his fists and tendrils kept her from bringing her weapon to bear. She flew backward, temporarily escaping his rush.

"You face hell!" he screamed, throwing his tendrils at her and wrapping her up again.

Fighting against the erratic pull of the tendrils, she rocketed straight for him, aiming her blade at his heart. The sword grazed his side, collecting more of his blood. She held onto it while falling to her knees in defeat.

He grabbed her by the neck, choking the breath out of her. Grunting, he lifted her up and slammed her into the ground with all of his remaining force. A flash of light blinded her for an instant. The flesh around his hand and along his forearm melted from the heat her skin radiated.

She screamed in pain as the light emanating from her dimmed. The heavy clang of her sword slamming against the floor sent a wave of fear across her face that he relished. Breathing heavily, his fingers dug into her neck as his black tendrils clamped around the rest of her body. Stinging pain overloaded her senses.

"Cl..Clara," she gurgled. "Don't.."

"Don't what?" Zyne asked through gritted teeth.

"Don't fall," Jailyn managed. Zyne had been right about one thing: she shouldn't have kept the truth from Clara. If she failed to defeat him here, Clara would be his forever.

A few beads of sweat crawled down the side of Clara's face after a tough battery of questions asked by the executive sitting across from her. His office was fairly large and sporadically decorated with iron sculptures. Remembering to breathe, she toned down the desire to tap her foot.

The executive, dressed in a black suit with a pair of glasses resting on his clean face, glanced over her resumé again while maintaining a proper posture in his leather chair. A few agonizing moments passed before he laid the summary of her professional life in front of him.

"You are very brilliant on paper, Miss Raime," he said plainly. "You should be very proud of your academic accomplishments. They have afforded you an opportunity to join our elite team. I believe you may have what we are looking for. However, there is only one man at this company who can determine that, and he will continue this interview in his office. If you are still up to the challenge, that is."

"Of course," she replied, having trouble containing her excitement.

"Excellent," he said while hitting the page button for his secretary, who quickly entered the room. "Please escort Miss Raime to Mr. Zyne's office. He should be expecting her."

He scooped up Clara's application packet and handed

it back to her. Clara took it with trembling fingers before shaking his hand and exiting his office.

The secretary guided her silently through the quiet, sterile halls to the central elevator. They both entered, and the secretary pushed the button for one of the top floors.

"Nervous?" The secretary politely asked.

"First real interview out of college," Clara replied.

"You are doing fine. Win over Mr. Zyne and you will have won the company."

"Thank you."

The doors opened to reveal an empty lobby with a coffee table surrounded by leather furniture. Large paintings of moody landscapes adorned the walls. She looked back to the secretary for instruction.

"Just enter and leave the rest up to Mr. Zyne," the secretary said.

Clara stepped off the elevator. The doors closed behind her, leaving her to her chosen fate. She walked into the center of the lobby, trying to take in the aesthetics. After a few minutes of nervous anticipation, she finally took a seat on one of the couches.

A click brought her attention to a door just to the side of the elevators. The handle tilted, and Arthur Zyne stepped through the door with a bright smile. He walked over and extended his hand. Clara stood up and shook it firmly. The sharp business suit he wore added an element of professionalism to his randomly spiked hair and beard. Of course, no one would openly question the style of anyone as powerful as him.

"Clara Raime, I presume," he said, letting go of her

hand.

"Arthur Zyne," Clara uttered breathlessly. "It is truly a pleasure to meet you."

"Since we both hold to the courteous conventions of our time," he said with a wide smile, "then I shall say, 'The pleasure is all mine.' Please accompany me, if you will."

She followed him back through the door and tight hallway that wrapped around the outside of the lobby. He led her to a door that would have been directly across from the elevator if not for the wall between.

"I have only one rule for my office. This is my personal place of business, and as such, I require everyone who steps through this door to leave behind all forms of pretense." He looked into her eyes with absolute sincerity. "If you cannot submit to my request, then please leave."

He walked through the door, leaving it open. She took a step forward and stopped; a warning sounded in her heart. This was the moment that would shape her entire destiny. She longed to enter and take what was hers, but an uneasy wave rolled through her. Whispers from her mother, imploring her to leave, drifted through the air.

She closed her eyes, taking in a deep breath. Her mother was dead and she could not afford to allow such grief ruin her future. This interview was all she had left. Whatever uncertainties that dwelt within her heart would only bring regret if she gave in to them.

"Clara," her mother's voice whispered.

Clara stood before the doorway, shutting out her mother's echoes. The last thing Arthur Zyne needed to discover was that she heard the disembodied voice of her dead mother.

"Clara, do not let go of who you are!" Her mother's voice resounded in the hallway.

"This *is* who I am," Clara responded, striding into the office with a renewed determination to achieve her life goals.

Zyne stood over his prey like a spider with an insect trapped in its web. Jailyn looked up at him helplessly. Her sword lay a few steps away from her grasp, its silver blade reflecting the tension between them.

"Now that you have released your wrath, let's have a nice chat," Zyne said, watching her struggle against his tendrils.

"Just finish me and take what you want!" she screamed at him through the stinging pulses riveting her body.

Zyne pulled up a stool and sat down in front of her. His tendrils looked like deformed snakes trying to escape his disgusting nature through his forearms. She turned her head away. He grabbed her chin and forced it back around.

"Vengeance," he began, "How can you even claim it when you are the one who left the reservation?" He laughed quietly at his own joke. "Though, no one really leaves, do they?"

She looked at him in silence, trying to will more of the Faith into her body. The suffocating grip of his tendrils made it impossible. If he wanted a game of words before destroying her, she would not oblige him. She held her defiant stare.

"If only Clara could see her mother now," he said after

a few moments of silence. "She always hated you for your passive nature. Just imagine how her perception would change if she could watch you, fighting until the bitter end. And..." He leaned in closer and whispered, "It will be bitter."

He signaled his pet to come to him. She stepped over his tendrils to sit on his lap with her arms reaching around his neck.

"This is all I want, Jailyn," he said, resting his forehead against his pet's. "Unwavering devotion. Look into her eyes; see what you have been missing."

Zyne pulled the sunglasses from his pet's face. Jailyn tried to turn away, but caught an unmistakable spark in the woman's eyes. Gray like a cocoon, they swirled around with mystical grace. Jailyn squinted, looking deeper until she discovered what Zyne meant for her to see. Horror spread through her. Zyne smiled at her realization.

"The interesting nature of hybrids is that they are anatomically distinct from either of our races and possess dual spiritual properties. This, dear Jailyn, is Clara's Shade."

Jailyn peered into the empty shell of her daughter. Zyne told the truth. Clara's soul was indeed tied to the manifestation sitting in his lap, though she questioned whether or not Clara's true sentience accompanied it.

Jailyn lashed out at him with her words. "This is why we have our eternal struggle, Zyne. You earthly Shades, outcasts from your dark realm, destroy all that is beautiful in this world."

Zyne laughed at her, pulling Clara closer to his chest.

"I believe you are right," he replied.

"I see a dim projection of my daughter in your lap, but

where is her soul? Even you with your power, you cannot override her will."

"Ah, now we get to the entire point of my 'diabolical' scheme." He gently pushed Clara off his lap and let her stand at his side. "You are right," he continued. "I cannot control her. She has to make her own decisions."

"Yet you hold her like a mannequin."

"You and Nathan are the ones at fault here. Both of you have lived so far outside of who you really are that you have blinded yourselves to the very nature of the universe. We live outside human comprehension. We are not like them and cannot live like them. You both forsook this when you found your 'love' for each other.

"Clara has already made her choice. You want to pretend that time flows linearly around us and that strings of cause and effect must lead to her choice, but that is simply not true. If you had not fallen from your true purpose, then perhaps she would be standing by your side. But, just as you left her alone without explanation, so she now leaves you."

Jailyn looked into Clara's twisted smile. She felt the emptiness and longing that could not be satisfied with the life she and Nathan wanted for her. Half Shade and half Illumin, Clara's power remained dormant all this time while she and Nathan carefully watched over her. The same lust for power that drove Zyne now fueled Clara.

"Now you can see it," Zyne interjected. "You hid Clara away and chained her to a mortal existence when her very nature is incompatible. Love--that human emotion you sought with Nathan-- is the very thing that drove you to this selfish decision. We are immortal beings, Jailyn. We cannot be human."

"Then why do you try?"

"Because it is my ultimate struggle." He smiled wryly at her. "I can easily control the universe, but I can never control the human heart."

Sunlight poured into Arthur Zyne's corner office through the large windows that bent around it. He leaned against his dark, glossy desk, watching Clara enter with her application packet in hand. She looked around the wide space, taking in the famous paintings attached to the walls. Three separate pockets of furniture broke up the room, and a tall bookcase covered an entire wall with a multitude of information.

"Please, take a seat, just not in front of my desk," Arthur instructed.

"How about over here?" she asked, walking to the trio of leather chairs closest to her.

She sat down and laid her packet next to a bronze sundial on the small table in front of her. Arthur joined her and scooped the packet into his lap, quickly flipping through it. She watched his eyes dart over the pages before stealing a look at the sundial. Unlabeled tick marks surrounded the fin, glinting off the sunlight. An angled shadow sectioned off the time, provided one knew each tick mark.

Her eyes met his as he closed the packet. An inviting

smile wound across his face.

"How does it feel to be one of the most qualified candidates interviewing with us today?"

"Like a dream."

"Interesting. However, this is one dream you have created for yourself. Tell me, why are you here?"

Her heart beat a little faster as she concentrated on saying the right words. "Mandrake is the pinnacle of this industry, and I want to be a part of its future growth."

He smiled at her, lightly placing his fingertips on her packet.

"You are who these pages say you are, but remember, you must be real in this room. I can easily pick you over the other candidates, simply because none of them would have shown up the day after their parents had been murdered. Now, aren't you really here to learn the truth?"

Surprise flashed across her face. He leaned toward her. Her foot tapped against the carpet, giving her a few seconds to think.

"How did you know that?"

"Look inside yourself. You have always known you weren't part of the society your parents lived in. Haven't you ever wondered why?" His smile faded.

Astonishment bound her to her seat. She felt like he had read her mind.

The room darkened as if a cloud were blocking the sun, though she could see no clouds. Shadows crept around the office in the corners of her eye. Her skin tingled as if the very air were charging with electricity. Quiet whispers from her mother told her to run, but she refused.

"Don't be afraid of who you are, Clara," Arthur said. "Remember what we accomplished yesterday and you will understand why you are here. You already know the truth."

"Run, Clara!" Her mother's voice shouted audibly.

"Yes, run from the truth, Clara," Arthur looked into her eyes. "It's what your mother did, and you remember what happened to her."

"What?" The warning she had heard while entering the building rang in her head.

Arthur pulled the sundial toward him, twisting it so its faint shadow rotated around. "Time doesn't concern you anymore. *When* things happen isn't quite as relevant as *why*. Imagine this sundial represents your life."

He ran his finger over the tick marks and continued, "You can see everything: your past, your future, your purpose. Unfortunately, your parents tried so hard to be a guiding light, but all they did was cast a shadow over you, locking you into a single point in time. They hid the rest of your life from you when you should have been free to see it, free to experience it."

Yesterday's foggy memory instantly became clear. She jumped up, covering her face with her hands at the horrible images rushing back to her. She screamed and the room darkened even further. She backed away from Arthur against a wall and slid to the floor.

She pulled back the sleeves of her suit to look at the scars running along her forearms, scars she didn't remember. Her hands were clean, but she relived the memory of covering them in her parents' own blood.

Zyne skulked around to get behind Jailyn, kneeling to speak into her ear, "Look at your daughter now. See the future you have given her. While you may not like what you have made her into, she will be ever so grateful in the coming millennia."

Jailyn reluctantly looked up at Clara. Jailyn had failed her as a mother by keeping her away from the world that found her in the end. Now, she would walk the earth a slave to Zyne and whatever else he molded her into.

"Clara, I am sorry you had to find out the truth like this. Believe me, your father and I love you dearly and were protecting you," Jailyn said to deaf ears.

"Clara's not really in at the moment. Leave a message and she will call back," Zyne whispered, placing his hands on Jailyn's shoulders. "Think of this as a cathartic experience for her."

Blue light returned to Jailyn's eyes. She ignored the stinging pain crawling through her and channeled the Faith once again. Her sword rattled on the ground and slid toward her.

"Run, Clara!" She screamed while pushing against Zyne's tendrils.

"Show her the choice you've made, Clara!" Zyne yelled, glaring up at her." Show her the truth she hid from you!"

Clara slammed her foot on the hilt of her mother's sword, stopping its journey. She reached out toward the stage, and the axe flew through the air into her hand. Jailyn writhed around trying to free herself, but to no avail. Her daughter swung the axe into her chest.

A black mist seethed out of Clara's skin. Her axe broke her mother's sternum, and Jailyn screamed from the pain. Blood pooled around her on the floor.

"These mortal shells were never made to last anyway, Jailyn," Zyne said calmly into her ear. "You are my prisoner now."

Clara struck again, tearing further into Jailyn and spilling more blood. Zyne laughed, standing up and stretching out his hands. The tendrils pulsated around Jailyn's torso, sending out throbs of burning pain. Jailyn heaved over, smelling her torn flesh. The axe swiftly fell into her upper back, sucking the breath out of her.

Her sword lay within reach, but her body had lost too much blood to fight back. She slowed her mind and accepted her fate. Clara and Zyne continued to ravage her mortal shell. Eventually, she would redeem herself and see Clara again. Zyne wouldn't be able to hold her forever.

"Pick up your mother's sword, Clara. Take your future back from her," Zyne commanded.

Clara tossed the axe aside and picked up the sword, drawing it in front of her. She stared at the silver blade, splattered with black blood.

"You are more than he has told you, Clara," Jailyn whispered. "Remember who you are."

Clara's frosted eyes faded into their brown hue for a second. False hope taunted Jailyn as Clara turned the sword around so the tip of the blade hung just above her mother's chest. Jailyn watched the blade slide into her own heart.

Whatever blood remained inside trickled from the cut. The pain running through her heart reached fever pitch; darkness swallowed her.

Clara fell to her knees beside her mother, still clinging to the sword. A few tears dropped from her eyes. The entire room went still as she pressed her forehead against the ornate handle. After a moment, she went to pull herself up, but her feet slipped on her mother's blood. She let go of the sword, and her forearms caught the sides of the blade on her way to the floor.

Zyne reached down and helped her back to her feet. He snatched the sword out of Jailyn and threw it to the side. The skin left on his hands smoked again from touching the Illumin weapon. His tendrils retracted into his arms as Jailyn's body dissipated into ash. The two Shades stood in silence.

"Now we need to pull some pedestrians off the street to mimic your parents' bodies and satisfy the police. Plus, I do enjoy the way you handle that axe."

Clara smiled at his approval, unconcerned by the crimson stream pouring from her arms.

Clara curled up against the wall with her hands clasped around her knees. Tears flowed down the sides of her face, soaking into her suit. She couldn't remember how long she had sat there, but the sun now approached the horizon.

The memories didn't feel real, but at the same time felt strangely tangible on a deeper level. Slowly, she accepted their truth. The anguish on the faces of her parents just before they died burned a permanent image into her mind. Initially repulsed by her actions, the joy that she had felt when driving the axe into their flesh returned, transforming the memory until it marked the exact point in time when she had liberated herself.

Clara smiled with tears in her eyes at the thought of liberation from her oppressive parents. She looked up at Zyne, who was looking out of his window over the silhouetted city.

"Your destiny lies with me," he said without turning around.

"Destiny," she whispered to herself.

Her entire life flashed before her eyes. The ridicule plaguing her adolescence mixed with a renewed animosity toward her parents' ideologies. Everything she hated in her parents converged on her. A warm sensation spread through her body, emanating from her heart. Suddenly, she saw her future streaming alongside her past.

She couldn't even attempt to explain what she saw. Language lacked the depth to reveal the duality of vision buffeting her mind. At its most temporal, it felt like living in a hall of mirrors with each mirror playing out a different scene of her life. All her past memories came to life before her eyes.

On instinct, she stepped forward, walking through her life, beginning at birth.

The farther she looked the darker and more warped it seemed. Her future appeared as a grand vision clouded by the time separating her from it. At its end, she could barely make out her parents rising up against Zyne and her.

She pulled herself off the ground to stand by Zyne's side, watching the sun dip behind the towers at the center of Shreveport. The warmth within her grew to a burning sensation the closer she got to Zyne.

"What am I?" She asked.

"A hybrid of light and darkness, Illumin and Shade. Your parents kept many secrets from you, the most important being that Nathan is a Shade and Jailyn is an Illumin. Your physical birth may have been two and a half decades ago, but this week has been your spiritual birth into the world previously denied you."

A reminder of her spiritual birth played across her mind. Like an out-of-body experience, she watched herself lying helplessly on the floor of her parent's home with terror spread across her face. What was she scared of? As she looked down into her own eyes, she knew that wasn't really her, just her body, a body that needed to be broken to release her true self.

She stepped into the living room over the broken glass. Her body turned to run, but she swung the axe in her hand against its side. The pain across its face filled her with joy. Soon, she would be free, free to join Zyne.

Terrified and confused, her body curled around the axehead. Clara jerked it away, watching the blood spill from the open wound.

Clara bent down next to her own ear and spoke the

words she remembered hearing, "Your vision is too narrow, but only through this pain will you expand it. Tear your heart in half and bury your soul."

Now she understood the meaning of the statement. This was her choice: to either stand with her parents or join Zyne. There would be a cost no matter which she chose.

Jumping down from the coffee table, she walked out through the front door into the daylight. She had already made her decision.

The memory died. Clara blinked away a tear in her eye, mentally returning to Zyne's office. "What now?" she asked.

"You come and work for me. As you have probably guessed, my company is only a platform used to keep me tied to this physical world. This city is filled with my enemies, Illumin and Shades alike. Stay with me and we will rule this world."

"What of my parents?" she asked, trying to make sense of her newfound ability to see into future events.

"Haven't you seen their fate?"

"I want you to say it."

He laughed and turned to her. "They have their revenge against me. But it doesn't matter-- you are lost to them forever."

He spoke truth. On the edge of her vision, she could dimly see the restoration of her parents and their subsequent crusade against her and Zyne. She couldn't make out the exact time or place, but Zyne may not want her to see that far just yet. His touch heavily warped her mind, shielding it from the brunt of these new sensations. Strangely, she knew to trust his judgment.

A door opened around the corner and Drake walked into the office.

"Drake, what are you doing here?" Clara demanded.

"It's okay, Clara," Drake answered.

"Sorry to deceive you," Zyne began, "but Drake is not real."

Zyne walked between them and held his hand before Drake's heart. A dark stream flowed out of Zyne's palm, surrounding Drake. Drake smiled before dissolving into the air.

"Drake was my creation to fully test your loyalty. My original plan was to use him against both you and your parents to pull you toward me, but you completed that task by yourself."

Clara felt more loss empty from what remained of her heart. Zyne rushed to her and grabbed her hands. A new fire burned deep inside her for her true love. Strangely, she felt this even before Zyne spoke.

"What I found through him is something inexplicable. I found that we have a future together. Remember our moment together on the sidewalk yesterday after you finished with the pedestrians?"

A familiar emotion, spreading out from her heart, impaired her rational judgment. She looked into Zyne's eyes and again felt the peace from yesterday. She instinctively ran her fingers through a familiar path in his beard, though she knew it was the first time.

"I do know you," she uttered softly.

"You sacrificed your life with your parents for us," he replied.

She stared at him, taken aback by the emotion exploding inside of her. She felt like they had known each other for decades. While technically it was true, they hadn't yet lived through them.

"I already know my entire destiny and our fate. What is the point of living?"

"To be alive," he replied cryptically.

He gently pulled her back to the window as night fell across the city.

Clara stared blankly at the two white caskets holding the mangled remains of her parents. The funeral had happened so quickly, the shock of it all consuming every piece of sanity she could gather. As the preacher droned on with his packaged sermon, her mind raced into strange fantasies.

She imagined her parents climbing out of their caskets, scaring the funeral guests away with the sight of their mutilated flesh. The guests try to run, but her parents descend upon them, biting into their chests and ripping out their hearts. They turn to smile at her, blood dripping onto the burgundy carpet. She smiles approvingly back at them.

Reality swept down on her. She found herself turned around in her pew looking absentmindedly at the small crowd spread out across the country church. Perhaps a third of the sanctuary was occupied, but only a handful were true friends of her parents. The rest were mostly distant family attending solely out of obligation. At least they tried to be supportive in offering their heartfelt condolences.

The preacher trudged on like a metronome, leaving her with her thoughts. Life as she knew it was finished. This funeral marked the final point of humanity in her life. She was determined to bury her soul with her parents and live on, preferring the emptiness to the knowledge of loss.

Thoughts of her parents' betrayal through their constant deception stirred conflicting emotions in her heart. Her love for them fought against a bitter, rising hatred that frightened her. Memories of her life flashed in her mind, providing incriminating evidence against her parents in their posthumous trial within her heart.

She latched her hands around the edge of the wooden pew, digging her nails into its underside. Her life had been a choreographed dance by her parents to keep her from learning the truth. They had worked diligently to shield her from it, but destiny, it seemed, had visited her anyway. However, it had no sense of proper timing or regard for human relationships. Without her parents, she was truly alone.

The preacher finally completed his remarks and called for everyone to bow their heads in prayer. The brief silence drew Clara's eyes to the caskets. Glistening light bounced off their reflective surface. Faint whispers from her parents called out to her, telling her how sorry they were.

Just as the preacher began praying, she quietly stood up and walked toward the front. No one but the funeral director in the back noticed her. Running her hands along the polished wood of the caskets, her entire body trembled with grief. She fell to her knees and rested her forehead against the last connection she had to her former life.

"I'm sorry, Mom, so sorry," she whispered between quiet sobs. "I know this isn't what you wanted for me, but I have to carry on your legacy. Dad, I-" She stopped and felt Zyne's presence charge the silent air.

Turning around, she looked at the faces of the funeral guests, now offering her their pity as a silent acknowledgement of her connection to the dark figure standing in the doorway. The preacher walked down from the podium to kneel beside her. Zyne's stoic frame gave her no guidance for the situation.

"Clara," the preacher said with a southern voice flowing like water. "We came here to honor your parents, both of them. This funeral party may look small, but it is meaningful. Look at their faces and see why they have come."

Ancient eyes, masking the Faith through transient, human form, revealed the preacher's goal.

"You will find only Illumin here, darling," he continued. "They look after you while the Shades offer everlasting death. Your patron in the back may sway you with words of honey; however, in the end, you will not find comfort."

"And you have seen this?" Clara asked.

"No," he admitted. "There was no need to see beyond this moment."

"Don't lie to me, not now. Everyone here has seen how this will play out." She stood up, placing her hand on his shoulder. His eyes pleaded with her, but she was immune to his offers. "My future cannot be altered. Zyne and I are-"

"Nothing is certain, Clara, even for you," he said, trying

one more time.

She smiled and shook her head. "The tears on my face now are all that I will shed for you and my parents."

She turned her back to the caskets and walked to meet Zyne at the doorway. He was her destiny.

Confined

by
Jason Craft

1

The Red King hid behind his last line of defense, fearing the oncoming soldiers. The battle had been swift and vicious, leaving him trapped against the edge with nowhere to run. Carved from bone, he stood tall and proud, stoically accepting his fate in what would become his final resting place. He was pinned between two impending attacks, and an enormous finger reached down and hovered above his head for a moment before finally toppling him over.

Daniel watched Zyne retract his hand from the chess board, accepting his defeat. Zyne smiled, his eyes deepening into solid black. A sudden burst of fear tore through Daniel. He pushed fiercely against the impulse to run, reassuring himself that Zyne would not hurt him.

"You continually amaze me, Daniel," Zyne said.

"Well, you are a worthy opponent," Daniel replied, hiding a shaking hand under the table.

They both sat around a small card table with the hand-carved, bone chess set between them. Mountainous shelves of used merchandise surrounded them in Daniel's shop, Dark Raven Pawn. The thick glow of the moon drifted toward them through the glass doors at the front of the store.

Zyne crossed his arms and leaned back in his chair, keeping his smile. "Sometimes I wonder if you are trying to find leverage against me."

Daniel chuckled at the comment, pulling glasses away from his weathered face. Short, white hair sat atop his head. A full, gray beard grew from his jaw line. Middle-aged, Daniel felt much older due to the constant interaction with the ancient beings that frequented his shop. It seemed unfair that the timeless one sitting across from him felt young and vibrant.

"I can only beat you in chess, my friend. I'll leave the game of maneuvering against your empire to better men." Another pulse of fear followed his lighthearted comment.

"You really are the only human I know that can stare death in the face and just laugh at the absurdity." He looked down at Daniel's hand tapping against the table. "As always, I apologize for my effect on you."

"Eh, I'm used to it now. I try to think of it as a sort of ultimate rush." He offered a genuine smile while his heart raced inside him.

"That comment alone is why-" Zyne immediately stopped talking to stare at the ceiling. Surprise dashed over his face as he stood up. He spread his arms out as if trying to catch invisible rain drops. A dark cloud seeped from him, dimming the lights. He took several deep breaths.

Anxiety intensified within Daniel, accompanied by nausea. His heart raced ahead of his breath. He jumped up and backed into the store's jewelry counter. Heaving over, he turned around and fell to his knees, trying not to vomit.

The air in the shop swirled around Zyne like a black

tornado. Daniel shut his eyes tightly, grinding his teeth against the unnatural force crawling through him. Disembodied whispers rode the torrential air.

"I don't believe it," Zyne whispered as the wind subsided and the room brightened again. "I thought we had a pact between our races, Daniel."

Daniel looked up at him through the weight of nausea. "Surely they weren't so foolish as to bring one of the relics into the open."

"For your family's sake, I hope not," Zyne said, standing over him, offering a hand. Daniel grabbed it and Zyne pulled him to his feet. "I will let you know what I find out."

In an instant, Zyne exited the shop.

Rumors were always circulating about the location and nature of powerful relics hidden throughout the city. Some had been forged by the Raven family in recent history, others by ancient Native American tribes. Until now, neither Shade nor Illumin had broken the pact between them by using one. If Zyne could be touched by this one's power, whoever tapped into it was a danger to the entire city.

Daniel looked around at the disheveled mess caused by Zyne's involuntary outburst. He would have to spend the last few remaining morning hours cleaning up. Steadying his body, he sat before the empty chess board. Chess pieces lay strewn across the floor.

D'Nas leaned against his knee from his high perch on a rooftop in downtown Shreveport. His azure eyes scanned the streets below. Gusts of wind teased his short, blond hair. He wore a white tank top overlaid by a shoulder holster nestling his gun, and black cargo pants. The edges of a tattoo written in ancient script peeked from his neck and the back of his left shoulder.

"What are we dealing with that it would have enough raw power to bathe the city," he said, mindlessly thumbing the detective's badge clipped to his belt.

"Maybe if you would quit hiding up here, we could find out," Gabriella replied with a smile. She sat a few paces down from him with her feet dangling over the side of the building. Her brown, wavy hair was pulled back into a simple ponytail. Gauged earrings opened her earlobes. A few more rings curved around the top of her ears and another around her right nostril. A pair of dark-rimmed glasses framed her face.

"It's all about perspective. Up here, with the whole city at my feet, I feel as if I can reach out and touch this hidden shadow. Down there, I feel too much like one of the humans, oblivious."

"At least we hope they are oblivious," Gabriella added. "For all we know, one of them could have triggered the whole event."

He directed his gaze several blocks down in the direction of the river, where the dome of a public garden center sat proudly next to a casino. He pushed out with his ethereal senses, searching for a particular soul. He was in luck-- one of his favorite groups was meeting today. With a smile he walked toward the side of the building.

"What are you doing?" Gabriella asked. She stood and

turned toward him. He saluted before jumping into the empty alley below.

Blue light surrounded him as he fell. Halfway down, a pair of large wings spread out from his back, slowing his descent. He landed gently on the concrete, looking around to ensure no one saw him. The light emanating from him faded as he transitioned back into his human form. With a flutter of wings, Gabriella joined his side, scowling.

"Why do you do that? One of these days someone is going to see you."

"But not today," he said, smiling.

She rolled her eyes and walked past him. He rejoined her side and they left the alley and strolled down the sidewalk.

Though the group may hold some answers, D'Nas still felt a bit directionless. The power discharge that woke him in the middle of the night had felt prescient at the moment, but its lack of holding power left no clear path to its origin.

He looked into the eyes of the pedestrians scurrying to work. Most wore business attire, carrying on normally. Nothing out of the ordinary caught his eye. He did notice a few Shades passing by, trying to avoid him. They weren't a problem, though. After all, the relic might have passed over their senses. No one knew yet exactly how far-reaching the effects were.

Eventually he and Gabriella came to a stop outside the garden center. The calm flow of the Red River just beyond the round building quietly filled the air. He followed the stone path leading around the outside to the courtyard in the back.

Just as he had sensed, the person he wanted to see was

gearing up for the day with her group. He reached out and felt their strong emotions leaking out. They were in a heightened emotional state and would only require a slight nudge to give him answers. Of all the humans in the city, these were the easiest to manipulate.

"Really, D'Nas? Do you have to do this now?" Gabriella asked, realizing whom he came to see.

"Actually, yeah. We need to see if she, or her crazy following, knows anything. Besides, you know how much I love the 'Cult of Lea.'"

Gabriella rolled her eyes and followed him down a flight of stairs shaded by a canopy of trees. As they entered the courtyard, the morning sun beat against them, giving a small taste of just how hot the day would become. "I hope she at least lets me dip my fingers into the fountain."

"Now that's the spirit," D'Nas responded.

Lea Brannon, local author of several books dealing with supernatural encounters, sat on the edge of a large fountain before the fans surrounding her. A cascading waterfall rolled over a few tiers of red stone ledges into the fountain behind her.

Despite being in her seventies, she gave off a youthful exuberance that her followers all simply adored. D'Nas found their blind adoration disgusting.

The twenty or so fans crowded around her feet, content just to sit on the grass and look up at their living saint. D'Nas and Gabriella took a seat at the back. The group acknowledged them with fleeting glances, mostly at their side arms. Lea ignored them completely, intently listening to one of her fans describe a personal encounter.

"We shouldn't have survived," the middle-aged woman said, deep into her story. "After we got out, our entire car was glowing. I heard a flapping sound and looked up just in time to see an angel flying away. The car had quit glowing before the police arrived, so they obviously didn't believe me. They said we were both lucky to be alive and that our head trauma caused us to see things. But I know what I saw."

"Of course you saw them," Lea explained, "The angels constantly watch over us. Hold on to that memory, dear. While you have seen the force of good that works for us, there are other forces in this city that would take that away from you." She turned toward D'Nas. "Isn't that right, Detective?"

All eyes shifted in his direction. He instantly became aware of just how much bulkier he was than the rest of them. Lea's eyes drilled into him. Gabriella shifted around to smile at him.

"Absolutely," he managed. "You know what else is really strange? The news. You always see these types of amazing survival stories, but no one can ever explain the true forces behind them. No one dares breach the subject of angels."

"Or demons," the storyteller added.

"That's right," D'Nas replied. He subtly altered their emotional state to accept his thoughts without question. Revelation spread throughout the crowd while Gabriella frowned at him. He winked at her before continuing with his captivated audience.

He lowered his voice to hushed tones, "Just think about all that could have happened last night. Angels were probably covering the sky, protecting all of us as we slept." He dramatically looked around to see if anyone was spying on them. "None of us will ever knowbecause 'they' don't want us to know. We are just sheep expected to follow a nameless shepherd. It is all part of their plan for control."

He let his 'deep' insight settle, knowing only this group would take such an inane notion seriously. At this point, even he didn't know what he was talking about anymore, but the entire group still nodded in agreement with each other after noticing Lea's furrowed brow. Lea just stared at him in shock. It was all he could do not to burst out laughing.

Lea looked around quickly before whispering, "I felt it too."

Everyone leaned closer to Lea. Gabriella rolled her eyes.

"What did you feel?" D'Nas asked, halfway seriously.

"Evil." The huddled group gasped in unison.

"Then it has already begun," D'Nas said, standing up with wide eyes. The crowd looked at him in astonishment. He held a worried pose before running back up the steps with Gabriella chasing him.

He made it to the street and briskly walked a few blocks before collapsing in laughter onto a bench. Gabriella rushed up and punched his massive shoulder.

"You are so cruel." She glared down at him, trying to suppress a grin.

"You know it's funny," he replied in between bursts of laughter.

She gave in and let out a chuckle, "It's still not right."

"But it is funny."

"Not really. She is beginning to see into our world. That is not supposed to happen."

"Look," he shifted back into a serious demeanor, "We can take that up with Darrus later. The important thing to note is she did feel whatever that was last night. Unfortunately, I could not tell if she knew from which direction it came."

"I'm surprised you were able to read her through your antics." Gabriella glared at him.

"Alright, killjoy. Did you sense anything I missed?"

She let out a frustrated sigh. "No."

"Then let's keep looking."

They traveled in silence down the street past a cluster of newspaper vending machines. D'Nas grabbed the back strap of Gabriella's holster and pulled her to one of the headlines catching his eye.

"Hooka Killer's Whereabouts Remain Hazy," D'Nas read aloud, staring blankly. Gabriella waited on him to speak.

"We missed something," he said.

"What? With the outcast killings?"

"Yes. Strange how a Shade and an Illumin disappear, and then only a few days later someone unlocks a relic."

She looked at the headline with him. A picture showing the nightclub encased by police tape was embedded in the text of the article.

"We need to go back there," D'Nas said, tapping his fingers against the front of his badge on his belt. "We need to catch the 'Hooka Killer' at some point anyway," he remarked.

"I don't think this relic is some trinket forged by the Ravens." She added, "I haven't felt such power since Cortés first set foot on the New World." Gabriella looked off at the horizon and shuddered. "I never wanted to feel that again. Those were dark times, and this morning felt as if they had returned."

Half an hour later, they were both standing in the main room of the Hookah Palooka. Outside, police tape still warded off the general public. They were both familiar with the crime scene, as their department had scrutinized and cleaned up the entire place.

D'Nas knelt down over an empty spot on the floor where only a few days ago the mangled body of a human female lay. He remembered looking into the empty sockets where her eyes had been burned out. He had known it wasn't Jailyn, but he had to let the police think it was to keep them away from the supernatural aspects of the case.

Whoever had been responsible had scrubbed the place fairly well. There were probably only a few Shades in the city that would have gone through the trouble of cleaning up these murders. Previously, he thought Jailyn's and Nathan's self-exile had taken them off the radar of both the Illumin and the Shades, so it had seemed unlikely that they would have been attacked.

For all he knew, Jailyn herself could have set this up as a way to escape with her daughter. Clara hadn't been seen since the murders, and Nathan would certainly have followed Jailyn until the very end. Only now, with the loose relic, did the case warrant another investigation.

"Where did you go, Jailyn?" he asked of the empty air.

"What?" Gabriella said from across the room.

He shook his head, reentering the present. "Nothing, just trying to remember what had happened. We glossed over this so fast; I can barely remember working it."

"She abandoned us. We were just returning a favor," Gabriella reminded him.

"Those bodies," he paused as images of the mutilated flesh raced in his mind, "Who did they belong to? Did we ever finish cross-referencing them with the missing persons reports?"

"Yes, but no missing persons matched the bodies--at least none thus far. You know how that can go."

He stood up and paced around the room, listening to his rubber soles thud against the hardwood flooring. Forging human bodies wasn't unprecedented. Jailyn could easily have created the deception; it fit her profile and her motives. He regretted their sloppy investigation.

He walked over to the small stage in the corner and sat down on the stool in its center. A remnant shadow of a powerful presence lingered in the corner. He was sure he hadn't felt that last time. He closed his eyes, trying to fixate on it. A stream of impressions slowly entered his mind.

Watching. Remorse. Helplessness. Relief. New life.

The room swirled as if he were in a daze. He blinked a few times to shake off the vision to no avail. He began to catch fleeting glimpses of a Shade interrogating a hostage in the center of the room. A black shadow stood over a terrified Illumin, ready to strike.

Without thinking, he stood up to intervene, but darkness rose out of the floor and swallowed him. He looked around as the room fell away. He screamed, only to hear the echo of his own voice. Wings spread from his back, blue light shimmering futilely against the darkness. A pulse of fear gripped him, holding him in place. The Shade, now towering over him with menacing red eyes, reached down at him with a clawed hand. He yelled a battle cry and swung his fist at his enemy.

A lithe hand grabbed his wrist, pushing it outwards and twisting him completely around. Vertigo settled inside him. He felt himself slam hard onto his back, crying out with open eyes. Multicolored ribbons dipped from a high ceiling. Gabriella stood over him with her boot pressing into his throat. Her wings were fully extended and shining so brilliantly it hurt his eyes.

"What was that?" she asked.

"Residual memories," he gasped.

"From whom?" She kept her boot on his throat.

He closed his eyes, picking up the memories again. "Not sure. I saw a Shade torturing an Illumin, Jailyn, I believe. I wanted to stop him from killing her, but felt so helpless. He seemed familiar..." he trailed off, placing the Shade in his mind. His heart sank. "Zyne."

"What?"

"Zyne took Jailyn here. He concealed it fairly well, but these were probably the memories of one of his pets."

Gabriella let go of his wrist and removed her foot while

offering him her other hand. He took it and she pulled him to his feet. His wings ached slightly from breaking his fall. A small crater remained from where she had thrown him into the floor.

"Let's go," she said.

He stood for a few more minutes to fully regain his bearings before they both headed back to their unmarked police cruiser and sped away toward Mandrake tower.

They stepped off the elevator into the small lobby to wait for Arthur Zyne. The arrogance with which he gave himself a first name as a way to blend in unnerved D'Nas. Most Shades hid from the public eye, but not 'Arthur Zyne.' He happily broadcasted his exploits to the entire world.

Gabriella took a seat on one of the leather couches and picked through the magazines neatly laid out on the coffee table. D'Nas leaned against the wall next to her, staring at the elevator as if it would hasten Zyne's arrival. Eighteen minutes passed before the elevator finally opened and Zyne greeted them with a smiling face.

"What a surprise," Zyne said, marching over to D'Nas and offering his hand. "I don't regularly have such high-profile visitors. What can I help you two officers with?"

D'Nas just looked at his extended hand for a moment. The last thing he wanted to do was jump through Zyne's hoops.

"This entire floor is empty and you still want to go through the business formalities?" D'Nas asked incredulously.

"Sure, why not? If I have to deal with your accusations, at least let me set my own terms."

"Like the terms you offered Jailyn?" Gabriella interjected with an opened magazine lying across her lap.

"Ah, I see. Well, I know this won't be easy, so please have a seat. Coffee?" Zyne kept up his business persona.

D'Nas shook his head and took a seat next to Gabriella. Zyne sat across from them and placed the tablet PC he carried on the coffee table. His eyes were menacing black coals.

"I gather no one slept well last night," Zyne offered, getting straight to the point. D'Nas appreciated the directness.

"What's your angle this time, Zyne?" D'Nas asked, matching Zyne's challenging stare.

"Why do these things always have to be about me? You leave the Raven family with free reign to use unlimited power against us and then wonder when a relic goes off without your prior knowledge."

"We have a pact. Neither Shade nor Illumin will unlock any relic," Gabriella jumped in. "If anyone in this city is going to cross that line first, it is going to be you."

"That may be true from your perspective, Gabriella, but I only represent a modest percent of our total presence."

"I never knew your kind could be so 'modest' in its own self-assessment," D'Nas said. "Where is this relic?"

"Again with the assumptions." Zyne's anger rose and the light in the room dimmed slightly. "The truth is I don't have it. If I did, you both would probably be dead right now."

D'Nas felt Zyne's smile morph into a challenge. The three of them remained silent for a few moments before

D'Nas finally spoke.

"You're lying," D'Nas declared. "We both saw your handiwork with Jailyn's and Nathan's murders. Jailyn left me a long time ago, but I'm sure she had enough fight left in her to stop you."

"Oh really?" Zyne raised his eyebrows at her. "How do you figure that?"

D'Nas said matter-of-factly, "The human mind is incapable of processing supernaturally traumatic events. I missed them during the original investigation, but today I picked up faint remnants of whichever pet you had accompanying you that day. Through her, I felt more than just your power at work."

"First of all," Zyne retorted, smile fading. "*She* isn't my 'pet'. She is a part of me which explains why you felt more at work than me. Secondly, you didn't seem to care about Jailyn at all until today. That was personal business I had to settle. You both were right to leave the investigation where you did."

Zyne seemed different to D'Nas. Perhaps he really did believe his pet was more than a slave. Regardless, it didn't matter. They needed to know about Jailyn. He looked at Gabriella.

Gabriella frowned, "Then you do hold Jailyn."

"To be specific, yes, but that is unrelated to the real reason you are here, isn't it?"

"Actually, that completely relates to the reason we are here," Gabriella countered. "We know you couldn't have taken both Nathan and Jailyn alone. So, we find it extremely coincidental that the outcasts, both of whom have prior histories with you, go missing right before a relic awakens."

"So, even after watching the rise and fall of human civilization you still don't believe in coincidence, Gabriella?" Zyne asked. "Everything must happen for a purpose; except, in this case, you don't know what that purpose is. At least you have your precious Faith to rely on.

D'Nas felt Gabriella flare up from the venom in Zyne's words. He reached out and rested his hand on her shoulder to calm her down. She remained fixated on Zyne, holding herself back from attacking him.

Zyne stared at her. "Perhaps if you two weren't so engrossed in your own mission against me, you could see further into the world we all share." Zyne picked up his tablet PC and tapped away on its screen. "I am a very busy man, so if you will please exit quietly, we all can get back to work."

D'Nas looked at Gabriella, who silently pleaded that they continue their questions. D'Nas shook his head, sensing they would get no more information out of him. The two detectives stood up, followed by Zyne, who again offered his hand. This time D'Nas forcefully grabbed it and shook.

"Now I am really curious. If you don't know who holds the relic, who does, and what kind of havoc are they going to cause?" Zyne said, giving them one last smile.

D'Nas led Gabriella back to the elevator before she could release her building anger.

Once the doors shut she let out a loud exhale, "Thanks."

"I should have let you learn your own lesson and attack him."

They both laughed, trying to shake off the residual power

from Zyne still clinging to them.

Zyne scrolled through some news feeds on his tablet PC, grateful to be alone for a minute. D'Nas and Gabriella were absolutely exhausting. Plus, they arrived right when he should be hearing a direct report about the relic everyone was scrambling after.

He had deployed several of his agents throughout the city to find out about it. He was certain they would discover the source before any of the Illumin picked up on the trail. Shades have always had an innate attraction to the subtleties of raw power.

Finally, his phone rang and Clara's shining face and name appeared on the caller ID.

"Hey babe," he answered.

"You aren't going to believe this," she replied, pausing for a dramatic effect. "Zombies."

"Ok Ripley, please, tell me more."

"I don't have a clear picture of the situation, but there are genuine, re-animated corpses walking around out here."

"Really. Have you found the relic?" He shifted forward in his seat.

"Not yet. I feel its power in short bursts that quickly fade away. It is almost as if it is intentionally trying to hide from me. However, I am fairly sure that it is following some kid out here. Everywhere he goes, the zombies appear."

Zyne thought for a moment. "Head back here immediately while I gather a team to assist you."

"What do I need a team for?" she asked skeptically. "I am sure I can find the relic before noon."

"Well, our good friend D'Nas dropped by today asking about my part in this, and I told him that we have everything under control. I worry he may interfere, and you will need backup in that case."

"Shouldn't he still be looking for my parents?"

Zyne felt her unresolved issues bleed through the phone. "No, he really just wants to look for ways to fight me. Apparently it's a crime these days to run a legitimate corporation."

"I will see you soon then. Bye."

"Bye."

He ended the call and stared down at his phone for a second. *Where else would D'Nas go if he were tracking my footprint in this mess?* he thought.

Searching through his contact list, he found Daniel Raven and called him.

"Hello?" Daniel answered, obviously preoccupied with a few customers in his shop.

"Real quick, Daniel. You will probably have a special customer drop by today."

"I realize the attachment to the ring, but I can only offer five hundred for it," a slight pause followed his strange answer before he came back on the phone. "Sorry about that Arthur, you know how this business is. Anyway, a visitor?"

"Yes," Zyne said without levity. "D'Nas is coming out there and I thought you would want to know."

"I do. I'll make sure to take good care of him..." Daniel's voice trailed off. "Ok, five hundred then? Please see my associate at the register and he will take care of you." Zyne heard Daniel adjust the phone, accompanied by scuffling shoes on cheap tile. "Ok Arthur, I'm back. Anything else?"

"Wheelbarrow Creek is probably lost," Zyne responded. "Some kid has unlocked a relic that is raising the dead. I intend to send out a kill team for him."

"Murdering an innocent kid?" Daniel asked in a hushed voice.

"Power such as this must be contained, no matter the cost."

"I understand," Daniel said before ending the call.

Zyne had to get a handle on the zombie situation before it exploded out of control. Any relic with enough power to raise humans from the dead could threaten him. It didn't matter who started this--he must die, innocent or not. Power just corrupts the innocent more quickly, though he only wanted to justify his actions for Daniel's sake.

Fortunately, Clara had grown into an extremely capable killer.

D'Nas parked the cruiser in front of Dark Raven Pawn. The shop was only a few miles from downtown, tucked away on the side of a road that wound through an area of thick pine trees. Only a few other businesses dotted the roadside, mostly specialty shops catering to nomadic clientele traveling home from work.

The detectives' boots crunched through the gravel parking lot on their way inside. A tight corridor of shelves displaying various trinkets focused their sight on the counter that occupied the middle of the shop. There a young couple haggled with Daniel Raven over the price of a home stereo receiver. A few other customers milled around trying to find hidden bargains.

Gabriella walked over to a wall adorned with several guitars. She ran her fingers over a few of them before taking down a bass guitar with a solid black body trimmed in silver. She whipped the strap over her shoulder and began to thump at the strings. D'Nas smiled at her, imagining the sound the guitar would make through an amp.

"Just like riding a bike," she said.

"And only slightly less boring than a harp," he jabbed.

"Can I help you folks?" Daniel inquired, walking toward them.

"Yes," Gabriella looked at him. "This bass is labeled 'Ibanez,' but it certainly does not play like any Ibanez I have ever touched."

"Custom model," he replied with a wink. "If you were ever caught in a fiddle contest with the devil, this would be the instrument you would want to have."

"Well, since you brought up the devil," D'Nas segued, "Can you tell us what your family was doing last night?"

Daniel looked behind him. One of his employees was attending the younger couple with their receiver purchase.

"I assure you, no one will hear what we are really talking about," D'Nas said as he sent out an invisible pulse to insulate their conversation. Gabriella kept her fingers lightly dancing over the bass.

"You both should know I don't keep up with any of that these days. I just run this shop and try to stay out of everyone's way."

"Which explains why this bass has such a powerful resonance," Gabriella said. "I hope you aren't implying you directly aid your friend now."

"How could I even hide that from you?" Daniel said defensively.

"We need to know what relic is out there and its purpose." D'Nas sparked up a blue tint in his eyes for effect. "We came to you as colleagues, but we can always treat you like a suspect, if that is the game you wish to play."

Daniel quickly glanced around the room again before responding, "I checked the archives last night and found no record of it."

Gabriella rolled her eyes at him and continued playing in silence.

"I did, however, see its effects firsthand," Daniel offered. "I was here with Zyne when it went off. The entire room spun from its mystic power, with Zyne lying helpless at the center. This alone sent me searching through the archives. Whatever it is, it's rogue and off the books. I can only surmise that another Raven must have planted it and erased its existence."

"You have no idea as to its purpose?"

"You can sense that I don't." Daniel scowled at him. "And before you ask, Zyne has nothing to do with it. He was as surprised as I was last night. I think this rogue element hurt his pride more than anything else."

D'Nas stared into his eyes and felt the truth in his statements. He nodded to Gabriella, who reluctantly put the guitar back on the wall. "Thanks for your help. I don't know why you like playing with fire, but when you get burned, don't call us."

The detectives walked back outside, giving a passing wave to the employee behind the counter. The sun greeted them with its hot rays as they headed back to the cruiser. Opening the car door, D'Nas saw Daniel exit the shop and head over to them.

"You have something else?" Gabriella asked.

"Yes. Zyne may not be the cause, but Clara was able to track down the real source this morning. Turns out some kid is running around Wheelbarrow Creek raising the dead with this relic in his pocket. I'd guess she was drawn to its power, as most Shades are."

D'Nas recoiled at the mention of Clara. He had completely forgotten about her. What did she have to do with Zyne?

"Strange," Gabriella said.

"I believe you are the ones playing with fire here, D'Nas. All of you forgot about Clara and let her grow up under the ideals of her parents. None of us here agreed with them, but by exiling Clara along with them, we effectively sparked a new flame that Zyne thinks he has control over. I wonder how that will pan out for you." Daniel snapped back around and returned to his shop.

A chill settled over D'Nas from Daniel's words. "We should never have left Mandrake tower," he stated.

They both hopped in the cruiser and sped back into town.

Daniel wiped the thin layer of dust off his glasses and returned to his shop. Signaling for Ryan to keep tending to the customers, he headed straight for his office in the back. The door shut with a firm click, and he pressed his forehead against it, wishing he didn't have to make this next phone call. But, it had to be done.

Creaking plastic sounded as he sat back in his old office chair behind his desk. He pulled out his phone and dialed the only person in the Raven family he trusted anymore.

"Hello?" Hunter answered after what seemed like a long set of rings.

"Hunter, it's Daniel."

"I can see that. Caller ID."

Daniel laughed, hoping that was a joke. "Don't get smart with me, kid."

Hunter made his tone more serious. "I assume you don't want me to tell Dad about this call?"

"Correct." Daniel got up to peek through his blinds into the shop to ensure Ryan was still doing his job.

"So, interesting days at the shop then?"

"Yes, now listen, Hunter." He eased back into his chair, placing his glasses on his desk. "I need your help, and, as always, keep this between us. There is a boy in Wheelbarrow Creek that I need you to rescue. He goes to school with your cousin, Cindy."

"Rescue from what?"

Daniel gently massaged the bridge of his nose. "I hid a Relic with him and I think he has unknowingly activated it. Now Zyne and the Illumin are out trying to find him. Just now two Illumin were here asking me about it. I pointed them back at Zyne to give you enough time to finish this. This is a family matter that I would handle myself if I wasn't already between Zyne and the Illumin."

Silence hung in the air.

"Okay," Hunter finally replied. "I assume I can drop by to properly equip myself."

Daniel smiled with relief. "I have just what you need."

"See you soon, Uncle."

An hour later, D'Nas and Gabriella sat in their cruiser a few blocks down from Mandrake tower, watching its doors. The air conditioner kept the summer heat from penetrating their improvised stake out. After reporting the information Daniel gave them to the rest of the department, a few agents had been deployed to Wheelbarrow Creek.

D'Nas tapped his fingers against the steering wheel, ready to leap out and attack Zyne's fortress at any moment. Zyne probably wouldn't have let them just walk in again, so they were forced to wait on his move.

"Where did we go wrong with Jailyn?" he asked, after his mind switched back to thoughts of Clara.

"You mean where did she go wrong? *She* left *us*. Not the other way around."

"Did she? Or did Nathan corrupt her?"

"Jailyn made her choice and suffered as a result. I have no remorse over that," Gabriella said, running her fingers along the inside of the door window.

"Clara is the real victim, wrapped up in this struggle, Zyne her only guide. I hope it wasn't her memories I felt. Though it would be just like Zyne to force her to watch him desecrate her mother."

Gabriella sighed. "Once again, Jailyn made her decision and it destroyed her family. We aren't here to live normal lives. We have a mission to watch and protect the mortals under our wings."

They both looked toward Mandrake tower. They felt five shades leave from the front and enter a van.

"That's our target," D'Nas said, pulling the cruiser onto the road in pursuit. He made sure not to drive in front of the tower for fear that Zyne may sense them.

D'Nas wound through the city blocks, careful to keep the van just out of sight. The shades it contained tried to reel in their bloodlust, but enough of it leaked out that D'Nas had an easy trail to follow. After a few minutes, the van reached the edge of downtown and took a road leading in the direction of Wheelbarrow Creek.

With the traffic around them spreading out, D'Nas clicked the cruiser's hidden police lights on and sped up to catch the van. It slowly pulled over into an alley. D'Nas parked on the street, blocking their exit. He looked over at Gabriella and offered all the visible strength he could muster.

"You ready?"

"Always." Blue sparks shot from her eyes as she

slammed a magazine into her sidearm.

The alley hid the sun's rays, casting everything in shadow. They left the cruiser and approached the van with their guns pointed straight ahead. The driver's door opened and out stepped a woman with frazzled, auburn hair and brilliant, blue eyes. D'Nas recoiled, unable to push away the vision of Jailyn in his head.

"Is there a problem, officers?" the woman asked.

Gabriella prompted D'Nas to respond.

"Clara," he finally managed.

"Yes." Clara waited with her arms crossed.

Gabriella darted her eyes between them before interrupting the silence. "We have reason to believe you are involved in an attack against the humans in Wheelbarrow Creek. Unless you can prove otherwise, we will be forced to confiscate your vehicle."

"How little you truly know," Clara responded coldly. "If you really cared about what is going on out in Wheelbarrow Creek, you would let us handle it."

"That is not how this works," D'Nas finally conjured up enough voice to speak.

"Quick to escalate? One last time." Clara added strength to her own voice. "Let this one go. If I don't finish this, we will all be overrun."

"What did he do to you?" D'Nas asked rhetorically.

Clara's eyes dilated until their entire sockets were black. "He set me free."

Clara jumped up and somersaulted onto the top of the van, leaving an indention. The back doors exploded outward, giving D'Nas and Gabriella a split second to get out of the way. Four large shades jumped outside, brandishing sledge hammers. Black tendrils grew out from their arms and wrapped around their weapons.

Blue light radiated from the detectives as they unfurled their wings. The Shades lunged at them with swinging hammers. The detectives leaped into the air and hovered above them. They trained their guns on the targets below and fired off several rounds.

Streams of silver light rained down from the gun barrels onto the Shades. They growled in pain as black liquid spilled out of them into the alley. Three hammers shot into the air. D'Nas twisted out of the way, careful not to touch the tendrils that drew the hammers back down. He snapped his attention to the other Shade who darted up the side of a building, quickly reaching his height.

The Shade launched out at D'Nas and caught him mid-air. The hammer slammed against his chest just before the Shade wrapped him up. They both crashed into the building on the other side of the alley. The Shade anchored them to the wall with his sticky tendrils and drew his hammer back, preparing to smash it against D'Nas's head. D'Nas gave him a swift head butt and pushed out with his arms.

He wriggled out just enough room to slide down as the hammer collided with the brick inches above his head. He struggled to put his gun to the Shade's chest and fire. A silver lance tore through the Shade and he went limp. D'Nas pushed off the wall with his feet, sending the Shade plummeting to the ground. He searched for Gabriella.

A Shade lay still at her feet with his tendrils still wrapped around her torso. She wielded a stolen hammer against the other two that dueled with her. Her gun lay several paces behind her. Lining up a kill shot, D'Nas remembered Clara.

As if summoned, Clara reached from behind him and grabbed his wrist. Pain riveted down his arm and he reflexively let go of his weapon. His gun clanked against the pavement. She turned him around to face her as they both hovered above the alley. Clara smiled as D'Nas's own fear reflected back at him from her dark eyes.

"Forget the relic," she whispered. "It has nothing to do with you. We only intend to stop its power from spreading. What do you think would happen if anyone actually tried to use it?"

All D'Nas could see was Jailyn speaking to him, and he unsuccessfully tried to shake the image from his mind. "Zyne would enslave this entire city if he could. Just as he has done with you."

D'Nas shifted his weight and used his free hand to grab her throat. She laughed at him, letting go of his wrist. Gabriella kept fighting below them, slowly turning things in her favor.

"At least Zyne believes in honor," Clara said, struggling against his grip. "He isn't the one who forges relics against the terms of the pact."

"Obviously there has been a mistake. No human blood needs to be shed while we investigate the matter."

"Yes, there has been a mistake."

Clara stuck her hand into her pocket. D'Nas slammed her into the wall, watching pain flicker through her face. She dropped the trinket she had pulled out. The sharp resonance of metal hitting concrete told D'Nas exactly what it was.

He looked at the ground. Jailyn's coin rotated around as it settled on the pavement.

Clara spread both her hands and the coin flew into the air like a white rocket. She reached out and snatched it mid-air as it formed into the familiar dagger D'Nas had not seen in years. She stabbed at his chest, catching him off guard.

A searing pain forced him to let go and fly backward. Clara stayed with him and forced the blade further into him, clearly showing her enjoyment at his pain. She twisted it around and pulled it back out. The edges of his vision blurred as he lost feeling in his wings. He tumbled down and smashed into the concrete, next to the Shade he had dropped earlier.

Gabriella danced around the last Shade left standing. Two lay at her feet. D'Nas could see she had mostly freed herself from the tendrils that remained wrapped around her. Clara jumped down on top of him, blocking his view of Gabriella. She pointed the dagger directly at his throat. The glow from it radiated a heat that warmed his skin.

"You shouldn't be able to do that," he mustered.

"That's your flaw, arbitrarily casting the world through your own narrow lens. I have been set free," she said, the glowing dagger combating the dark cloud that surrounded her.

A shot rang out, and D'Nas and Clara turned to see Gabriella kneeling down, holding her gun out. The last Shade stumbled against the wall before toppling over.

"Sleep through that," Gabriella said while spitting at her fallen enemy. She fought against the remaining few tendrils snaking around her.

"Have fun catching up," Clara said to D'Nas before standing up.

She jumped in the air and spread out a pair of black wings that cast even darker shadows in the alley. With a swift stroke, she flew toward Wheelbarrow Creek. He clutched at his chest, grateful Clara left him. The wound had already closed, but the dagger's power still lingered. Never before had one of the Raven weapons been used against him. At least now he could empathize with his enemies.

He pulled himself to his feet, holding onto the wall for support. Gabriella rushed to his side.

"I'm ok...just need a minute," he assured her.

"I think a minute is all we have," she replied.

D'Nas felt his strength return as the Shades around them began to move. He motioned to Gabriella and they worked quickly to bind them. Thin filaments of light stretched out from their hands and surrounded each of the Shades. That would hold them for a few more hours anyway.

"We need to stop Clara before she kills that kid."

"No," he said through gritted teeth. "Zyne has overstepped his bounds. Enough with all this sneaking around. Time to take the fight directly to him."

"What? Earlier you held me back from doing just that." She locked eyes with him, trying to calm his building rage. "Clara is going to kill an innocent kid. We can deal with Zyne afterward."

"Let him die; if we don't stop Zyne now, it won't matter. He took Jailyn and now wields Clara like a knife. He won't stop until he controls this entire city."

He snatched his proffered gun from Gabriella's hand

and holstered it. Her eyes narrowed.

"We are here to protect these people, not the city," she said forcefully. "Let Zyne have the city. If you don't see the value in that one kid, then perhaps you only see things the way Zyne does."

His fists shook until he turned around and slammed them against the wall. Brick pulverized into dust before him. Flexing arm muscles propped him against the wall while his head hung down.

"I could not stop Jailyn, but I can protect her daughter from Zyne's manipulative touch," he yelled at the ground. With that, he took off running back to Mandrake tower, leaving Gabriella alone.

A flash of light hid his wings as he reached the end of the alley. Only a few miles of sidewalk and light pedestrian traffic separated him from Zyne. He ran back toward downtown. His feet moved only slightly faster than a human's, as he didn't want to attract too much unwanted attention.

It felt as if it took forever to get through all the crosswalks, but he eventually found himself staring up at the reflective sides of Mandrake tower again. D'Nas caught his breath and looked around at the rest of Shreveport's skyline. The sun had finally climbed high into the sky, blessing him with its hot touch. The humidity condensed around his skin, giving the impression he was actually sweating.

He knelt down and concentrated on channeling the Faith. It swirled around him and focused his intentions above. Blue light poured out of his eyes and surrounded him. A few onlookers stood frozen at the sight of him. His large wings spread into the material world.

He ignored the shocked expressions of the pedestrians around him. The cold steel of his gun reassured him of his plan and eased all doubt. He looked up at the window of Zyne's office at the top of the tower.

"For Jailyn," he whispered before exploding upward.

The ground fled from him as his blinding reflection followed him up the glass side of the tower. He shot just past Zyne's window and looped back around to bring him parallel with the ground. Bursting through the window in a rush of light, he filled Zyne's office with melted shards of glass. Zyne turned from his desk as D'Nas rammed into him. D'Nas carried him across the room and slammed him into the wall with his full force.

"Your reign is over, Zyne!" Fury burned through his words. He pulled the trigger of his gun, and a stab of light barreled through Zyne's chest.

Zyne went limp before him, crumbling to ash. D'Nas looked around, stunned.

"You are a fool, D'Nas," Zyne said, appearing from a black cloud in front of the shattered window. "I warned you to leave this alone, but you persisted."

D'Nas brought up his gun, but a whip of tendrils flew out from Zyne's arms and wrapped him up, restraining him from pulling the trigger. D'Nas struggled against them, using his wings to fly backward. Zyne held him in place like an energized kite.

D'Nas dropped his gun after a surge of pain forced his hand open. He flapped his wings, trying to reach the window. Zyne kept the pressure against him and drew him back. The tendrils shortened until D'Nas found himself face to face with Zyne.

"Jailyn was not your fault," Zyne said. "She abandoned you. Let it go."

"As long as your kind inhabit this city, I will never let it go."

"Is that really what you want? I brought down Jailyn. Do you really think you can defeat me here in my own fortress?"

"I am compelled to protect this city at any cost." Light flared out from D'Nas's eyes.

He twisted back and kicked Zyne squarely in the jaw. For a brief second, the tendrils eased their grip and D'Nas wrestled his left hand free. He jumped toward Zyne and landed another blow to his head. Zyne stumbled back and waved his tendrils around.

D'Nas dodged them, trying to step inside for another hit. A jerk to his right side threw him off balance. Zyne's hair grew into long spikes as he knelt. After D'Nas recovered his footing, Zyne launched up at him head first.

Zyne's spikes ate into the same spot Clara had attacked earlier. D'Nas shuddered at the renewed pain. He felt himself weaken for a second that Zyne used to wrap up his legs. D'Nas's feet moved out from under him, and he found himself face first on the floor. He pushed up with his free hand, trying to grab the air with his wings.

"I think we are done here," Zyne said mockingly before kicking the back of his head.

"I'm sorry, Jailyn," D'Nas managed.

"You can tell her that yourself. After Clara returns, you will be joining her mother in her own personal cell." He lifted up D'Nas's head so he could see the city's skyline.

Wind kissed his face with regret. "Right here in the heart of beautiful Shreveport."

D'Nas's senses dimmed until all he was left with was the mild laughter of Zyne as he stood over him.

D'Nas opened his eyes to see Zyne working at his desk across the room. Dull pain pulsated through his body. He sat on the floor with no bindings holding him down. He moved to stand up, but his muscles wouldn't comply.

"I would wait a few more hours before you try that," Zyne said, never looking up from his computer.

D'Nas leaned his head back against the wall, trying to get his bearings. Zyne's eclectic taste in art filled the room. Of course, the real prize was the bookcase that covered an entire wall. Who knew what knowledge hid among its volumes?

Condensation dripped down his face. The sun waned low in the sky, spilling its final drops of summer for the day. Zyne looked over at him, smiling at his acknowledgment of the heat that permeated the room.

"You know, I would have turned on the AC, but..." Zyne turned around in his chair and gestured across from him at the missing glass before raising his voice. "I don't think it would do any good."

D'Nas scowled at him as the click of a door sounded to

the side of him.

"And here we are," Zyne said, walking over to his guest. After pausing to see who had entered, he continued, "Well, this is an exciting development."

D'Nas looked to his left and saw Clara walk in, caked with dirt. She dragged a limp body behind her and laid it at Zyne's feet. The body moved slightly, and D'Nas saw familiar wavy, brown hair. He looked more closely and his heart sank as he noticed the gauged earrings. Gabriella!

"The relic was tied directly into the guy's flesh. Once he died, it disintegrated," Clara reported.

"Those Ravens, they really don't want us to have anything, do they?" Zyne asked, winking at D'nas. "Now, what do we do with these two detectives?"

D'Nas cursed himself. If Zyne really didn't gain control over the relic, all of this was for nothing. Helplessness etched along the back of his mind. Zyne would lock him and Gabriella away until the end of time.

Gabriella struggled to her hands and knees. Zyne walked over and pulled one of his office chairs over and helped her into it. She glared at him with pain in her eyes.

"Can't we just call this a truce and go our separate ways?" Gabriella asked weakly.

"No," Zyne spoke forcefully. "All I asked was for the both of you to leave this alone. You can't keep this city under control without me. I could have stopped this whole crazy Wheelbarrow Creek thing much earlier, but you had to interject your own ideals into my plan. You probably wouldn't have even been able to find the relic if you had not been tracking Clara."

"What is going on out there, Gabriella?" D'Nas looked at her for strength.

"Death," she replied.

D'Nas bumped the back of his head against the wall in frustration. Zyne was always thinking several moves ahead of them.

"What else do you want with us?" D'Nas asked Zyne.

"An example. The rest of the Illumin need to know how valuable my services are."

"I thought Clara was the only example you needed--manipulating an innocent life and binding it to your will," D'Nas said, looking into Clara's dark eyes.

"I have made my own choice, D'Nas," Clara shot back. "I see the world for how it works, not as you think it should work. Zyne and I have a shared vision."

"Well, I can see you two still have some unresolved issues," Zyne interjected while walking to the door. "I'll just go and check on a few other areas of the company that need my attention."

After he left the room, Clara remained still a few more moments, looking down at the battered detectives. D'Nas saw the shadow of her mother cast on her visage. Somewhere in the cold exterior was a reasonable being. A revelation sparked inside his mind.

"Have you thought about why your mother exiled herself with your father?" D'Nas asked.

"I no longer think about my parents at all. They left me defenseless and, as a result, here I am." She waved her arms around. "Locked in battle."

The resemblance to her mother grew stronger.

"Your mother and I protected this city together for years." He watched the genuine interest wash over her face. "We had captured your father and were holding him for intel purposes. Your mother handled most of the interrogation, but instead of coming out with answers, she came out with a new perspective. Your father's desire to become human had infected her as well."

Out of the corner of his eye, he saw Gabriella begin to glow. He kept Clara focused on him.

"Clara, your very birth was a miracle. All of us were astonished, to say the least. Your parents called you their 'love child,' saying it was their love for one another that made your existence possible. That was why they tried to raise you as human, because you represented much more to them than their own mystical backgrounds. Everything you have learned until Zyne forced his leash around your neck was at the hands of mortal humans."

Gabriella shuffled in her chair, attracting Clara's attention.

"You are still too weak to take me," Clara warned. She fished out her mother's coin and twirled it in her hand.

D'Nas continued, "Your parents saw how important humanity is to us. Humanity is the reason we fight, the reason we exist. Your parents wanted you to empathize with these mortals so you could figure out your own path. The only thing they couldn't see was Zyne's retribution."

A tear fell from Clara's eye, quietly splashing onto the carpet. D'Nas forced himself to his feet, hoping he wouldn't fall back down. His limbs felt painfully stiff. Chaotic emotion poured from Clara, signaling she was breaking. Gabriella stood up and worked herself around the room, crunching glass under her boots.

Clara's eyes reflected sharp regret, gripping her mother's coin tightly in her hand. D'Nas kept his eyes locked with hers, trying to steady the emotional storm inside her. He instantly remembered the feeling from the Hookah Palooka.

Gabriella came up to his side and offered herself as a crutch. D'Nas let her support most of his weight, as he felt too weak to stand much longer.

"Just go," Clara whispered. "You don't matter to Zyne anyway."

"Thank you," D'Nas replied gratefully as he and Gabriella backed away toward the shattered windows.

Gabriella's wings sprouted from her back as the two of them moved closer to the ledge. A feeling of dread loomed over D'Nas. Clara just stood there, crying softly.

"How touching." Zyne's voice carried through the air.

Gabriella jumped out and flew over the city with the sun setting in the distance. D'Nas looked back and watched Zyne tenderly embrace Clara.

Daniel finished cleaning his shop after having sent his employees home a few hours ago. Alone with the stale air, he disconnected his mind from everything that had happened over the past few days. It wasn't his choice to immerse himself with the secrets of the city--he was born into it. By his account, he should at least be able to choose his own level of involvement, and, at times like these, he connected with the philosophy of blissful ignorance.

He took one final pass through the shop before bringing out the familiar chess board and setting it up on an empty card table. He carefully ordered the lifeless chess pieces onto their designated squares and stared at the miniature battlefield. Daniel marveled at how each piece followed a simple set of rules, but, together, they formed an incredibly nuanced system. One piece could make an errant move and cost its side the entire game.

An intense wave of fear charged through him, sending his skin crawling. The sudden ring of the door jolted him around to meet the smiling face of his oldest friend walking around the corner.

"Good to see you too, Daniel," Zyne spoke quietly.

"Some week, huh?" Daniel said, trying to keep his heart from speeding away from him.

"You know how women are," Zyne smirked.

Zyne took the empty seat across from him, and they began their scheduled game. After mulling through their typical conversation topics, Zyne finally arrived at the thought weighing Daniel down.

"At least no one else secured that relic. I would hate to fight against one of my own brethren at this point," Zyne remarked.

Daniel looked up at him, trying unsuccessfully to mask his reservations. Zyne stared into him, conjuring a swarm of terror inside his head. Daniel adjusted the glasses on his face and quickly made a move on the board. The back of his throat went dry.

"There are so many other pieces moving here, Zyne, that it is easy to get lost in what is really going on."

Zyne countered his chess move and crossed his arms.

"We have both been tricked," Daniel said through a blank stare. "Another party has entered our arena and hidden the relic from you. The boy's death was only a small distraction to mask the relic's movement. It is also painfully obvious that this other party has help. And not from the Illumin."

Zyne turned back to their game, and they went a few more turns in silence.

"Has it really come to this?" Zyne asked rhetorically. "It must have been a convincing trick to fool Clara. How long will this game last?"

"Until we are all left bleeding out in the streets."

Zyne laughed at the comment. "And I thought I kept ahead of the curve. Check."

Daniel moved his king back to safety. "Clara, like all of you, can be manipulated by our hands and our blood."

"Then this game is not over."

"I hope you treated D'Nas well."

"He has Clara to thank for his release," Zyne replied. "Women never know what they want."

Daniel smiled, unsure whether or not Zyne even understood what he was saying. For a moment, he thought he saw doubt in Zyne's eye.

"Checkmate," Zyne declared triumphantly.

Daniel congratulated him for the small victory, knowing the relic had stirred more arcane power than Zyne realized.

Zombie Delivery Services

by
B. L. White

Matthew Gillard was a quiet boy, born 18 years, 11 months and 23 days before the real zombie apocalypse.

The only preparation he had for any of this was a fake zombie apocalypse, found in a computer game named *D3ad Living*. It was a cooperative affair, meaning that three friends could connect to the game over the internet. They fought as a unit, which threw hordes of pixilated zombies their way.

Mild-mannered boys and a few girls played as the characters Jax Ultim, Sophie Stevens and Sergeant Grizzled: three survivors in a world gone dead, with the living dead. Such was the fate of any who bought *D3ad Living*.

Night and day, Matt made the living dead, dead again, using a variety of methods: shotguns, rifles, axes, pitchforks. Any and every tool found in the game was used in saving the virtual world alongside his friends, George and Trish.

The three of them conquered the virtual zombie outbreak from the safety of their bedrooms found, in the case of Trish and Matt, in their parents' houses. They lived in Nowhereville, USA, or Wheelbarrow Creek, as the locals called it. Truth be told, no map-maker ever found the small town. A little dot usually appeared near Natchitoches, but the town was actually 76 miles farther north, along the outskirts of Bossier City.

They were lost to the world.

Matt sat in a computer chair, wheels entangled within the folds of dirty laundry. He himself was dressed in an old shirt and shorts, talking to his friends via headset, looking at their avatars through the game. His character took on the appearance of a grizzled old man. His user name, *Doormat_77,* floated above the old man's head. George's character, Jax Ultim, had more muscles than humanly possible. The name *Geo_21* floated above the pixilated head. Trish's character, Sophie Stephens, was dressed in a tight, pink and busty shirt, a little black skirt, and red high-heeled boots; rather inappropriate attire for a zombie apocalypse. The username *Trishcabob* hovered over bobbing red curls.

Watching the in-game character Sophie Stephens reminded Matt of his crush, local cheerleader Cindy Raven. He imagined saving Cindy from a horde of zombies, planting one sweet kiss before blowing the living dead's daylights out. She would be in her cheerleading outfit of course. His hands brushed against an envelope that contained his deepest, heartfelt love for her. Someday he'd have the guts to send it off.

This bittersweet thought occurred to him nine hours and two minutes before the actual Z-Day.

One hour later, the three adventurers found themselves fighting their way through a corn maze. Trish's busty vixen held off a zombie attacking in the rear as Matt followed George's lead in taking out a tall giant one.

Matt's bullets didn't seem to be making a dent. George

had to shout at him, yet again, headset crackling between words, "Conserve your ammo Doormat! Wait for his eyes to blink... Okay, NOW!"

Trish spoke to them in a sort of bored slur, "You guys. I'm getting overwhelmed. I'm surrounded." She audibly yawned and then said, "They're right on top of me. I can't get them off. Anyone there?"

The giant zombie grabbed corn stalks and tossed them at the duo. Matt said, "I'm kind of busy here Trishcabob. Can you use a flare?"

"Not when I'm on the ground with their feet stomping on my head. George can you do anything?"

George threw his gun down and grabbed a chainsaw off to the side. "Not now sweet cheeks. I've gots me a zombie to gut out!" He then charged at the giant zombie, timing it just right, to catch it in mid-blink. "I'm a man!" George yelled while cutting off one arm, then the other.

Matt maneuvered his character over to Trish's character, shooting the zombies off of her.

Trish sighed, "Thanks for the help—a little too late though. Unless you have a defib, I'm toast."

Matt said, "As a matter of fact, I do." After he killed a few stray zombies, he switched to the defibrillator and brought Trish's character back to life.

George shouted in waves of static, "Did you see that? I wasted that giant thing!"

Trish spoke up in scorn, "All I heard was some idiot shouting 'I'm a man!' while I sat here bleeding to death."

George had his muscle-bound character rev up the chainsaw, "Hey Trishy. I think you still have some zombie goo on you. Why don't you come over here and let me wipe it off."

Trish spoke in haltered tones, "Oh, grow up!"

"I'm a man!" George said as he chased Trish's character all over the corn maze.

"Stop it George! I said no; now knock it off!"

"Not 'tell I cut a piece of you for my collection!"

Matt maneuvered his character toward a barn off in the distance. "Hey guys, I think I found a safe house."

"George, you get that thing away from me!"

Matt said, "Guys, are you listening to me?"

Trish's character ran past Matt into the barn. George followed, chainsaw biting into Matt's character, taking a quarter off his life bar.

Matt's demeanor turned from mild to pissed off, "Cut it out Geo! You almost killed me!"

George cornered Trish and made to slash her with his chainsaw. It sputtered to a stop mere inches away.

"Ran out of gas? Guess you aren't a man anymore." Trish said scornfully.

George replied, "Just 'cause it's out of juice don't mean it still won't work." He started stabbing her with the empty chainsaw, bloody blade clipping through Trish's character but doing no damage. Trish pulled out her magnum and pointed it at George.

"You don't have the guts to shoot me, Trishcabait."

Matt tore bloodshot eyes away from his computer screen and looked at the clock on his cell phone. It was almost midnight. He ran his character inside the barn and shut the door. This automatically closed the game session, saving their progress.

George spoke up then, "Why'd you turn it off? We just got here."

Matt replied, "I have work in the morning Geo. The zombies can wait."

George said, "Your snub-nosed boss can wait, Doormat! We almost made it to New Orleans! The zombies there are the size of cars!"

Trish interrupted them both, "Stop being yourself, George, and think of others for once. Matt actually has a job that makes money... unlike some people."

George replied in anger, "Thanks for the buzz-kill, Trishcabait."

Trish replied more angrily, "I know what you mean when you call me that! Matt told me it had something to do with jail bait. I'm almost 18 years old!"

Matt disconnected from the Vapor gaming network, leaving his friends to fight it out. Ever since Trish and George broke up, it had been a two-month, non-stop argument. George, an eleven-year-old stuck in a college drop-out's body, wanted non-stop fun and then some. Trish, a thirty-year-old stuck in a high school senior's body, wanted stability and love.

If it weren't for *D3ad Living*, they wouldn't even be talking to each other.

Matt shut his computer down, navigated through piles of dirty laundry, sat on his bed and took off his shirt. His eyes lingered on the letter near his computer. On a whim he got up to retrieve it. He checked the address for the hundredth time and opened it up. It was the usual unrequited love letter containing such endearing phrases like always looked at you from a distance and never had the nerve to ask you out.

He'd have to change the part about joining the Marines, and leaving town, for that matter—mother's orders.... He placed the letter near an ornate wooden box on his night stand. Then his eyes focused on that box. Mother's intrusive words replayed in his mind like an annoying tune: *Never put it on; don't even touch it. Never put it on; don't even touch it. Never put it on; don't even touch it—*

He looked at the engraving on the box. It was written in some form of Aztec script. Nearby was a translation into Spanish and beneath that, a second translation into English. He opened the box and pulled out a large skull-shaped pendant. Something *never to be worn in life*, as the translated Aztec text professed. He read the rest of the poetic riddle:

Never to be worn in life
Never to be mourned in death
Always to be scorned from light
Always hide the taker's breath
From the scent of dreamer's night
From half a Raven's lust for wrath

His mom had hidden the amulet from Matt, hoping it would be forgotten. Matt remembered many significant things in his life: the first time he made a goal in soccer, the first time he saw Cindy Raven (it was 3rd grade and she had the brightest scarlet bow in her hair), and the first time he saw the pendant skull. Matt found it in his fourth-grade year under his mother's bed while searching for Christmas presents. But before he could reach inside, his mother shut the box tightly and shouted at him, "Don't you ever look at Father's stuff! Never put it on; don't even touch it!"

That was to be the last time he would see it. High and low he had searched for it, until it really did become a forgotten thing. It was a day ago when he stumbled across it in the attic, mixed in with some old hand-made dolls... the last place he would have searched.

But he was searching for other things then, planning to run away. He had just been in a fight with his mother about joining the Marines. She just wouldn't have it, told him he had a *destiny* and a *purpose,* whatever that was about. The jewelry was dear to her; that was certain, yet she kept it up there with all the dusty boxes.

Never put it on; don't even touch it.

Matt touched it then, held it up to the light. It felt alive and inviting. He shrugged and placed it around his neck, preparing for the feel of cold stone. Throbbing warmth touched his chest.

Matt lifted it away and took another look at the ancient jewelry. The amulet seemed to be looking back; the carved skull had eyeballs stuck in the wide-open sockets. Gnarled, bony hands touched a broken forehead. Aztec style tendrils fell out of the top, carved so life-like and real. Very different from anything he played with in a video game. He rubbed the dirt off the edges of the thing. Aqua colored stones were set in each tendril, frozen forever in place. He never had the chance to count the stones as a kid. He thought there were more than fifty of the things. Now he saw that there were only thirteen... a bit of a letdown really, especially if he wished to sell it.

Matt stared at the garish thing for what seemed like hours. He imagined every aqua stone a wish to be brought to pass... if only he knew how to make the thing work. What would he do with thirteen wishes?

But it didn't work... a reluctant gift from an estranged father, the hated man who left him alone with a mother still in love. Matt's plan was simple: pawn the hideous thing and use the money to leave Wheelbarrow Creek. At least then his father would amount to something in his life.

Mother said he had Dad's raven-dark hair and thin, pointy chin. Matt used to imagine his father appearing one day to take him far from the small hick-town of Wheelbarrow Creek. He imagined living in one of the high-rises across the river, deep in the heart of Shreveport.

That dream had faded long ago, replaced with more adult ones... Cindy Raven held gently in his arms... her beauty lulled him into a deep sleep, and in that sleep he dreamed of zombies.

The amulet glowed a bit, as if caught on fire. At the stroke of midnight one of the aqua stones cracked. Every Illumin and Shade in Shreveport felt a stirring then, some more than others. It was seven hours and forty-five minutes before Z-Day.

Matt awakened with a start. Was he late for work? He checked the clock. It was 6:30, nearly one hour before the alarm. He couldn't sleep though... then he remembered, very vividly, the nightmare that had woken him up.

A demon with long, dark hair hunted him in the woods. So many roots on the ground—what if he fell? His foot snagged on one of them; he fell, tumbling to the gnarled ground. He reached forward, hitting something hard. A tall monolithic stone stood before him, much like that of a headstone. Other monoliths were planted deep in the ground. Was he in a cemetery? A glowing skull protruded from the stone above him, saying, "Make a few wishes to free me from this grave, Matt. Touch my death before she can give you hers. Mine is gentler."

He couldn't move; terror had paralyzed him. He looked back at the demon and saw a beautiful woman instead. She was impossibly close: hair transformed into frizzy auburn. The amber brown eyes gazed outward, gently set within a soft, tempting face. It was a bittersweet feeling; his greatest fear replaced with enchanting beauty. Why had he been afraid? He looked ahead. The stone skull wasn't glowing anymore. It was, in fact, retreating inside the headstone. "I tried to warn you," it said before completely disappearing.

Words replaced the skull on the tombstone: "Here lies Matt Gillard, too wise to live and too dumb to die."

When Matt looked back his hair stood on end. The beautiful woman was a foot away, catching him with those large amber brown eyes. Up close they became black shadows of rage, thirsty for murder. It was the demon!

The demon lifted him and shook him until he wore out. Snaky hands felt like ice all over his body, filling him with shivers and a fever of the plague. He became a marionette doll to her, shadowy fingers biting into his flesh, panting breath whispering into his ears in a deep, sensual voice, "You're dying Matt; dying to be touched, felt up by Death herself. Your life is only one joke after the other. I am the punch line!"

Even in memory the nightmare gave Matt chills.

"It was only a dream," he kept saying to himself, "It was only a dream. Nothing ever comes out of my dreams."

He lay back down, content with the knowledge of his safety, his psyche conditioned by society to ignore the unknown, ill-prepared to face what was to come.

Another nightmare came to him in his dreams: dead animals on the side of the road, re-animating to life, feeding on the living. His chest burned as he took it all in. He had to find George and Trish. They had a job to do; zombie animals to kill.

A pride of zombie housecats approached him. He looked around for something that would help him, anything really.

Even a pitchfork would do! At that thought, a pitchfork appeared in his hands. The first cat attacked him. He stabbed the cat and threw it against the wall. Two more came at him. He kicked one, inciting a screech, stabbing the other four times before throwing it through a window.

His mom entered the dream, a zombie-Mom screeching in high-pitched tones. He hit his own zombie-Mom three times with his fist to make her stop. He was debating on whether to stab her or not when she screeched a fourth time. He looked deep into her empty eye sockets: they read 7:45 am. The screech became a long beep that woke him up. Zero hours and zero minutes to Z-Day.

Matt was in the middle of the room, alarm clock blaring. His sweaty palms held a pitchfork. He didn't own a pitchfork. Something was burning on his chest. Shaking fingers touched the glowing amulet. They fell away in surprise.

Widening eyes looked down at his chest. The ancient amulet had fused to his skin! Gingerly, Matt touched the flesh on his chest that was melding to the pendant. It felt rubbery and dead.

Then he noticed two aqua stones had cracked on the amulet. He never should have put it on. Mother was going to kill him!

His mom began pounding on the door in rhythm to his migraine. The pitchfork dropped from his hands.

"Matthew, that's the fourth time I've heard that blasted alarm clock! Get up before you're late for work!"

Matt sat on his bed in a daze, looking at the amulet that grew into him. He heard a faint whisper in his ear, like druids mumbling. He couldn't understand what was said over the blaring alarm clock and his shouting mother, "Matthew Alfred Gillard! Do you want me to come in there myself?"

Matt's mind came into focus then, lightning fast. He shut the alarm clock off, threw on his work clothes, and went for the door, just as it opened.

Matt's mom stood two inches shorter than him; yet somehow, in Matt's fuzzy logic, she was much taller.

"So you finally got up, I see," she said in that accusing tone of hers, "Even put on your dirty uniform I see."

"Mom, I don't have time for this. Have to be at work in 15 minutes!"

"Never any time for your mother. Might as well stand here and wilt away while you play your video games."

Matthew grabbed his nametag and keys and made to leave. He idly touched the amulet through his shirt, hoping it wasn't glowing at the moment. She barred the door, looking up into his eyes with a pair of her own emerald orbs. "You're almost 19 years old young man, a high school graduate! What are you going to do with your life?"

Matt sighed audibly and mumbled, "I wanted to be a Marine. You put a stop to that."

"Was that backtalk I heard from you?"

"It was nothing mom. I just want to make it to work."

He made to pass her. She held him back with a firm hand… two inches away from where the amulet was fused to his chest, "What is *that* doing here?"

At first Matt thought she meant the amulet. Cold sweat dripped off his pointy chin. Then he remembered the pitchfork lying over the pile of dirty clothes on the floor.

How could something he had just dreamed of appear in the world of the living? He reached down and touched the farming tool. It felt normal enough, so he picked it up. His mom was tapping her foot, impatiently waiting.

He shrugged and said honestly, "I have no idea."

"Well here, let me have it."

Matt held it back from his mom. He needed to study it.

"Matthew, give me that pitchfork before you hurt yourself."

Matt did not want to give in to his mother, but he couldn't ignore those steely eyes. He stood over his mother, handing her the weapon. "It's a friend's tool; I was going to give it to him at work."

His mother grabbed the pitchfork and stared him down, "Don't lie to me, Matt."

Something lurched inside of him, and a curse word leapt unhinged from his mouth. He tore the pitchfork away from her. He'd never once cursed in her presence. For the first time in many years, his mother was speechless.

He walked to the front door and grabbed his chest in pain. The amulet was seething with heat, but when his hand touched the amulet, it was icy cold. He lifted his hand away in surprise, accidently ripping his magnetic name tag and dropping it on the tiled floor.

His mother came behind him then, placing a cool hand on his forehead. "You're really getting hot. Maybe you should call in sick."

Matt sighed. He didn't feel well, but something deep within was urging him to get out of there. He had things to do, people to see.

"Matt, I know I've been hard on you… it's just that… it's just that I don't want you to leave me. I don't want us to grow apart." She placed a hand on his pitchfork.

Matt began to feel sorry for her. He was about to say as much when the amulet pulsed alive, kicking against his sternum. Another thought entered his head: his mother was keeping him from pursuing his dreams, to be a Marine and fight for God and country.

"It's too late for that."

He tore the pitchfork away and marched out the door.

Matt worked as a delivery man for *Talon Dry Cleaning Services*. Not the best gig in town, but it paid for the car note and the car insurance. A dry-cleaning route was very easy, unless you missed a delivery order—then you had to drive back with your own car, apologize profusely to any offended customers, and hear an earful from Randy, the jerk of a boss that ruled Matt's life from eight to four.

Besides that, it was all simple routine: drive here, drop off clothes, pick up clothes, drive there, put a reminder note on the door that you "were in the neighborhood and missed them dearly," move on to the next house, rinse and repeat, over and over until your dreams died of boredom. It was a good job though, a safe job… whatever that meant.

He liked to ride with '80s death metal on full-blast,

windows open wide. Matt turned a corner, banging his head in rhythm to the chorus:

> *Gotta go make it right!*
> *Gotta go fight the fight!*
> *Gotta see the stakes are high!*
> *This shirt is ripping tight tight tight!*

At a red light, something rank caught his nose, like moldy cabbage mixed with doughnuts. Hurriedly, he shut the window. At that moment he felt a prickle of fear and apprehension coming right around the bend.

Then he saw it. Nothing much really—just a little raccoon stalking a homeless man on the side of the road. The beggar held up a cardboard sign that read, in bold, black letters,

THE END IS NEAR

Matt drove on once the light changed. He watched the scene unfold through the rear-view mirror. The bum was comically using his sign to beat off the raccoon. Then Matt saw the blood on the raccoon's side. Surely a cardboard sign couldn't do that? Then he saw the coon actually bite the man. Rabies?

A car horn brought Matt's attention back up front. He slammed on his brake, mere inches from the blue sedan.

His music blared through the speakers,

> *Only thing I see tonight…*
> *Is you and me fighting the fight!*

He drove the last two blocks and pulled into the parking lot, right next to the delivery van, more than fifteen minutes late. The cacophony of drilling guitars, wild screaming and double bass drums shut off as soon as he turned his key to the off position.

He was just about to leave the car when he noticed a book in the passenger's seat. He didn't remember putting a book there. He picked it up, saw the cover, and immediately threw it down. The cover picture of a gray skeleton looked back at him, empty sockets gazing at nothing. *The Soulless Cometh to Dine* was displayed in narrow, broken lettering at the bottom. KINGSLY HATECROW held a place of honor in tall silver letters, like a macabre crown above the skull-cap.

When Matt was a kid, he had attempted to steal the book during Uncle Ned's snoring repose. Ned woke up suddenly and caught him. "You can have it if you dare, Matt," Ned said, "Horror books are worse than movies though; they use all your imagination up just to bring the monsters to life. Once that happens, you can't put it on pause."

Matt never got past page 147. Even to this day he didn't dare touch it. In fact, he firmly remembered throwing the book in the trash bin.

What was it doing in his car? Matt took his keys out of the ignition and looked back at the floor. The book was gone.

Mr. Randy greeted Matt with an angry glare from behind the counter. Matt squeaked past the man's wide, unforgiving frame and clocked in, then went on to begin his duties. A meaty hand held him back. Mr. Randy's tobacco breath spoke, an inch from his ear, "Did your dog chew on the alarm chord again?"

"It was the cat this time, Mr. Randy. Won't happen again."

Both meaty hands held Matt's shoulders, forcing him to look up into blaring nostrils, and, beneath that, a hairy black and gray mustache. It twitched comically up and down above lips that stated with a southern drawl, "I like you, son, but... what's this?"

The boss's eyes and eyebrows narrowed, looking at Matt's chest.

Matt could feel the amulet's cold touch against his sternum bone. If his boss saw this through the shirt he would think it was some sort of hipster thing. There was nothing written against it per se, but *Talon Dry Cleaning* forbade tattoos and male piercing... a hunk of stone fused to skin would *not* bode well.

Mr. Randy thumped him just left of the amulet. Matt hunched over from the pain on his tender skin. "Forgot your nametag. That's two strikes Matt! One more and, well, I don't know if you watch baseball, but..."

"Yes sir, sorry sir." Matt couldn't help but grin with relief.

"What's that boy? You think this is funny? I don't think you understand how a Raven-owned business is supposed to run." Mr. Randy started counting off his fingers, "On time, in full uniform, and squeaky clean. If you can't do the first two, you might as well do the other."

Mr. Randy swiveled Matt around until he faced a broom and mop. "When you get back from your delivery run, I expect you to mop the floors 'til I can see my reflection." The boss left him at the ding of the bell, all smiles and anecdotes to the customer that just walked in.

Matt gave his boss an angry scowl and then checked the manifest: 12 deliveries. With an audible sigh he went outside and drove the delivery van around back. A younger version of his boss's smiling, mustached face was plastered on the ancient vehicle's side. Beneath *Talon Dry-Cleaning Services* smaller lettering read, *Raven's Crave'n Your Dry-Clean'n Needs.*

Matt always wondered who had written the little jingle. It didn't even make much sense! How can you *crave* someone's dry cleaning needs? On bad days he day-dreamed about finding the ad person and shooting him point blank in the head... right after shooting his boss, of course. The only good thing about the Ravens would be the beautiful daughter of Talon Dry-Cleaning's owner... that being his crush, the raven-haired, cheerleading beauty Cindy.

Matt pulled the van up to the front of the store. He walked inside and found Randy inside jawing to some costumer about the upcoming football season, "Dallas has a good chance to actually win this year. Though our Saints will put up a fight like they always do!"

Matt grabbed some clothes off the rack and went to the van, only three more trips to load his van with all the day's deliveries.

Inside the store again, Matt heard Randy reply to a question, "I wouldn't doubt it, though I bet balls to doughnuts they'd take their second string quarter back from them if they could because he'd be—blah, blah, blah." It was all nonsense to Matt. He gladly closed the front door and hung the second batch of clothes inside the Boss-mobile (as he called it).

Then he noticed the bum.

He was walking slowly toward Matt, about 35 yards away, favoring his left leg—dragging it actually—along with a sign that read, *THE END IS NEAR.* Matt ignored him and went back inside for another load.

Randy laughed incessantly, "Don't you know it! LSU's wide-receiver just ran straight past him on the final play. It was nearly 30, scratch that, a 35-yard run before he hit the zone for a good ol'-fashioned Louisiana touchdown!"

Back outside, Matt noticed the bum had dropped the sign and was almost ten yards away, staggering towards him like a crazy drunk. Then the stench hit Matt's nostrils: something akin to moldy lettuce and skunk droppings. The summer heat wasn't helping much.

Matt immediately thought of finding something, anything to protect himself. Heavily-starched clothing dropped to the ground as his fingers encircled something solid. He looked down and saw the pitchfork strangely materialize right there in his hands. The bum didn't seem to mind it poking into his ribs. He was staggering and drooling, much like a zombie did in the video game. He began to think this man had more problems than just being homeless. Matt barely kept himself from throwing up.

He met the bum's eyes and said, "Go away."

The bum relented and walked on. Matt followed him

for a while, pitchfork poking his back, just to make sure. He thought about calling 9-1-1 to report him, but the bum staggered on and away from the premises, moving slowly toward the *Brazen Beauty* hair salon. He wasn't Matt's problem anymore.

Something deep inside whispered silky smooth words to him. He looked down at his chest and shook his head to clear it. Then he remembered the starched clothes on the ground. Matt threw the clothing and the pitchfork inside the van, and then went back for one last load.

"I'm telling you he's my best pick! Knows how to lock 'em down the line. Throws as straight as an arrow! Nothing like seeing that good ol' boy light it up with a pass play."

Matt grabbed the last batch of clothes and made to leave.

"Hey Matthew." His boss's deep voice rumbled.

Matt froze and turned around.

"Don't forget your manifest." Mr. Randy tucked it under Matt's arm and went back to the counter.

The morning was young as Matt drove the van down Femafields Highway toward Glendale community. The van's radio was a broken thing, turning on and off of its own accord, on full blast even, like something possessed.

Worst of all, it played only a single country station. In Matt's own words, country was "the worst offence to music since cave men hit rocks together."

His boss had only laughed when Matt asked to have it fixed. "99.9 fm KING Kountry is the best station around. You need some good ol' U-S of A music in your bones, wasting away as you are."

Matt hated it with a passion. A hundred plus hours of it coming on and off only increased that hatred. All he could do was grin and bear it.

Break my heart Texan
I know it is vexin'
To know Ted's relaxed
When you're not around.

Break my heart Texan
Life surely is vexin',
Just get your legs waxed
And I'll come back around.

The song ended with a twinge of the steel guitar. Disc jockey Jethro Jeepers spoke in a natural drawl, "You, sir, were just listening to 'Texan Vexin' Heart' by James Yearbrook. His little number topped number five on the charts. Number four is coming up after this news update... It appears angry citizens are taking to the main street. A sort of haphazard strike I guess. It all started with the homeless. One even mentioned how a bum bit into him... weeell, I gotta tell you th—"

The radio thankfully cut out as Matt pulled into Glendale Community to make his first drop of the day. He parked the van near a brown two-story house, third one on the left. He hung the clothes on the front door, checked it off on the manifest—only 11 more houses to drop off clothes, and an extra ten to see if they have any clothes to pick up.

Next was a yellow house, fifth on the right, down Gray Maters Lane. He almost hung the clothes on the front door, but then remembered his boss telling him the customer wanted them on the back door. He went out back and tried to ignore the bark of the Rottweiler behind the next-door-neighbor's chain-link fence.

Matt tiptoed through the muddy grass, gave up and just smashed through it. He hung the clothes on the door, went back to the van, and checked it off on the manifest... ten more to deliver, ten more to check.

His eyes paused on the next victim of Talon's services: *Atwater, Freda.*

Matt gave out a long sigh. He pointed his van right, took a few streets and left Glendale Community behind. Talon Dry-Cleaners had many routes. The ones in Shreveport stopped every few blocks for a drop-off. His van was the only route in Wheelbarrow Creek, a small town across the river with lots of countryside. This meant many long drives between stops.

Ten minutes later had him facing a tall hill and, at its tip, as far as Matt knew it, the oldest house in the parish. Three stories high and badly in need of repair, the Atwater estate home creaked about, losing its age-old battle against gravity.

Most customers only asked that you hang up their dry-cleaning on the front or back door. Mrs. Atwater requested that you knock on her door until she answered, so that you could personally hand it to her.

Matt assumed living in the middle of nowhere made her paranoid… because a robber would drive twenty minutes to her house and wait in the bushes just to steal her freshly-pressed church clothes. Matt rolled his eyes.

The customer was always right, though. No employee with a job could argue with that.

He knocked on the door. Forty-five seconds later the blinds on a nearby window parted. Matt conjured up a smile and a wave. The door opened to reveal Mrs. Atwater's ancient frame, hunched over. She was gibbering as usual about her long-deceased cat.

Matt handed her the dry-cleaning and went into his conversation on auto-pilot as she droned on about her dull life. "Here you go Mrs. Atwater.... I'm terribly sorry about your loss Mrs. Atwater.... Perhaps you should get another cat Mrs. Atwater.... I didn't mean that…. No cat in the world could replace your Percy."

It was then that Matt's auto-pilot ears went haywire. "What was that you said, Mrs. Atwater?"

Her gravelly voice spoke as high as it could, "It's what I've been trying to tell you. My Percy's come back to life and he's trying to get at me! I just don't know what to do about that."

Matt stood there stunned. The grandfather clock behind her tick-tocked in the background, keeping time for no one. Mrs. Atwater's cataract pools stared at him from behind wide-brimmed glasses. He could see she was more worried than usual and really did believe her dead cat was alive and out to get her.

"Well, Mrs. Atwater, I don't know what to say about this. Perhaps you're just going through a time of mourning. Maybe you *want* to see your cat alive and—"

"Young man, the only time I want to see my Percy again is in heaven. My cat's alive and certainly not well. He's been viciously attacking all my other cats, poor dears. Tried to get him to stop." She lifted her right hand, still holding the church clothes. "Look at how he bit me!"

Matt saw the bite marks on her arm. Something whispered at him to get out of there. He took a few steps back, trying to hold on to reality. "Maybe it's another cat. Some cat that looks like Percy but—"

"No, no, NO! I know it was him! Only way I could stop him was to cut him up myself." She pulled the door open all the way, revealing a bloody left hand hooked around a large red blade. She took a step toward him, "My strength just isn't as good as it used to be. I only stabbed him once, but it sure felt good!"

Matt stumbled backward.

"Why are you stepping back? I won't hurt you. You're not Percy."

Matt stepped farther back. Mrs. Atwater's eyes were blazing now. She threw her freshly-pressed dresses into the well-manicured flower bed. "You come by here every other day, young man. I see you looking down at me, all high-and-mighty, too young to speak to little ol' Mrs. Freda." She aimed the bloody knife at him, "You think I'm crazy, don't you?"

"No ma'am. I don't think any such thing."

"Just some crazy old basket case asking for nothing less

than a few moments, just to share her life with someone, anyone that will listen before she nods off to heaven. All you do is come here, drop off my clothes, and run away scared of talking to me, scared of talking to an old, decrepit lady!"

Matt was really backing up then. Her sweet, grandmotherly disposition was gone, vanished and snuffed out, replaced with something less-than-human.

Then he heard a hiss and a growl. Turning around, he saw Percy surrounded by ten other cats. These were not the laugh-out-loud, hold-me kittens he often saw on the net. They were something else entirely—mutilated, decrepit things with skin hanging from their teeth.

Matt didn't have to think very hard to conjure up the pitchfork.

Mrs. Atwater dropped the knife and started dragging her feet toward him, very much like the bum he had encountered back at the store. That same nauseating stench hit him then.

Freda Atwater's sentences became an incoherent garbled mess of grunts and sounds: "Won't die me, won't love, won't talk or do, or say or pray me a shiver."

The almost skeletal Percy attacked him first. He moved his fork swiftly, stabbing him in mid-flight. He still tried to scratch at him, still alive, still dead… somehow both at the same time. Mrs. Atwater attacked next. He threw Percy right in her face and ran to the van. Mrs. Atwater chased him, fighting off the many cats biting at her and each other.

He'd never seen an old lady move so quickly.

He started up the van and backed up to turn around. Mrs. Atwater slammed into the driver-side window. All the while KING Kountry blared at him:

I don't think she loves me, I don't think she'd care.
All that she misses, my plaid underwear.

Matt slammed the gas pedal and flew down the hill. He grabbed his cell phone and dialed 9-1-1.

All he got was the busy signal.

Traveling 70 mph down the country road, rocking and shaking about, he checked the manifest to get the number for his boss at the store. It was about that time he realized he'd only given Mrs. Atwater two of the three items listed. Mr. Randy would have his hide if Matt didn't deliver the third dress, that is, if Mrs. Atwater weren't trying to kill him.

Matt had no idea what to do then. He needed help and he needed it fast. He needed someone who always knew what to do. The problem was he didn't have anyone like that. He threw down the manifest and picked up his cell phone. Matt dialed George's number. Close enough.

Earlier that morning, while Matt was facing off with his mom, George was catching his zzz's. Even on Z-Day, the man without the plan was caught quite unawares.

George's roommate Carlos was the early bird, up two hours prior to him, spending one of them trimming the bushes. Carlos was a quiet man, barely speaking above a whisper—a perfect match for center-of-the-universe George.

The one safe place away from George was Carlos's garden. Carlos came from a long and proud Mexican lineage, going as far back as the Aztecs. Most Mexicans celebrated the ancient Aztec holiday, Day of the Dead, on November first. But that was how the Catholics in Mexico celebrated it. He was a true Aztec at heart and knew that the first of August was when the proper Day of the Dead festivities began. So, he celebrated the death and new life of his relatives by placing wooden skulls in his garden, which was also the hiding place for a local dog's playthings. Coincidentally, a few days prior, the neighbor's black lab had caught a squirrel. After messing with it a bit, she had placed its carcass in Carlos's flower bed for safe keeping.

As Carlos listened quietly for his visiting dead relatives to speak to him, the flower bed rustled beneath him. He shuffled back in surprise. Nothing prepared him for what was to follow. Wooden skulls throbbed and shook until a squirrel carcass rose up amidst them and leapt at Carlos's neck. Carlos felt intense pain at the bite, and then caught a whiff of the smelly carcass. He nearly puked. An alien sort of rage swelled up from inside him, causing the mild-mannered young man to snap.

He thought of all the times George would borrow money and never give it back, all the times George ate food clearly labeled *Carlos*, all the times George hit on Carlos's girlfriend. Carlos took it out on the poor zombie squirrel, ripping its head off its neck and impaling it on the end of his trimmers.

He felt tired then, dopey, and strangely satisfied after

slaughtering the thing. He left the body where it was, amidst a slew of wooden skulls, and stepped inside to take a nap on the couch. Infected blood from his neck wound dribbled down, intermingling with clots of dust on the un-vacuumed carpet.

George got up at 9:16 am with a mild headache, nothing a college drop-out couldn't handle. He slipped on his Darth Vader slippers and walked the meter distance to his PC rig, built inside a *Star Trek*, cubed-shape Borg vessel, and logged onto Vapor Gaming Network. Two messages popped up. One of them was another invite to join an online gamer clan. This one was called *Breaker_Scags_Unlemited* (at least they spelled "scags" correctly). The second message read as such:

To: Geo21

From: Trishcabob

Subject: Sorry about last night

Sorry about last night, I mean, this morning. I didn't mean to be mean. Guess it's kind of hard when you broke my heart like you did. I know it's my fault for ignoring you like I did. We should meet up sometime and talk—

Blah blah, I'm young and foolish so pity me, blah blah blah was all George heard. With three swift clicks, he chose and deleted both of them. Then he turned on the 3D specs of his $1500 , 22-inch monitor, put on his $75, state-of-the-art 3D glasses over his $175 headphones, loaded up *D3ad Living,* and signed on as Geo21.

Fifteen minutes later, Geo21 was fighting his way through

a campaign, babysitting some 13-year-olds or n00bies as he called them, over the mic. Their characters were sloshing through a junkyard of flooded cars when a hopper-infected zombie jumped Geo21's character and yanked him away. The n00bs were too busy shooting zombies to notice him.

George thought they were snubbing him on purpose; there was no way anyone could be that stupid. He told them all of this of course, and much more, anonymity empowering his racial tendencies. One of the players looked everywhere but right above his head where the hopper-infected zombie nested, eating out Geo21's guts.

He gave up getting their attention, and guzzled down the last gulp of last night's Miller Light. It was about that time the scent of dead skunk entered his nostrils. Before he could grimace at the smell, his door flew open wide. George turned and glanced at Carlos standing there, swaying back and forth… just like a zombie.

George held up the empty beer bottle, planning to say, "Hey roomy, would you kindly bring me a brewski?" All he got out was, "Hey roomy—" before Carlos took the bottle and smashed it into his head, breaking his 3D glasses and headset in the process.

Face down in dust-ridden carpet, George lifted his head slowly, looking at a blood spot on the floor. He felt the side of his face. He lifted his hand away; it was covered in blood and bits of black plastic. He had known Carlos to be very quiet… nothing above a whisper really. George felt dizzy and confused at the situation.

The pain was just starting to settle in. Carlos was screaming incoherent phrases at him, "Hate me hate you hate all. Your mom isn't here and neither am I! Taking time to mock me with, you are horsing around, only horsing around!"

George spoke haltingly, the once-mild headache a jackhammer of pain. Reality was hard to settle in here, "Wow, that was... what was that?!"

Carlos went further into his rage then, grabbing George's 22-inch, 3D deluxe, OtherWorldly Inc, $1500 computer screen, ripping it away, wires and all.

George screamed at such an atrocity, finally going into shock.

Carlos muttered, "Don't know my name, even now me," before raising the screen above his head to smash it down onto George.

George kicked his roommate in the leg. His screen fell in slow motion then, before cracking with a dull thud on the corner of the dresser. George gave out a blood-curdling scream, got up and administered justice with another kick to his roommate's side. Carlos grabbed George's leg, forcing him down with him. He then tried to bite at his toes, hidden behind Darth Vader slippers.

George grabbed the first thing he could, which just so happened to be the $3000 PC rig, fit nice and pretty inside a *Star Trek* Borg ship, custom-made from New Zealand Unlimited PCs. George ripped it off, chords and all, and slammed it into Carlos' cranium.

At that moment his cell phone screamed his favorite heavy metal song:

None can stop the end, the last,
Unless it's death whose fingers' grasp
All the dreams of haunting past.

Only thieves get slight reprieves,
Stealing time away from death,
Making murder one a myth.

Yet the reaper is their keeper,
Taking all to end, to slaughter,
Until they breathe their very last.

Matt was driving 80 mph when he called his best friend; the phone rang six or seven times before it went to George's voicemail. While AT&T methodically told him about cell phone options that would never be used, he yelled, "Come on Geo, this is serious! I don't have time for your crap right now!"

George's sarcastic, annoyingly peppy voice came on then, "Hey It's George. If you're not a hot broad, don't bother leaving a message. If you are a hot broad then leave a number and I'll pick you up at eight."

Matt got a call-waiting notice from George and switched over, "George where have you been? We need to talk and fast! I just got attacked by undead cats! I know that you don't like the Stop-n-Go-Nutz ever since Trish got a job there, but I'm going crazy here!"

George's voice sounded very different from the cocky voicemail message, deeper than usual, sad even, "I killed my roommate. I can't even remember his name, and I killed my roommate. I don't even know his mother's name. Don't even have her number. I've got to call the police."

"George! Snap out of it! You can't call the police. 9-1-1 is busy right now! Listen, I got attacked by one of the sweetest old ladies I know. I need someone to talk to, to clear my head. Meet me at the Stop-n-Go-Nutz."

Matt heard someone blubbering and sniffing on the other line. "George? Are you crying? Pull yourself together man; I need you to help me figure this out."

George only responded with tears. Matt had never heard him act so sentimental.

"Geo21, get your butt in gear! You're the leader of our clan. I need your leadership now!" George stopped crying at those words. "I'm sure that whatever happened, your roomy's fine."

George looked at the bloody pile of his roommate's body. The way his roomy had come at him—violent and deadly, just like in *D3ad Living*.

Matt's whiny voice said, "Meet me at the Stop-n-Go—"

"Nutz... I heard you the first time, Doormat. I'll be there. And Matt. Call your mother. I think we have a zombie apocalypse on our hands." George hung up the phone.

It was at that point Matt realized what George had said... how he killed his roommate... cried... George never cried... told Matt to call his mom... proclaimed in that hollow voice of his... those dooming words... Z-Day was here.

If it weren't for the strange dreams, the mysterious pitchfork, the Aztec amulet fused to his chest, the crazy cat lady attacking him, Matt would have called it all nuts. Yet somehow it all made perfect sense. His wildest dream had come to life!

He thought it would have felt better. In his dreams he imagined mowing down hordes of the walking dead. Reality was a rather bland, frightful affair. Just like graduation a few months back. All he felt was numbness and a certain haunting dread creeping up, an undeniable truth that coming of age wasn't all it was cracked up to be.

Whitman was a retired drill sergeant. Wheelbarrow Creek had dubbed him General after he retired from the Army twelve years back. History was his only love and gasoline his greatest hate, which is peculiar to say for a man who owned the Stop-n-Go-Nutz gas station. He had nothing personal against gas itself, just the station that held it. Such was the price for purchasing the historical site of Stalwart Hill.

Since it was the only gas station in that area, Wheelbarrow Creek's venerable mayor wouldn't allow Whitman to shut the place down to turn the hill into a historical landmark. So he either had to buy the station and the hill with it, or Feather Black Drugstore would come in and destroy 150 years of Civil War history. He would not allow his forefathers' deaths on that hill, runaway slaves trained into bleeding soldiers of the Union army, to be disgraced and forgotten.

So General Whitman managed the store, put up with the smell of gas and the horrendous name (also part of the deal), and, in return, had the profound reward of helping the long-dead heroes of his kin stay at rest. What angered him most was how every patron that ambled in couldn't care less. They didn't want to hear his stories of the brave 58th. They just wanted their gas and cigarettes.

Bitter thoughts of such an aimless generation entered General Whitman's mind between puffs of his cigar. The KING Kountry radio station blared on through the ancient store. They were playing one of his favorite honky tonk tunes:

> *Don't be mislead,*
> *My poor heart's not dead.*
> *I just be thinkin' it's time, you should know,*
> *Now I know…*
> *And I say no.*

A tall farmer walked inside the store, red hair bursting into shaggy curls at the top.

General Whitman scratched at his wiry gray hair and hobbled over, "How's life been treating you, Red?"

"Oh just fine, General, except for my wife. She keeps getting on me to pick up that package, and I keep having to remind her how slowly things move in the Wheelbarrow. She just doesn't listen, tells me a little grease can go a long way in fixing a squeaky wheel. Speaking of which, have you heard that strange sound outside? Like some sort of distant buzz."

"I'll look into it. Got everything you need?"

"Nearly so, General, nearly so."

Whitman looked around for his employee to manage the counter. She was quite the astute worker, usually never gone from her place. He called her out, "Trisha!"

He found her in the back, wearing those ridiculously tall high heels. She was sweeping the floor, very slowly, over by two boys, one of whom was patched up in the head. They just so happened to be taking up room at the only diner's table in the joint, and they had no drinks. She shook her head at something they were saying.

He hobbled on over and caught her reply, "This is the worst prank you guys have pulled! Zombie apocalypse! Oh for crying out loud! And don't even try to make me feel sorry for you George. No doubt the head injury's a fake."

General Whitman butted in, "Trisha I ain't calling you twice now. Go ahead and get that customer."

Trish was about to leave when the boy without the head wound, a skinny looking scarecrow of a thing, grabbed her arm and said, "We aren't joking, Trish." Then he started tapping at his chest. "Just let me show you something, and you'll see." Trish looked into the boy's earnest eyes and seemed to waver in her disdain.

Whitman cut in, "Better leave my Trisha alone before I throw you off my property!"

Trish looked up at the old man, "It's okay General. These people won't hurt me."

Whitman pushed her along, "Don't tell me how to run my store. Now take care of that customer and I'll take care of them."

The general was about to tell these young folk how to treat a lady when his favorite radio song cut off.

Disc jockey Jethro Jeepers came on, his usual gag-ridden voice replaced with one of somber repose, *"We interrupt Fred Amsterdam's number two trendsetter, Knowing You Know to Know, on 99.9 fm KING Kountry, to give you this special report. Reports are coming in from all over town of people suddenly getting angry and attacking friends and strangers alike. I know this sounds like one of my pranks, but it ain't. And to prove it, I'm switching us over to Channel Eight Wheelbarrow Creek News.*

The familiar voice of local news anchor Ms. Brenda Sullivan took over, *Around 8:00 this morning, reports started pouring in. Angry citizens, claiming mutilated road kill had bitten them, are attacking men, women, and children, and biting them in turn. "It's not rabies or mad cow disease," local science teacher Mr. Warner says. His advice is to stay indoors.*

Mr. Warner may be overreacting though, to keep suspicions of his science fair cheating techniques on the down low. More of that story at 5:00, only on Channel Eight Wheelbarrow Creek News... this just in... what? Um, we'll be back after these messages.

After a few seconds of dead air, Brenda's voice came on, talking to someone off set; hints of her southern drawl were creeping in. "Are you kidding me? You don't pay me enough to report this hogwash! Okay fine, but after this I'm moving to Texas! This hicksville town is too small to have its own news organization anyways. For crying out loud, I almost graduated from Berkley! Well you tell the mayor to go, to go... what?! I'm still on the air?"

More dead silence... Ms. Sullivan came back on, professional voice, if a bit shaky, returning with her. "Ladies and gentlemen, this may sound crazy... I don't know how else to put it. Bereaved citizens at Ester's Funeral Home are saying their dead relative, a Jebediah H. Smithy, came out of his coffin during the funeral service and started attacking his grandchildren. He was finally shot in the head by his daughter, a Sophia Stephons. We have that daughter live on the line; only on Channel 8 Wheelbarrow Creek News, best and only news station in town."

The sound of distant screams came on, with it the crackled throbbing of something hitting against the telephone receiver. A raw, hollow voice spoke out, *Hello? Is anyone there?*

Ms. Sullivan replied, trying to sound professional, "This is Brenda Sullivan, Channel Eight. Can you tell me what's going on?"

The woman on the other end began to cry, rubbing her chin on the receiver loudly. "My father was dead. I loved him so much. He was dead this morning. I saw him in the coffin last night as dead and handsome as ever... but dead! I just wanted him to hold me again. To give me that smile of his!

When he came to, I thought for a second it was all a

dream. He hadn't died at all! He was alive and I was just waking up from a dream. We were at church and everything was all right! My kids, poor Jonathan and Timmy, they missed him so much. Well, they started running at him. About that time I noticed something wasn't right. The way he walked, that blank look in his eyes, that awful rotten smell… it wasn't my father at all!

Then he started reaching out to my kids, and then he started pulling roughly at them, and then he started biting them! I can still hear their screams!" The phone clicked into dead silence.

Ms. Sullivan came back on, southern drawl in full force, "Well that was um… that was just something now wasn't it? It appears we have something of an, of an epidemic on our hands here, something that can animate dead organic tissue. I can't believe I just said that. My advice: stay away from anything dead and wait for the police… or perhaps the National Guard."

General Whitman shut off the radio and noticed other people had walked in. They were all glassy-eyed, looking straight at him, just like new recruits did before taking their first parachute jump from a plane. He was about to say something when he noticed a sound… like a million bees buzzing away. It was very faint and yet… somehow very loud. The more he listened, the more familiar it became.

Many times he had heard it at Fort Blakely. Recruits with disciplinary issues digging holes, only to fill them back up and dig elsewhere. Short jabs and shovels stabbing the dirt. 1, 2… 1, 2, 3.

Something outside was scraping the dirt.

Matt hadn't heard the radio news; he could barely think as it was, mind wandering to the book he had stolen from his uncle. Passages from *The Soulless Cometh to Dine* sounded off in his head, as if he had read it yesterday... necromancers raising the dead, binding century-old bones together, foraging them into a strong fighting legion of death walkers. So vivid was the book's description that he had had nightmares for days afterward. One passage in particular struck him with terror:

Like bleeding hearts of lambs to the slaughter, I watched the death bringer's coal black eyes gaze, numbing me where I stood. It was the night before Dia de los Muertos, or Day of the Dead. This Hombre de los muertos was about to make those ancient relatives come back for real. One swift stroke of his thin-as-blades-fingers could cut my soul in half. I felt feeble and powerless before him. He grinned widely, stretching his face so tight I could see his cheek bones bulging out. He spoke to me then; under a black breath he said, "Mira me señor como resuscito los muertos."

He turned his back to me, so sure of his strength and power. I was mesmerized, completely in his spell. Quietly he spoke his incantations; like a lover he cooed and flirted with the bones. His voice rose in power; the bones rattled at his command. One by one they awakened and became living beings.

Something tiny shattered in Matt's chest as he thought of this. His imagination ran wild... dreaming of skeleton armies.

The inner voice grew stronger. It whispered that he should look toward Stalwart Hill. He saw something there crawling out of the top. It took a while for him to recognize it as a skeletal hand, stabbing its way out of the surface. First the zombies, and now this…

The unnatural was becoming so very natural.

He stepped toward the window and watched as a horrific sight unfolded. Others joined him slowly, silently, until General Whitman, attempting to calm everyone's nerves with a halting speech, came over.

Whitman saw them then, the 150-year-old skeletons of his forefathers, crawling out of their Civil War graves on Stalwart Hill.

"What the hell?" one patron asked.

Whitman's lips started shaking. He spoke in a loud, drill sergeant whisper, "The 58th brigade of the Union army, previous slaves trained into soldiers, had done their duty in holding that hill. Not a one of them survived the rebel onslaught. All those brave men gave their lives for my freedom. In return, their dead bodies were piled on that hill, left to feed the buzzards. And not a one of you gave a damn! Now, watch them rise up. Watch history arise from the grave and murder us where we stand!"

Matt felt a fearful pulse in the room. Everyone was high-strung with trepidation at such an atrocity coming to life. Many of the men in Wheelbarrow had come in to Stop-n-Go-Nutz for a cup of coffee, only to find monsters waiting to devour. Was it the end of the world?

Randy Evens, an oil rig worker, rather large around the middle but swarthy to the core, asked the obvious question. "What are they going to do to us, General?"

Whitman looked at the citizens of Wheelbarrow Creek and said, "Didn't you hear me boy? I said *they want to murder us where we stand.* All we need to do is exercise our second amendment rights and murder 'em back!"

As one, the men left the store for their guns, cleaned and ready on racks in the back window of muddy trucks. Only the family men drove away. The rest had nothing to drive to, nowhere to go. Single men working for the next paycheck came back fully loaded. Matt, Trish and George were already being drilled and yelled at by Whitman, setting up ammunitions from the general's own personal stockpile of guns.

Whitman pulled out his double barrel and marched the men out front. They lined up, just like a normal day at the practice range. By then the skeleton army was marching its way toward them.

Matt was trying his best to keep it together. He never did finish that book, left forever marked on page 147. It seemed so hopeless to win against an army of skeletons. How could you kill something long-since dead?

Red fired the first shot. The recoil from his buckshot flung back copper hair. A skeleton went down, shoulder dissolving to powder. It staggered up and kept coming. General Whitman held up his arm, "Hold your fire! Let's hit 'em all at once! On my mark... ready... NOW!"

As one they shot, a cacophony of sound and lead, cutting through twenty-five skeletons, century-old bones turned into dust. Hundreds more came after them. Twenty yards away they shot again, another twenty-five down, another hundred to replace them.

Ten meters away General Whitman hollered, "Fire at will!"

The five Jackson brothers expended their ammunition and ran as one to face them off, using their riffles as clubs. Two skeletons went down with every blow. One skeleton stabbed his jagged fingers into a Jackson brother's back. Its bones shattered into dust. This greatly emboldened the brothers. The skeletons were too feeble to be of any real threat. Whatever voodoo power was holding them up couldn't stop 150 years of natural erosion.

One of the skeletons threw itself at a man's face, cutting it with grainy lacerations. The man opened his mouth to scream; brittle bone turned to dust flew down his wind pipe. The man fell to the ground, writhing under bodies of skeletons as they turned into waves of dust. Two others fell beneath the skeleton army, heavy dust piling up and keeping them down, crushing them.

General Whitman called out, "Fall back inside men!"

Three more went down as they retreated inside the station. Skeleton after skeleton pounded against the glass, giving up animated life for the chance at smashing in the window.

Men were already running out of bullets. It didn't matter—too many skeletons for lead to make a difference. Skeletons rammed into the glass with a swoosh, like shovels in sand: 1, 2… 1, 2, 3. It was only a matter of time before the piled-up dirt would shatter the window.

General Whitman was actually happy, flashing his pearly whites in a toothy grin. "My ancestors sure know how to bring it… even after 150 years!" He turned and looked at the men, coughing up dust. Wide eyes looked back.

Whitman couldn't help but grin even more, "Looks like the end boys. You've fought well, but I think it's time to give this place up to them."

Ol' Red went to light a cigarette. Whitman grabbed his lighter and said sternly, "You know the rules Earl: no smoking in here—unless it's me!" He went to his counter and pulled off four valves. The smell of gasoline saturated the cramped room. He turned and looked at Matt. "Well, what are you waiting for?! Get the hell out of my store!"

Matt looked at the front windows. They were beginning to crack beneath the pounding dirt.

"Not that way! Out back!"

Matt, George and Trish went to the back. Three or four men followed behind. General grabbed a gasoline can, uncorked it, and started pouring out a trail leading the back way. He looked at the rest and said, "You can stay if you like, but I'm not going to die for this hellhole." Everyone scrambled out the back way, some carrying six-packs of beer, just as the front glass shattered. Waves of sand poured inside, and behind those waves, the skeletal remains of the 58th brigade.

Matt led them out, only to find a line of skeletons closing in. He held his arms out as if waiting to receive something. A pitchfork materialized in his hands.

In deft motions, Matt waved the fork back and forth, cutting through ancient skeletons one at a time. They fell into piles of dust, unable to get beyond the arcing swings of the pitchfork. He cut a path for the rest to follow. No one questioned how the pitchfork appeared from thin air... they'd seen enough unnatural things; one more didn't matter much.

About a hundred yards away General Whitman stopped, pulled out a cigar, and lit it. "Ever seen an explosion?" When no one answered he added with that familiar grit of his, "Well, it ain't like the movies, so drop those asses to the ground!" They fell as one. He dropped the lighter and fell with it, shielding his face. Fire trailed inside the store, bursting it open like a shaken can of beer. Dust and flame flew everywhere, throwing smoke and debris high into the sky.

Matt closed his eyes with head held low to the rattled ground. His ears felt the shockwave as it passed by at the speed of sound. This was nothing like a video game. He lifted himself off the ground and looked at what was once the Stop-n-Go-Nutz. Flames and rubble were surrounded by piles of ash mixed with dust. A few people around him sent up a howler, and then dead silence. Whitman was asking around for names.

He spoke with a sigh then, "We lost six men, boys. We're going to have to do better than this if we want to get rid of the spooks in town! Any trucks that survived the blast are hereby confiscated by the Union army of Wheelbarrow Creek! Let's take it to 'em!

The hollering came back in full force then. A few were passing out some beers. Whitman started choosing lieutenants, all the while making sure everyone only had one drink.

Matt just sat there, ragged breath, parched lips... just like boot camp for the marines. What a day, he thought. This morning he was a nobody delivering dry-cleaned shirts to other nobodies. Now he had been drafted into a makeshift army with a cause to take back the town. Who knows, thought he, By day's end, I just might have the courage to finish reading that book, climb Mount Everest, or even send that letter to Cindy. The hint of a grin creased his lips.

His phone buzzed, as mad as a disturbed beehive. He checked the name... it was Mom. So she was okay! He released a sigh of relief and pushed the receive button.

"Mom you're doing all right!"

"Matthew! Thank God you're okay! I've been trying to reach you."

Matt was grinning then, "Yeah, I think everyone in this town is trying to reach everyone."

"Where are you?"

"I'm at the Stop-n'-Go-Nutz, or what's left of it. We just blew up a ton of skeletons! I've joined the Wheelbarrow Creek army and we're going to take this town back from the zombies!"

Shadeskin

by
B. L. White

Clara's coarse, black wings cut the harsh wind. Dark strands of hair fell over a stark white face. Her enhanced senses had led her toward the relic's birth of power.

Pitch black eyes gazed down, tracing the amulet's source; a residue of power trailed back to a residential area where it rested within the heart of a red-brick, white-trimmed, two-story home.

Upon hitting the ground she reigned in her lust for power. Black wings folded back inside, scraping against a stone soul. Dark hair shriveled into frizzled strands of light auburn. Black eyes transformed to amber. She walked toward the house in question and knocked. It took a few seconds before she heard footsteps through the walls. The voice of a middle-aged woman was talking to someone on the phone.

Clara's hypersensitive ears caught the woman in mid-sentence, "—don't know about you joining a ragtag army like that Matt. Come back home. I've called your father. Yes I know. He will explain everything when you come here: why I have kept you so close to me… why he was never here while you grew up… we have an important role to play in the days ahead." The woman who opened the door was a bit shorter than Clara. She had graying hair and rosy cheeks. A horrified look crossed over her face, "Oh my! You look like you've been chased by an army of those creepers! Please come inside young girl!"

Clara looked down and noticed for the first time how disheveled her clothes were, an unforeseen side effect of flying through the air. Perhaps this is why the Shades I've met wear tight clothing. She made a mental note to don similar attire in the future. She stepped inside and took a moment to clear her throat. The woman took that as a sign to get a glass of water.

Clara could hear her in the next room still speaking on the phone, "Son, you get on back here. We'll figure it out together. I have to go; a straggler just came in from the outside, no doubt hiding from the creepers... I don't want to hear a word about zombies and skeleton armies. This isn't one of your video games! This is real living, real terror!" A beep signaled that the phone was cut off.

Clara took this moment to think about how best to manipulate the situation. She replayed what the woman had said to her son named Matt earlier and concluded: an estranged father must have hidden the Relic here. I'll try to retrieve it with as little fuss as possible.

She glanced around the hallway and saw a family crest hanging over the entryway. The name Gillard was written in flowery letters.

The woman, whom Clara surmised was named Ms. Gillard, entered the hallway with a glass of water and a yarn blanket. Clara's face took on the shocked expression of one who had experienced something traumatic. The blanket was wrapped around her and the drink placed in her shaking hands.

"There, there now," said the woman, "let's go to the couch and have a seat."

Clara allowed herself to be led onto the couch. The woman sat next to her, placing a hand over her shoulder. "Tell me, dear. What happened?"

Clara's voice sounded cold and distant, "No time to explain. He told me to come as soon as I could."

"Who dear?"

Clara looked deep into the woman's eyes. She touched her hand, allowing the Illumin side to soothe the woman's fears. The woman's eyes responded with a relaxed look.

"Your estranged husband is my employer, Ms. Gillard. He has been detained fighting those… creepers. He sent me here to retrieve the relic."

Ms. Gillard replied in a drowsy sort of way, "Estranged husband, you say?" Clara touched her again, more strongly than before. Ms. Gillard's eyes grew drowsier.

"I really don't have time to explain, Ms. Gillard."

The woman yawned in reply and said, "Of course, I'll go to the attic and retrieve the amulet for you."

Clara's senses noticed the residue of the relic's power did not lead up to the attic. "Ms. Gillard, I know that the relic isn't in the attic. Please be honest and prompt with me. He doesn't want to be kept waiting."

Ms. Gillard froze in place for a few seconds. She whirled around, "What is his name?"

"Who? My employer?"

"My estranged husband, as you called him."

"You really want to test me now? I've fought through hordes of creepers to get here. Your son's name is Matt. He wants to join the Army."

Ms. Gillard deflated, "Did he really tell you we were married? And he thinks it was the Army Matt wanted to join?"

"He told me many things that I can't speak of right now."

Ms. Gillard grasped Clara's arms, "Well, he was lying! I haven't heard from him in more than a decade! He left me alone with a number to call if anything crazy started happening. I called it. He said he was coming, promised me! You have to get us out of here!"

Clara felt a smoldering rage growing within. Her amber eyes immediately dimmed to coal black. "I don't have time for this." She got up and promptly walked through Ms. Gillard, throwing her aside like a ragdoll. Her senses were tuned to follow the essence of the relic's after-glow. It led upstairs into a young man's dirty bedroom. There it should have been, resting on a grimy bed. She threw the bed sheets aside, dug her fingers into the mattress, and then threw it across the room in rage. The relic had been birthed alive in this very room, on this very bed; yet, it was nowhere in sight.

She closed her eyes and reached within time to see if she could discern something, anything, about the relic's birth. It was too powerful though, fudging the lines between past and future. She opened her eyes and saw a letter on the floor. On a whim she picked it up... it was addressed to a Cindy Raven... what did the Ravens have to do with this?! The letter was crumpled and placed in her back pocket.

Whoever had awakened its power was gone. She let out a blood-curdling scream. Wings clawed out of her back. She launched through the ceiling and into the attic. Her hypersensitive eyes and hands searched desperately for any hint of the relic. None were found. Ms. Gillard was lying to her.

Clara walked down the stairs, brushing off debris and wood. "Ms. Gillard, I'm not through with you."

She sauntered back to the living room and found Ms. Gillard's body on the floor. She turned it over; rosy cheeks were replaced with a horror-stricken look. Was she in shock? Clara nudged the woman's body with her toes... no response. She kicked her... nothing. She bent over and delicately felt the heart... dead! Her only lead was dead.

Clara smashed through the nearby entertainment system. Her hair grew long and black once more. If only she hadn't gotten so angry. Then she saw Ms. Gillard's phone resting nearby. She picked it up and dialed the last caller, labeled simply, My son.

A boy's panting breath, drenched with fear entered her ear, "Mom! Are you there?! Is my dad really coming back?"

She spoke to this fearful child, "I have your mother, Matt Gillard. Come home now and she won't be harmed."

Matt shouted back, "Who is this? What have you done?"

Clara responded in a haunting tone, "I am your own personal death angel. I'll be her death if you do not bring what I want. Give me the relic and I will let your mother go."

The boy was panting even harder. She enjoyed every agonizing breath he made. So much pain and fear! She couldn't wait to see the look on his face when he found his mother dead on the dining room floor.

His breathing slowed, grew soft and then suddenly quiet. Something else spoke darkly through the receiver, "I am the amulet! None can own me!"

The phone went dead in her hands. She carefully placed the phone in her pocket. The boy was smarter than she thought... or was that something else at the end, someone else speaking through him? Either way, this someone didn't sound like he wanted to be reckoned with... this suited Clara just fine.

The relic's birth of power sent out a strong residue of power, so powerful in fact that she couldn't sense where the relic was at the moment. Her eyes caught something on the ground though, a nametag thrown haphazardly on the tiled floor. She picked it up and read: Talon Dry Cleaners, Matthew Gillard. A residue of the relic's power emanated from it.

Matt ended the phone call, moving slowly, like a dream. He didn't know what he had told the haunting voice on the other end. Whatever it was, it shut her up. He had to get to his mother, no matter what. He noticed his work van had remained untouched by the blown up gas station. He looked around for Trish and George. They'd have to really book it if they wanted to desert this army.

The general's make-shift, zombie-hunting army was the closest he'd get to joining the Marines... looks like mom would always win out in the end.

He saw them on the outskirts, Trish holding on to a visibly shaken George.

When he got there he heard Trish saying, "George don't walk away from this. We need to stick this out together." George didn't seem to be hearing her. He looked close to a zombie himself as he took another step away. "George, we need you!" Trish fell to the ground desperately, her voice barely above a whisper, "I need you."

George turned around with the most horrific look on his face, tears streaming down his cheeks. "I didn't sign up for this. I... I'm sorry." George ran then, far into the woods.

Matt picked Trish off the ground and wiped away the tears from her eyes. A feeling of boldness came over him and he said, "Let him go, Trish. We can take my van and cut him off on the road to the other side. Unless you have your car."

Trish just stared off into the distance, "Gone. They're both gone."

"Who else is gone?"

"George is gone... and my car... all gone." Matt looked back at the parking lot. Half of the cars and trucks were covered with dust and debris. The only thing that saved his van was the nearby dumpster.

Just then a man in overalls carrying a shotgun over his shoulder walked up and said, "Hello boy. Name's Joe. You the owner of the van there? Minuteman army needs it."

Matt saluted sharply, "Yes sir, right away."

Trish frowned and was about to say something. Matt held a finger up to her and walked toward the van. Joe was speaking all the while. "Gotta drive to Jake's Army Depot to pick up some ammunition. Might have to throw out the clothes to make room. I'm sure your customers won't mind, probably all spookified and such. Are you going to be okay driving?"

Matt nodded as he climbed into the driver's seat. Once Trish got in the passenger's side, Matt turned the van on.

Joe signaled Matt through the driver's-side window to back up. Matt just sat there with his hands on the steering wheel. Then he opened the window and called out to the man, "Sorry about this, but I need to find my friend and save my mom." Before Joe could respond, Matt spun out down the road, kicking up trails of the 58th Brigade's ashy remains.

It didn't take them long to find George walking on the roadside… much like a zombie. A dark blue car had pulled over. An older black man in a brown suit and tie was behind George holding a pump-action 12 gauge shotgun. The gun's butt was held against his forearm like an amateur. Trish frantically rolled down the window and cried out incoherent phrases. Matt pulled over just as the man took aim to shoot George. Luckily for George, the man was a horrible shot. The kickback threw the gun out his hands. George reacted at once, cowering on the ground.

Matt got out of the van, ran over, and picked up the shotgun.

The man fell to the ground, dumbstruck at what he had almost done.

Trish ran to George's side. Matt pointed the gun at the old man, "Why'd you try to kill my friend?"

The man was breathing hard, leaning against the blue car. He held his right forearm as he spoke in a deep, tired voice, "Thought he was one of them creepers. Creeping along, biting people, killing my family. One by one they took 'em. Then my family rose up to eat me. Had to run away, had to hide from my own grandkids."

Matt put the gun down, letting out a breath. He handed the gun back to the man. The man shook his head, "You keep it. These old bones have no idea how to shoot."

"Where'd you get it?"

"Stopped off at Jake's Army Depot. He's still there handing out guns to any who want them. I was his first, you know. He tried to tell me how to shoot it. Couldn't hear him over everyone shouting, all of them trying to take control of the city. Lots of sickos walking there, animals and humans alike, carrying this disease from who knows where." The man looked over at George, "Good thing I'm a bad shot though… could have really done that boy in. You tell him not to walk so slowly, you hear?"

Matt nodded and said, "We're going to save my mom. Do you want to come with us?"

The old man laughed then, "No sir. I'm finished with this. My family's all I had. They're gone. I gotta get out of here, gotta leave this town gone crazy.

Trish walked George back to the van. George pushed himself away from Trish and crawled in the back. Trish was visibly shaking at this point. Matt placed a hand on her shoulder and stepped inside the back door. George was taking clothing off the hanger, making a nest for himself in the corner. He sat there in the midst of the clothing like a frightened child. His center-of-the-world, jerk mentality had vanished.

Matt said, "How're you doing there, Geo?"

"I killed my roommate" was all George could say.

Matt placed the gun on the floor and said, "You killed a zombie, plain and simple. If you had done nothing, he would have turned you."

"Didn't mean to kill him though. I was just so mad, so angry that he would attack me. He destroyed my computer… do you know how much money that monitor cost me?"

Matt didn't know what to say to this. He glanced at his phone. They were losing valuable time.

George went on, "I just took the computer tower and WHAM! Slammed it on his head."

"George, you killed a zombie, not a person."

"That's not the point… I would have done the same thing to anyone... I'm just, I'm just a violent person. Guess all those statistics are right about gamers. We secretly want to watch the world burn."

"Was your roommate trying to bite you?"

"Yes."

"Did he even seem like himself?"

"No, not at all. He assaulted me with a beer bottle."

"So you were in fear for your life then?"

"Yes, but--"

"Sounds to me like good, old-fashioned self-defense. Something we'll be doing a lot of before this day is through."

George turned to Matt. His face lit up. "Carlos!" he said.

"What?"

"My roommate's name was Carlos. He was a good man, helped me out many times." His face darkened to a frown, "I never really thanked him though."

"Thank him now."

"Carlos. Thanks for everything," George whispered.

Matt placed a hand on George's shoulder, and then moved up to the driver's seat. Trish sat there, knees held to chest, rocking back and forth in the passenger's seat. She looked up when Matt sat down, eyes frantic with worry. He looked at Trish and said, "Go to him."

She ran to the back and held George close, like a mother cuddling her child. Larger-than-life George didn't seem to mind one bit.

Matt drove back on the road and waved at the old man, who was still sitting near his car. The sad old man got up slowly. Matt saw the dark blue sedan in the van's rearview mirror driving away in the opposite direction.

On the way home they passed three unusual happenings: a truck loaded with pre-teen boys holding guns, a crying man walking outside his trailer house with a bloody axe, and a Feather Black Drugstore on fire, raven-crested sign bending precariously towards the road.

As if on cue, a human with black wings flew overhead. The face was ashen white, surrounded by thin, long strands of black hair. A pent-up memory clawed its way out of Matt's mind: the dream of a woman, beautiful death, haunting him. Matt rubbed his eyes. The image was gone.

Two miles down, he pulled into his subdivision and squealed to a stop near his red-brick house. Rushing in with pitchfork in hand, he found his mom slumped over the counter, moaning to herself.

Matt said, "Mom? Are you all right? She didn't hurt you did she?"

His mom sat up, head oddly tilted, and turned around. Her empty eyes and lips drooled with saliva and blood. Even with a broken neck she was animated, zombified with a force strong enough to move her about to feast on her own forearm.

Matt ran out of the front door and slammed it shut, trying in vain to hold back tears. A flood of screams rushed out of him. His mother, oh how he hated his scheming and conniving mother... and now she was dead, murdered by someone he'd never even seen. Trish exited the van to comfort him, but he would have none of it. He ran to the side of the house, screaming at an unjust world.

Everything was caused by the amulet he wore, yet he had the unnerving sensation that it was wearing him, playing with his emotions and dreams. It was his father's fault for giving it to them. He ripped off his shirt. Everything wrong in his life was caused by Dad.

He looked at the pendant on his chest. There it stood, skull held by bony hands, aqua stones, three of them crushed, stuck on the top of the skullcap, all of it fused to his skin. He tried to rip it off; it refused to budge, though, like a gaudy masquerade mask. He didn't care; it would come off even if it killed him. He put his fingers over the thing and began to yank as hard as he could.

Something whispered inside his mind, You can't murder

immortality. A power shot through him, shook him to the core. He blacked out.

A dream came, suffocating his reason with chaos. He beheld a shadowy presence of cold stone enveloping him. The stones softened when touching his skin, as if they were made from a thick tar. It spoke, "You wanted to be closer to your father. This can be arranged."

"What are you?" Matt asked.

"I am the wish-maker, the night-watcher, the weaver of dreams."

"Did you cause this to happen?"

"I only cause what is dreamed, whether good or bad; you dreamed of zombies; the price of such a dream is animated carcasses, death incarnate."

Matt looked at the shadow in the amorphous head and screamed, "I wish for my mother to come back!"

The shadowy being chuckled a bit, "But she has come back. She's in there now... in the kitchen where you left her... at least for the moment."

A loud bang woke him up. Trish was standing over him, staring in horror at the pendant on his chest. He got up, feeling strangely better, powerful even. Then he remembered his mother....

Then he remembered the bang!

He shot past Trish. George was walking out the front door, holding the shotgun like an amateur. Before he could say anything, Matt slammed his fist into George's face. George fell with a clunk. Matt picked up the shotgun and pointed it at George.

George looked pathetic, holding his head and

stammering, "I had to do it, man. She was a zombie."

Matt screamed, "You should have waited for me. I at least could have made my peace, could have done something... maybe even pulled the trigger."

George was holding his hands up to the gun, "What's done is done, man. She's dead. Just like my roommate, just like Carlos. It's all self-defense, you know. She was coming at me and I had the gun up."

Matt moved the gun closer and screamed, "That's not the point! It was my call to make! You always think of yourself... your way of doing things, your path and your thoughts on the matter, to hell with anything else. She was my mother, man! I had a right to do something about it!"

"I—I'm sorry. I didn't know what to do. She was coming right at me... you know, self-defense and all."

"Use some common sense Geo! When you see me running out of the house... don't walk in. From here on out, I call the shots."

George got up slowly, "Fair enough, Matt. You're the boss."

Matt put the muzzle down and walked to the van.

George walked up to Trish and said, "We need to keep an eye on him. He might snap any minute."

Trish looked at George coldly, "All those years growing up. I had the biggest crush on you. How could I have missed it?"

George blurted out, before he could think, "What do you mean, Trishcabait?"

She slapped him in the face, "I told you to wait. But no! You just had to do it all your way." She walked over to a water hydrant and took off her impossibly high heels. She started banging the heels on the hydrant until they broke off. "Big bad George's gonna save the day," she said. She put on the heel-less shoes and walked to the passenger side of the van.

George wondered at the duo. Has the world gone mad? He thought to himself as he crawled into the back of the van.

Matt turned on the van and pulled out. The radio turned on—of its own accord—with Jethro Jeepers broadcasting in mid-sentence, —all over the city. Some are rallying around the post office joining the make-shift army. General Whitman is leading the crusade to take our town back! Here are some signs to look for. A fully infected man will probably be waltzing around like a crazed ol' drunk. But that isn't always how it starts. The first stage sets in when a person gets incredibly angry. Don't shoot 'em yet, now. We all lose our cool from time to time. Notice what is being said, though. If the angry tirades devolve into mumbo jumbo… then you got yourself a creep and he needs to be shot forthwith.

Matt's phone rang as they left the subdivision. Matt balanced the phone on his right shoulder while taking a sharp left turn, "Who is it?"

Mr. Randy's commanding voice came on, "You better be on your way back with my van. I don't want to have to fire you."

Matt hadn't expected this… didn't his boss know what was going on?

Jethro Jeepers' high-pitched voice professed, Onward Christian soldiers! Our make-shift army is marching from street to street shooting any and every creeper they find!

Might as well get your firearm and join 'em. They're at fourth and Willow this very second. I'll keep you posted.

"I don't have time for this sir. I have to use this van to help clean out the zombies from this town."

"No, Matt, I… I don't want you to do that. Come on over to my place. I have something for you, from me."

There was a certain odd intonation in the way Mr. Randy spoke, as if he were afraid.

"Sir, are you all right?"

"Matt, I'm fine; I'm just afraid—." The phone was moved away from Mr. Randy. A haunting voice said, "You wanted to play me, Relic. I will kill this man if you do not come to Talon Dry Cleaning."

Matt nearly screamed, missing a guy with a bat walking on the road by a few inches. "What do you want? Who are you?"

"I am your death if you don't give me what I want. But first I will kill your boss here. I might even be doing you a favor."

"What about my mother?"

"Your mother? Your mother's right here waiting for you to save her."

Matt was furious then… how could she lie so easily to him? "Put her on! I want to hear her voice!"

Mr. Randy's baritone voice quivered treble with fear, "Matt, don't try to reason with her. She has a knife to my throat and she's going to take me, kill me if you don't come back and give her what she wants. No, please don't."

What Matt heard next chilled him to the bone: his boss's final words intermixed with the sound of choking and gurgling blood, "No! Don't!"

Clara's sultry voice crooned, "Bring the relic to your work place or I will do the same to your mother." The phone clicked off.

"Hello? Hello?" All Matt heard was dead air, and then Jethro Jeepers' twangy voice spoke enthusiastically through the radio, Looks like our gun enthusiasts have things under control! Let's play some music to keep you company while you kill them creepers! This one never gets old!

A familiar steel guitar riff sounded. A drawn-out voice sang, Break my heart Texan, I know it is vexin', to know Ted's relaxin', when you're not— The last part of the chorus broke off in static as Matt's pitch fork materialized, embedded deep inside the radio.

George popped his head in and asked, "How did you make that happen?"

Matt could only reply with a mumble, "It was just a dream—the zombies, even this pitchfork."

Trish yanked the pitchfork out and placed it beside her, "That's not important right now."

George's eyes grew in size, "Not important? He just materialized a freakin' pitchfork from thin air! And you're not even curious as to how that could happen?"

"I'm very curious… but we don't have time to sort it out now. Who was that on the other line?"

Matt slammed on the brakes before a sea of abandoned cars. After a few deep breaths he said, "It was my mother's killer. Now she killed my boss—just slit his throat like it was nothing! My boss was a very big man. Death is sure to find me eventually, my very own personal Death Angel. I have to find her first. And then," he paused, "I have to kill her." Matt looked down at the relic. "Somehow everything is tied to this amulet of mine." He looked back at George, "Including my ability to conjure up this pitchfork."

Trish placed a hand on his shoulder and said, "We're here for you."

George merely jumped out of the back and said, "Well that's fine and all, but do you think we could get a bite to eat?" He was looking at an abandoned McDonald's.

Matt shook his head in frustration. "Sorry to disappoint you, George. We won't stop for food. Jake's Army Depot is right around the corner."

George spoke in that annoying know-it-all voice of his. "That's fine. I'll get the food, you get the guns."

"It isn't wise to split up. We only have one gun between us and you don't know what's inside there. Let's get more guns and—."

George cut in, "And then we'll get some food."

Matt stepped out of the van, getting irritated, "My mother has been murdered… twice! One time by you. This town is in peril! A woman calling herself Death is coming for us! And all you can think about is food?"

George got that cocky look in his eyes, "What about my mom, and Trish's? Are we going to check on them as well?"

Matt leaned the shotgun against a lamppost, walked over to George, got in his face, and yelled, "Your mother was not murdered!"

George got that cocky look in his eyes, "Hey, all I'm saying is we need to eat. It's basic survival instinct. Can't win this war on an empty stomach you know."

"We don't have time to deal with our empty stomachs! What we need to do first is survive!"

George held up his hands and backed up, "Okay, okay, we'll do it your way. I'm just saying I could really use a Big Mac right now."

Matt said simply, "Tough!" and moved on toward Jake's Army Depot. Trish followed behind timidly.

George eye-balled the shotgun, grabbed it, and ran off toward the yellow-arched sign.

Matt took twenty steps before he noticed something was amiss. He turned around just as George was walking beneath a ten-foot-high cartoon clown holding a sign that read, Kids eat free on Tuesdays! Matt's anger boiled over. The pitchfork immediately appeared in his hand. He made his way back.

Trish stood in the way. "Let him have his way, Matt. Jake will have more guns at the store."

Reluctantly, Matt retraced his steps and walked around the bend. Trish followed hesitantly behind.

All Jake heard was his chair, rocking back and creaking forth… back and forth. He sat there, just behind the bars of his front window. The "U" of GUNs had been smashed in. He'd done it himself. And there he sat, rocking back and creaking forth, smack dab in the middle of the "G" and the

"Ns". The stench of death surrounded him. Mutilated bodies were strewn about, mere inches from his feet. A desert camo scarf, peppered with dark splotches, covered his mouth and nose, yet did nothing to stop the stench. Arresting blue eyes, cold and calculating, watched a lame fly scurry across a pool of blood.

Half an hour after General Whitman grabbed most of the guns for his crusade to take the town back, a bloody mass of spooks attacked Jake's gun store. Good thing Jake had stayed behind to protect the place.

Good thing.

Some of the creepers wore familiar faces. Sally from the antique store down the street rested her pale, diseased cheek on the back track of his rocking chair. It lifted up... and then back down, in motion with the chair as it rocked back... and creaked on forth. He had had to shoot her, and when that didn't work, break her skull with the butt end of his full auto AR-15. Jake thought about Sally and the others, rocking back... the mutilated mess, creaking forth... He stopped for a bit to glance down at the itchy bite wound upon his forearm. Sally hadn't given in without a fight.

Good thing... It wouldn't be long now before... rocking back... before he joined them.

There was movement around the corner... he stopped the chair before the creak could settle in. More spooks no doubt; maybe they wouldn't see him.

He let out a tense breath. It was just a boy and a girl. The boy held a pitchfork. Maybe they'd pass on by. He wanted them to. It was too dangerous at his store. He being the chief danger.

They made a beeline in his direction. Jake swore.

Bad thing.

The morning had started as normal as ever. Then the angry mobs began to attack. Suddenly, Jake's gun store had become the popular hangout. The first unusual costumer was an old black man with a gaunt look in his eyes. He pointed to a pump-action 12 gauge shotgun. He didn't even know what to call the thing. Jake had refused the man. So the man went over and turned on the radio. That's the first Jake had heard of the mayhem. Then he watched in awe as several cars parked in front of his store. Men with fear in their eyes had come in seeking the solace only protection could bring.

Everyone wanted his guns, even the insanely liberal Methodist parson; and now—he gazed at the boy and girl walking his direction—these two kiddies wanted some protection. Thousands of dollars down the drain. All because of some damned apocalypse! He couldn't control the diseased rage welling up inside him, so he picked up his gun and started shooting.

Luckily for Matt and Trish, Jake had set the auto off; his diseased mind was also throwing off his aim.

They dove behind a car. Bullets hit metal with a loud thwack. Matt looked over the top. Jake stood up and wobbled along, swaying side to side like a drunk.

"Who's shooting at us?" Trish asked.

"Looks like Jake. He's been infected. Gotta take him out."

Trish held Matt back, "If he's got the disease, it won't take long before he drops his gun. We can take him out then."

Matt looked back, tears of terror streaking across his

hardening face, "He cannot kill the Relic."

With that, Matt jumped out from behind the car and ran straight toward Jake, holding the pitchfork like a spear. Jake shot back, missing him by many frustrating feet. When the gun ran out of bullets, Jake threw it down and yelled. Matt entered through the broken door and pierced Jake against the wall.

Jake's anger seemed to dissipate then. He looked gaunt and sad. Matt was crying as he pulled the pitchfork out. The blood made it slip out of his hands.

Jake fell to the ground and got up mumbling, "Don't know how to kill, how to kill the spooks. Gotta shoot them in the head. Gotta shoot them creepers dead. Shoot them dead in the head."

Matt picked up the AR-15 and aimed it at Jake's head. Jake lunged at him yelling, "Shoot them spooks!"

Matt pulled the trigger, bracing for the recoil. A horrifying click sounded. The gun was out of bullets. Jake threw the gun aside, along with Matt. He looked about ready to stomp Matt to death.

Trish appeared out of nowhere and pointed a Glock-18 right on the side of the creeper's head saying, "Cover your face Matt."

Matt did as commanded. A deafening bang sounded, followed by a dull thud. Jake fell to the floor on top of the other unfortunates. Trish just stood there holding the gun, frozen in time. Then she cocked her head, "I thought there would be more blood when I shot him. I was so scared there would be more blood. You know, like in the game."

Matt got off the ground and wrapped his arms around

her. She wept then, "I told you to cover your face because I thought you would get infected, with all the blood spraying, like that one scene in D3ad Living."

Matt saw all the bloody bodies, massacred and sometimes in pieces. What type of weapon had done this to them?

He shushed her, "It's okay. Everything's going to be fine. We have guns now. We can make it through this."

Trish looked up at him, teary eyes frowning intensely, "Everything is not going to be fine, Matt. We are not okay! Look around!"

Matt noticed the bodies anew. Somehow he'd managed to place them far from his mind. He realized then… this was the most horrific sight he'd seen in his life: limbs and a bloody mess, meat and crushed bones, barely recognizable faces.

The adrenaline left his body, replaced with the shock of it all. Then the sweet-smelling stench of decay hit his nostrils. His stomach lurched inside… he pushed Trish away and dry-heaved into a zombie's stomach.

It was Trish's turn to pat him on the back.

Matt had to get his mind off the carnage around him. He looked over at the Jake's gun and picked it up for a quick examination. "At least we didn't come here for nothing. This here is a full auto Colt Ar-15 Conversion with a butt stock and receiver extension, collapsible too. Here's a tango down stubby gripper beneath the barrel." He flipped the gun and held it closer. "See the sear pin on the other side. That's how you can identify an auto. Yup, I'd say a custom job done here, maybe by Jake himself; pre-'86 no doubt."

Trish followed Mat to the cleaner side of the store as he talked. It was nice to hear his voice, anything to keep her mind off the carnage. "What does all of that mean?" she asked.

Matt looked up with a glint in his eye. "It's a fully automatic machine gun, Trish, perfect for killing zombies."

"I didn't realize you knew so much about guns."

"YouTube helped me there."

Trish raised an eyebrow.

"I wanted to join the Marines so I thought I'd learn how to shoot."

"Have you ever shot a machine gun before?"

Matt laughed. "No. They're mostly illegal… unless it's been made before the Hughes Amendment in 1986." Matt looked at the Glock in Trish's hand. "I have shot one of those. It's a good choice for you." He held out his hand. Trish placed the gun in it.

"This here is a Glock nine-millimeter." He looked around for some ammunition and grabbed a box of magazines. "Put as many of these as you can in your purse."

Trish dumped everything but her cell phone out, replacing it all with magazines.

"This is how you load it," Matt said while pulling the barrel back and ejecting the half-empty magazine. He pushed the magazine in and pulled the barrel back, releasing it to zoom forward. It clicked in place. Taking the magazine out again he handed it to Trish and said, "Load it."

Trish looked at the gun for a few seconds then asked, "Which way does the magazine go in?"

"Face the bullet tip forward."

Trish immediately felt foolish for asking. She pushed the magazine in, bullet tip facing the front of the gun, and clicked the barrel in place.

Matt was grinning, "And that's how you prepare for a zombie apocalypse. Do I have to tell you to aim for the head?"

She was about to say something in response when she heard a strange, distant scream. Matt walked to the front of the store and saw George running toward them, his yelling high-pitched like a woman. He was carrying the shotgun haphazardly in one hand and a McDonald's to-go bag in the other. It would have been almost comical if not for the mass of zombies... if that's what you could call them.

It was more like a walking bloodbath. Infested creepers sprinted after him, running and biting into each other. Some had limbs torn off. Some ran aimlessly as blind men. The bigger zombies were thrashing the smaller ones aside. One of them was a creepified black bear with matted, torn hair and baring red teeth. It tore a human zombie to shreds until it was trampled on by the others. The remains of the zombie got up and bit at another one's foot. Another was trampled by the bloody mob. It was cast aside, crawling on toward them.

It all looked like a horrific meat grinder come alive. Thousands of bodies of the undead were attacking everything around, including themselves. Zombie dogs and cats were running along the outside, going blood crazy and diving into the bloody mob. One of the dogs ran after George. He turned around and shot it in the head, dropping the McDonalds doggy bag in the process. Other dogs left the mob to attack the twice-murdered carcass of the dog.

Matt wiped the puke from his lips, grabbed a few magazines, noticed they were for the wrong gun, grabbed a few by Jake's rocker, and tried to figure out how to put one in the automatic AR-15. By the time he'd found out, Trish had already shot two magazines of her Glock, shooting through the barred windows, into the bloody onslaught.

George ran inside and tried to close the broken door. He was blocking Matt's view. Matt yelled, "Don't worry about the door Geo! Move aside!"

George moved and Matt shot. The sound was deafening inside the enclosed space. He had to work hard at keeping the gun level as he fired it. Half the bullets shot above the bloody mob's head. In almost no time he emptied his magazine. While he changed magazines George took aim with the shotgun and shot a shell into two zombies about to run inside. The other zombies cut through them, literally tearing their own apart to get in. Matt yelled, "Hit the ground!"

Once George moved out of the firing line, Matt let them have it at point blank range. It was hard to miss this time.

Trish called out, barely heard above the cacophony of sound and stench, "Back here Matt! There's a way out!" Matt helped George up, just as the meat grinder of creepers drilled its way inside the gun store. They ran out back through a door that led to the alley. A few zombie dogs and cats were chasing them. George kicked a cat up. It was caught mid-air by a dog, golden retriever by the looks of it. Its leash made a jingling sound as it tore the cat apart. Matt managed to put in his last magazine. He made short work of the animals. Trish finished one of them.

Then the zombie bear broke through the door, undead cat and dog limbs spilling out with it. Trish tripped over her heelless shoes. The bear was lumbering towards her. George ran up and shot it point blank in the nose. Still it came thrashing at them; George and Trish were barely able to scramble out of the way in time. Matt conjured his pitchfork and launched it into the creeper bear's skull. It fell at last, two inches from Trish's face.

The rest of the zombies ran through the broken door. Trish's Glock was caught under the bear. She lay beside it in shock. George was pumping empty shots at the zombies, screaming at the top of his lungs.

Matt knew they couldn't outrun the lot. He would have to hold them off somehow. He placed a hand on George's gun. "You can't do any more harm here, George. Grab Trish and take her back to the van."

George saw the steel in Matt's eyes and nodded. He awkwardly helped Trish off the ground.

"Matt!" Trish said in fear.

Matt gave her a sly grin. "Don't worry." He held up the machine gun. "I'll kill 'em with this."

When George and Trish had moved around the corner he threw the empty gun aside and went for the pitchfork. Then he remembered he could conjure it in his hand. He thought as fast as he could... Pitchfork in hand. Nothing happened.

The zombies ambled closer.

Pitchfork in hand! Pitchfork in hand!

A whispering voice echoed within, Your creations are an aimless mass, badly in need of a leader. Let me show you what I mean.

Something jerked inside him, forcing his hands to let go of the pitchfork that had finally materialized. In jerky motions he walked—or, rather, was led forward by an unseen force—right toward the waiting zombies. His hands were held up and his mouth forcibly opened. The zombies were only a few feet away. Their stench was unbearable.

A power surged from within and erupted out of his mouth. "Stop!" he yelled.

The zombies stopped.

A smile forcibly crept across his lips. Tears of struggle dribbled out of his eyes. I am the dream catcher, the voice told him. You are the dream harnesser.

"I don't want to be anything, demon!" Matt yelled. "Leave me alone!"

The zombies responded by walking away. He was about to turn around when a thought crossed his mind. He turned back to the creepers saying, "On second thought, come back."

They came back silently and stood before him, as best as their broken bodies could.

"Kneel before your master."

The zombies obliged with a penitent pose, crushed faces held close to the ground. He felt a thrill of excitement. They were his to do with as he pleased. Then, as swift as it had come, the power left him. He felt deflated… alone… just like the same old Matt.

Without me, the voice whispered, you have no power over them. Remember that. The zombies started to stir, forgetting whom their master was.

Matt conjured up his pitchfork and dispatched them one

at a time. He felt nothing, no connection of doing right or doing wrong… just the stabbing.

The zombies were torn up so much they couldn't move. A writhing mass of undead bodies blocked the doorway back inside the store. Something was scratching on the other side. He didn't care to check what it was, didn't much care about anything anymore…

He pulled the pitchfork out and walked away.

Clara landed in a large crater of dust and ash. She had waited for the boy at Talon Dry-Cleaning for nearly 30 minutes. He hadn't come. Perhaps he had grown wise to her. She needed more leverage on him. She went to the next outburst of power, what used to be the Stop-n-Go-Nutz.

In the midst of gray debris a woman stood, glowing blue. Clara kicked a cloud of dust her way. Not a speck landed on the glowing skin sizzling with energy.

"So, Gabriella left the great and powerful D'Nas to challenge me herself?"

The Illumin looked at Clara, tears pouring out of her eyes, only to evaporate into vapor from the powerful light. "So much pain and regret. The relic must be stopped."

Clara's eyes fixed on her with a stone-cold stare, "This is why I am here."

"You are here to bring death. The boy is innocent!"

"Look around you! This is his second outburst. A whole gas station destroyed."

"We must contain him."

"No. I must kill him."

"You are just being Zyne's puppet."

Clara shot forward, shoving Gabriella hard into the dust. She was caught unawares as she fell.

"I am no puppet." Clara replied through gritting teeth.

Gabriella knew she couldn't contend with Clara's powers. She would make an attempt upon Clara's vanity. She pretended to be badly hurt, even letting the grimy dust cling to her. Something was hanging outside Clara's back pocket. If only she would step in close enough.

Clara stepped in closer and said, "Oh come off it. I didn't shove you that hard."

One more step and Gabriella would have the jump. She needed to keep her talking, "Illumin and Shade blood is flowing too strongly in you, Clara. You can't have it both ways. One day you will have to choose."

Clara made the next step, smiling. "I have already made that choice. Zyne is my destiny."

Gabriella sprang up, giving an uppercut to Clara's chin. While Clara recovered, the Illumin grabbed for the piece of paper in Clara's back pocket. Clara swung around, kicking Gabriella in the ribs. The paper flew out of Gabriella's hand. Clara gave her a beating then, viciously punching and kicking the Illumin into a bloody pulp.

Gabriella laughed, pain throbbing with every shake, "You may be more powerful, but you're an amateur when it comes to follow-through."

Clara's eyes turned pitch black with rage. "So says the Illumin beneath my boot!" She brutally stomped on Gabriella's back. It broke with a crack. Gabriella screamed as dust and ash clung to her open wound.

Clara's black wings opened out. With one swift push, she was 30 feet into the sky.

Gabriella reached deep inside for her Faith. Sinews reformed, reattaching her back bone. It was in times like these that she missed her natural form. She pulled herself up with a snap. Her skin charged up translucent blue, vaporizing any soot and dust. Then she reached down and picked up the piece of paper. It was an envelope addressed to Cindy Raven.

What role are Ravens playing in all of this? she thought.

Matt had led them to the nearest Feather Black Drugstore. After checking for zombies, a gnawing hunger began to take its toll on them. They made a hasty lunch of chips and coke.

Trish insisted they put on new clothing and clean off the blood. George complained that only a woman would think of clothing and personal hygiene at this time. Matt had to remind George that the blood on them was infected.

Trish passed out scarves to wear over their faces. She also found some tennis shoes to put on instead of the broken-off high heels.

Matt was nuking some burritos in a microwave he had plugged in. Trish sat nearby, nursing her sore feet. George was off exploring in the electronics department. The KING

Kountry radio station was on, Jethro Jeepers giving the latest news on Z-day: Main Street's been cleared up, and so have the surrounding areas. Whitman's taking his crusade out into the sticks. Seems the whole town got hit with the bug. First came the dead animals and road kill. From their bites the hobos got infected, getting raging mad and spreading the disease further. Now I know the Z word's been thrown around a lot today, but here I got a bonafide scientist who can attest to it being a mutated strand of rabies.

Matt shut the radio off. The skeptics were already trying to make sense of it. Matt knew the truth; deep inside, he knew the amulet had caused it all.

Trish spoke up then, "I don't know how those women do it. Female super heroes in high heels and bikinis, give me a break!"

Matt chuckled, "You mean like that time we went to Comic Con and you dressed as Sophie Stevens?"

"Minus the high-heeled boots!"

"You would have looked nice in those."

"They were too expensive… the real thing is very different isn't it, from D3ad Living I mean?"

Matt clicked off the microwave before it hit zero. "My mom didn't die in the game."

Trish looked up. "How are you dealing with that?"

Matt grabbed the hot burrito gingerly. "I'm finding the strength to push on for now. Did you finally reach your family?"

"Yeah. Mom and dad are fine, worried more about their 'little princess.' I told them I was in good hands."

Matt looked at her then; he had never noticed how

smooth and angelic her face was, sandy blonde hair done up in a cute little bun. The warm smell of apple-scented shampoo permeated the air around her, a pleasant change from zombie filth.

Ever since he and George had hit it off all those years ago Trish had tagged along, always trying to get George's attention. Matt had viewed her as one of the boys. Somehow she'd blossomed, though, into a rather gorgeous nerd. He watched her brush hair off her cheek as she put the other shoe on.

She looked up questioningly, and then asked, "Matt, when we were at your house earlier... well, I saw that skull on your chest, and it was glowing somehow. What is that?"

Matt clutched at the pendant beneath the shirt absent-mindedly. Should he tell her about the dream of the shadowy stones? Should he tell her about the voice inside him, how it gave him power over the zombies? He looked deeply into her brown eyes, larger than life. His mouth started moving, words spilling out like a confession, "My mother always had it; even as a kid growing up I remember her looking at it. It's very old, a pendant from the Aztecs. She said it was my father's, given to us for safe keeping. I should have never put it on. I—I was planning on pawning it after work, to get enough money to escape this place. That was before the zombies..."

"How did it get stuck on your skin?"

"I don't know. You may not believe this, but it sort of just melted into me... I hear, I hear voices, Trish. Voices calling to me, telling me things. I don't know what to do."

Trish came over and placed a hand on his. "You could

always pray to God."

"Pray? I thought you were an atheist."

She shrugged, "I don't know what I am after all of this: zombies, skeleton armies, Aztec skulls fused to chests; seems way outside the realm of science."

Matt squeezed her hand, "Thanks Trish."

"For what?"

"For being you."

Trish looked away with a slightly endearing look, one she usually wore when George was around. She looked back and said, "You know, I had a crush on you before George."

Matt was taken aback, "What? You liked me?"

She was smiling then, touching him tenderly on the arm, "Yup, I thought you were hot. But you wouldn't give me the time of day. All you thought of, all you dreamed about was Cindy Raven."

Matt brushed some hair from her face, "Well, how about that. Maybe you could, you know, have a crush on me again sometime."

Trish shrugged, "Depends. Like the roll of the die, anything's possible."

About that time George showed up. Matt and Trish separated from each other.

George didn't seem to notice and said, "Found something you guys might want."

George handed them each a pack of walkie-talkie headsets.

"What's this for?" Trish asked.

"Headsets to talk to each other, you know, in case we get lost fighting the zombies."

Matt looked perturbed, "George, we aren't going to fight any more zombies. We'll hole up in here until it's over."

George looked at them both smugly, "I know. It's just in case, though."

Matt shared a look with Trish. They both knew where this would lead. Matt had to put a stop to it, "George. This isn't a game."

George threw his headset down, "Don't you think I know that! My roommate's gone; I can't get a hold of my family! I just thought that…" He was looking frantically between them. His head dipped down, "Never mind."

Matt's phone rang. He just looked at it for a second. Mom showed up on the caller ID. Only one person had his mother's phone…

He pushed receive and said, "I know you killed my Mom, Death."

A very different voice responded then, a voice that would melt his heart into mush, send chills down his back… just to be in her presence, to see her dancing in that red and white cheerleading outfit. "Matthew Gillard? Is—is that you? Some woman has me. She's making me tell you things."

Matt sat down in shock, eyes closed in frustration, "Stay calm, Cindy."

"Matthew, she killed my brother. Not even our weapons could take her out. She's not a Shade, not that you'd know… she's something else. I know you don't understand that, but she wants me to talk to you, wants something from you. Don't let her kill me, Matthew… I, I don't want to tell him that."

Matt heard a slap and then a scream of pain. He stood

up frantically. "Cindy! Cindy, are you there?"

Cindy's voice was shaking as she said, "I'll—I'll do anything Matt. Anything you want. Just give her what she wants!"

Clara's sultry voice came on then, "You see, Matt; I'm not all that bad. You give me the relic, and I'll give you your dream girl."

"I am through with your games, Death."

"Sure about that, Matt? Long, wavy dark hair, ample bosom… I'm sure you could think of something to do with her. Put a knife at her pretty throat and she'll do whatever you want."

"Don't touch her! I'm, I'm coming over."

"Good, meet me near the levees… alone." The phone clicked off.

Matt sat down and placed the phone on his lap.

Trish came up beside him and put a hand on his, "What's wrong?"

"I have to go do something. Go somewhere."

Trish got up, "Okay, let's go."

Matt held his hand up, "I have to do this one alone Trish."

Trish grabbed him by his shirt and threw him against the wall, "You have just lost your mother! You keep getting these strange calls from some woman called Death, and now you say you gotta do this one alone? That's it? Get me out of the way so you can go kill yourself? You are not alone Matt. Now tell me, what's going on?"

Matt placed his hands on his face, tired of crying, tired of fighting, tired of losing people he cared about. "Cindy

Raven. Death has found Cindy Raven. Kidnapped her and wants me to meet her alone. Somehow she knew about my crush on her."

Trish said, "Okay… did you leave anything at your house that might give Cindy's location away?"

Matt held his head and thought deeply about it. His eyes looked up at the realization… his love letter: "My letter! I wrote a letter to her… never mailed it but it had her address on it."

"Okay, good." Trish said with a concentrated frown, "Now we know how she found out. We need to call the Ravens first; I'm sure her parents are worried."

Matt was shaking his head, "Death told me to do this alone; I can't bring in her parents."

Trish picked up Matt's phone and held it against his chest, "You will call Cindy's parents and let them know what's going on. Death's already killed two people; we cannot let her do this again."

"But how will they know it isn't me who took her?"

"You have no choice but to convince them, Matt; without help, Cindy's as good as dead."

Matt nodded his head and made the call.

Gabriella was in the Ravens' living room, talking to the family, warning them about Clara. When the phone rang she instinctively perceived who it was. Lightly, she leapt over the sofa and picked it up, "I know who you are relic boy: guilty or innocent?"

Matt's confused voice said, "What? I mean, I don't know what you mean."

She heard it then, in the way he spoke, the intonation of sound; beneath the veneer of confusion was a heart deep in pain of loss. The boy had no idea what was going on. "You've lost your mother haven't you?" she asked tenderly.

"Yes... Death took her."

Gabriella heard a certain disdain on the word "death" as if it were someone... he wasn't talking about death, he was talking about a person... Clara.

"Would you like to find out Death's name?"

Matt's voice spoke with overtones of determination and anger, "Yes!"

Clara sat in the bushes, the tall levee looming behind her, pitch black eyes watching Cindy squirm on the tree trunk. She was a feisty one, almost broke free a few times with that infamous Raven gadgetry, even tried to take Clara out with it. Clara's Illumin side kept her from being affected, though. Only a full Shade could be hurt by Raven weaponry.

Distant thunder boomed in the sky. A tall, bulbous thunderhead, colored pink by the setting sun, flashed its way slowly across the sky.

Cindy looked toward her captor; her fear shrouded by a façade of anger, "Do you even know who I am?"

"Yes." Clara replied dryly.

"Then you know my parents will stop at nothing to get me back!"

"Okay."

"I'm serious! We Ravens know how to take people like you out."

"I'm shaking in my boots, little girl."

"Just let me go and I promise they'll let you off the hook."

"Okay."

"What? You mean you're going to let me go?" Clara heard relief in Cindy's voice.

"Oh, is that what you said? Well then no, no I'm not." Clara's smile was rude and sarcastic.

Cindy shuffled her feet, "Well, you be sure not to lay a hand on me. If my pop finds out, he's going to—"

Clara smacked the girl lightly on the cheek, "Shut up. Or the next one will break your neck."

Cindy's cheek was burning red. Even that light tap had almost given her whiplash.

Clara's heightened senses picked up the sound of the van. "Oh, here we are. Your knight in shining armor comes to rescue his damsel in distress."

Tears came out of Cindy's eyes, "You're going to kill us, aren't you? After you get what you want. I'm going to die… just like Ronny."

Clara lightly touched Cindy's cheek where she had slapped it, "Now, now little girl, you just look all pretty in that cheer outfit of yours. I killed your brother because he got in the way. Don't make the same mistake."

"He was just bringing me home from practice... you didn't have to kill him!"

Clara sighed, "I wanted you to understand how serious I was. Now quiet down."

The van pulled into the levee's parking lot. A skinny young man walked out, alone.

Clara reined in her powers, black eyes returning to a healthy brown. She walked along the levee to meet him. Matt stopped 20 feet from her.

She held out her hand, trying her best to look normal, "Give me the relic, Matt."

Matt pointed toward the van, "It's in there."

"Well, go and get it for me."

"Where's Cindy?"

"Tied to a tree."

"How do I know you didn't just kill her like my mother?"

Clara was doing a good job reining in her desire to kill him, but this boy was causing so much trouble. Her curly brown hair was already beginning to darken, but she needed the teenage boy's cooperation in order to obtain the relic. "Your mother was a mistake. I didn't mean to kill her. I'm sorry."

"That's not good enough! What makes you think I can trust you this time?"

"You know, I could just kill you and take the relic from the van."

Matt laughed then. "Do you think I'm that dumb? Telling you exactly where the relic is?"

Clara frowned, eyes growing pitch black. She needed to take over this situation before it got out of hand. She extended the power of her aura, inciting the boy to fear her. He was protected by another power... not Illumin, another Shade... somewhere very close.

"Fine boy, have it your way. Your girlfriend's this way."

Matt kept his distance as she led him to the tree.

Cindy sat there tied up and crying. Matt wanted to run to her side immediately, but he held it all back, managing to say, "Don't worry, Cindy. I'm taking you home." He looked at Clara then with a deep-rooted hatred. So this is Death, he thought.

Clara relished the taste of his fear and anger directed towards her. So much bitterness, she thought, and yet so powerless to satiate it. "As you can see, Cindy remains unharmed. Now, if you would just give me the relic."

The thunderhead of a storm was over them now, hazy bits of gray falling from a distance became a rushing force of heavy rain.

Something daring took shape in Matt's eyes. Did he honestly plan to fight her? Matt brought something out from behind his back. Something like a gun, but the barrel was too large. Clara couldn't stifle the laugh as her hair grew dark and long, as thin as blades. Did he think to try to shoot her with that toy? Didn't he know who she was?"

Matt spoke in deep husky tones, "I know who you are Clara: half Shade, half Illumin, totally mad with power." He said all this while lifting the gun to her, and then high into the sky.

Clara's eyes went wide with the realization. Matt shot the flare straight up; it burned brighter than the rising moon. Amidst flashes of lightning a blue streak shot out of the thunderhead, falling directly onto Clara.

She barely raised a hand before the blue form of Gabriella smashed down, pushing Clara back until they hit with a thud against the levee's thick concrete wall.

Clara didn't have time to think as the vengeful Illumin pounded into her. Her black wings shot out, attempting to climb high into the air, to take back the upper hand.

Gabriella would have none of it… she kept beating her down. Something deep came out of Clara, a part of her she had ignored until now. Blue Illumin light sparked into her eyes, dark hair glowing with a blue hue. One hand drew forth a black flame, the other a blue one. She put them together right when Gabriella made contact with her. Illumin and Shade powers were never meant to mix. An explosion shot out, sending both of them flying apart.

The moment Gabriella hit against Clara, Matt moved toward Cindy. The knots were held tightly together. Matt cursed himself for forgetting a knife. Cindy was yelling at him to hurry up.

"I'm going as fast as I can. These knots are tight."

"Use my necklace," she said.

Matt looked into her sweet, dark eyes and then down her neck; the necklace was deep inside her chest. How was he going to get at it without…

"Just grab it," she said.

Matt apologized as he gingerly placed his hand down her neckline.

"Not that way, pervert! Pull at the chain!"

Matt's trembling hand yanked out as if it had been caught in a cookie jar. His face grew stern again, "How is a necklace going to—"

"Oh my gosh, all of you boys are alike! Think you know better than a girl. Just get the damn thing out."

Matt pulled it out, more delicately this time. It was a simple heart-shaped ruby set with gold and silver.

"Flip it in the air."

Matt obliged Cindy's request. While it was in the air Cindy whispered a strange chant. The heart liquefied into the short blade of a knife. Matt didn't question the happening. He'd seen stranger things. He grabbed it from the ground where it landed and cut through the cords. He took Cindy's hand and led her away with little time to spare as the Illumin and Clara exploded into each other nearby.

Matt and Cindy ran away, deep inside the trees.

Gabriella hit the ground hard. By the time she came to, Clara's dark blue form was careening toward her. Gabriella opened herself fully to the impact, using Clara's momentum to twist at just the right moment; with a normal Shade, this would have worked. Clara was too fast though; she anticipated the flicker of movement and compensated, throwing Gabriella, with all the force she could muster, hard against the Levee. Before Gabriella could even get up, Clara grabbed her face and slammed it against the concrete.

She moved close to the Illumin's ear and said, "Ever

heard of the Great Mississippi Flood of 1927? I was doing a paper on it once upon a time, before Zyne freed me from my mundane life. Turns out the levees couldn't hold back the river, couldn't keep it from rushing over. Normally this wasn't a problem, but you see, the nearby towns were built at a time when the river was low. The levees have made the river high... higher than the towns even... kind of like the ancient little town of ol' Wheelbarrow Creek here. You see, I expected your little Illumin mind to interfere with Zyne's work. That's why I wanted to meet over by the levees. Anything funny goes on and bam! With a slam of my fist, there goes the town! You wouldn't want to be the cause of so many deaths, now would you? Are you even listening to me, Gabriella?"

Gabriella pointed at something to the left of them. A small box of some sort was attached to the levee wall. Clara dragged Gabriella's face over to take a closer look. She released her at once, saying, "What the—."

The plastic explosives went off with a boom.

Cindy and Matt where half a mile away when the Levee broke. Amidst the lightning strikes they heard multiple booms, and then saw tons of water flooding towards them. Matt cried in futility as the Boss-mobile was washed away under a torrent of water. They ran as fast as they could to higher ground. Trees and boulders thrashed about behind them, water moving faster than they could run. Matt knew they wouldn't make it... then reality shifted.

Everything froze.

A dark, shadowy mass of dripping black stones seeped out of him, forming into a humanoid of liquid tar. "You don't have to die," it whispered to him, "All you have to do is make a wish and I'll save you."

"At what cost?" Matt asked.

The shadow grinned somehow, "Cost? You run futilely away from a tidal wave that will kill you and your little crush in an instant, and you dare to ask me about cost?"

Matt yelled at it, "Why should I trust you? You brought all of this about. The zombies, my mother! All of them gone. All because of you!"

The shadowy stone monstrosity tilted its head sideways. Out of the tar-shaped monster a stone skull emerged, tilted and glowing a faint red… just like the skull on the tombstone in his nightmare. Where was the demon, though?

The skull spoke more pronouncedly, "I thought we decided that your father was to blame for giving me to your mother, which allowed me to tempt you."

"What are you?"

"I am what you humans would call a Shade, nesting in that amulet of yours for thousands of years… waiting for the proper time to emerge. The usual course of action, for the Aztecs anyway, is to activate me over a dead body where I take on its features and form. Unfortunately for me, they feared my power too much to let me out, thought I was some death god or something. I really just make dreams a reality. Where I come from, dreams are as potent as death, so I can understand the confusion."

"Why are you here though? I'm no Aztec. I didn't call

you forth."

"Oh, but you did. The moment you placed me over your live, beating heart I was called into action."

"Why did my father give you to us?"

"To keep me safe… so that no Raven would open me to this world. He didn't count on you, though, little brat of his sticking his nose where it didn't belong. Such a little sin really. Pawning me out to the highest bidder! And it would have worked too, had you not touched me."

"What do you mean?"

"In these parts, only those with Raven blood can make a Shadeskin. And yet, I believe this will be the first time such a feat was accomplished by a half-blood."

Matt's eyes grew wide then. He looked at Cindy, who was slowly moving away from him. Was he related to her?

"Yes, Matt. That's right. Your father is a Raven. Half of his blood is flowing through your veins. But don't worry about Cindy. She's only a cousin to you, and a second or third cousin at that. It'll be fine. One touch with my power and she won't even care."

Matt looked back at him, "What do I do?"

The shadow laughed, "Humans are so cute; tell them their life's story and they'll follow you anywhere."

Matt looked scornfully at the being, tired of it all, "What if I say no? I can choose to die."

The shadow swirled around him, entering him just as the first bits of water lapped against his legs. An inner voice whispered, You don't have a choice Shadeskin. Look behind.

Matt did and saw his death: mile-high water ready to grind him to bits. He didn't mean to think it, but self preservation won out. His lips whispered, "Save me!"

Before he had even finished the phrase, a dark power enveloped him. He turned and lunged towards Cindy. It was like swimming in molasses, moving just as slowly as the rushing water. But the water was getting fast again. Time was speeding back up. He reached out and touched Cindy's arm just in time. Gallons of water came alive and flowed above them, over their heads. He held her close to him then, relic glowing, shafts of a dark light pushing away the water, cutting trees and bedrock in half, forcing them aside like torn parchment. Matt walked slowly and confidently up to higher ground.

The pendant's glow lessened, shafts of dark light growing ever faint. Matt seemed energized with Cindy held so close to him. She looked at him in awe, truly taken aback by such an unusual salvation. He looked down upon her, drenched wet in her red and white cheer outfit. He looked deep in her eyes. His were emboldened by the Relic, empowered even, to cause her to do his bidding. One touch and he knew she would do anything he wanted. He touched those pouting lips with wet fingernails and almost kissed her… almost kissed his cousin. Then another thought entered. He didn't want to kiss Cindy, didn't want to be with her anymore… he wanted Trish.

Cindy gave in to his power, though, melting in his arms, even trying to kiss him. When he released her… he knew it, in the way that she looked at him, fawned on him… she was totally his, forevermore his, and yet, he knew he couldn't love her. Not really.

She was just a crush.

A dark blue streak caught his attention. It wasn't Gabriella, though. Clara carried the Illumin's lifeless body into the sky. Then her eyes narrowed toward him. He turned back to Cindy. She was kneeling before him, eyes beckoning for his every request.

He knelt down to her and said, "Go. Run away. Live a normal life as you did before I came and stole your heart."

Cindy frowned at this, "I cannot! You are my life now!"

Matt shook his head, "No, Cindy, I was merely a nerd in love, and you are my cousin. I didn't mean to dream for this, for you I mean. I don't want any of it."

"But I love you!" Cindy cried.

He touched her tender face, "I am commanding you to leave me... NOW!"

With that shout she got up and ran away in terror. Matt ran in the opposite direction, leading Clara away.

Clara chased him deep inside the woods. So many roots on the ground—What if I fall? His foot snagged on one of them; he fell, tumbling to the gnarled ground... he felt a hint of déjà vu like this had all happened before. Then he remembered his nightmare, the stalking woman of death! He crawled away as fast as he could. A monolith stone stood before him. It was a gravestone. He looked around and saw other gravestones. He'd stumbled into an abandoned graveyard. He was lying in an indention where a body had once been buried, now long since turned to dust. Clara appeared between two trees. He grabbed the ancient gravestone like a lifesaver. Faster than light, she hit him. He flew through the air, back thrown against a tree.

"I should have known," Clara said, brushing dark

strands of hair aside. "Should have known you would be wearing the relic. All humans lust for power."

Matt's green eyes were blazing, "I am not wearing the relic. I am the relic!"

She took another step toward him, a snide look in her eyes… and froze in place. Something held her there. Matt looked down at his amulet. Nothing was glowing. Five aqua stones had broken, though. A flashlight turned on, shining in his face.

"You all right there?" A friendly voice asked.

Matt held up a hand to shade him from the glare.

A hulking shadow approached Clara's frozen body. Another person, the one holding the flashlight, stepped toward Matt. A shadowy hand appeared from the glare, "Name's Hunter. Cindy Raven's parents sent me to handle the situation here."

Matt noticed a golden raven cufflink near the man's palm.

Hunter said, "That's Trent over there. Careful with that!" Matt turned and watched Trent moving Clara's body aside and lift what looked like a bear's trap made of leather and jewels.

Hunter's voice cut through the darkness, "Okay, lay the fake amulet across her body. Once she comes to and grabs it, it will turn to dust."

Trent lay a body down beside her. It resembled Matt in every way.

"Yeah," Hunter was saying, "It took a pretty elaborate trap to set against a half-Illumin, half-Shade. Something like this hasn't happened in ages past. Well, aren't you going to take my hand?"

Matt turned back and saw Hunter's hand was still outstretched toward him. He shook it. The gold raven cufflink came alive and nicked him with a claw. Something screamed inside him, power he didn't even know he had swelled up... and then dwindled away.

"Easy now," Hunter was saying, "Had to restrain those powers of yours. Don't want another zombie apocalypse on our hands."

Matt felt limp in Hunter's powerful arms. "The city," he asked, "What happened to the city?"

Hunter replied, "Yeah, such a shame, really. Clara busted that levee clean through with her powers. All of Wheelbarrow Creek is under a flood."

"Trish! George!"

"Oh, don't you worry about such things. We'll take care of them. Won't remember a thing by tomorrow."

Matt heard the double click of car keys, and saw car lights flashing up ahead. Trent opened the back door and placed Matt inside. Hunter got in with him. Matt saw his face and demeanor for the first time; he was dressed impeccably with a black, form-fitting suit, handsome as a devil, but with a friendly disposition.

"Who are you and where are you taking me?" Matt asked, suddenly dubious.

Hunter took on the look of being personally hurt, "Now is that any way to treat your relatives? We're going to Shreveport to meet the rest of the family."

Trent drove the car down the country road... far away from the flood that swept over Wheelbarrow Creek.

6

Trish awakened the next morning full of questions. She only wanted the answer to one of them: Where was Matt?

She jumped out of her bed… no, it wasn't her bed. She was at Cindy Raven's mansion. Then it all came back to her. The zombies… the flood… where was Matt?

Cindy walked in, "About time you got up. We're just about to eat some breakfast. Grab one of my gowns and come on down. Oh, and, sorry about the darkness. Power's out. You know, from the flood and all."

Trish put something on and came down the stairs to the sound of laughter. Mrs. Raven was laughing at a joke George had made. Then she saw Trish. "Oh, it's so good of you to join us, dear! Come on over and have a pancake before George eats them all." George was being his usual devious self, winking at Cindy while pouring some syrup over a second helping of pancakes. "These pancakes are quite tasty, Mrs. Raven! Can't say I've had their equal."

Trish sat down, stomach grumbling.

"Sorry about the lights, dear," Mrs. Raven was saying. "The flood took them out, took half the town with it. But don't you worry, the Ravens are doing their part, bringing food and water to those in need. We'll put this town back together. And don't worry about your parents. They are on their way to pick you up."

Trish's mind was abuzz with questions, but she only wanted to know, "Where's Matt, Mrs. Raven?"

George frowned at this. "Who's Matt?"

Mrs. Raven laughed while taking some pancakes from the gas stove and placing them on Trish's plate, "Oh, you wicked boy! Trish is being serious here. Eat, dear girl, and I'll tell you all about it."

Trish was about to object, but then she smelled the aroma and her stomach grumbled.

It was the tastiest pancake she'd ever had. She felt full and safe... and a bit dazed. Cindy was sitting nearby, eating eggs and toast but no pancakes. Even Mrs. Raven didn't have them.

Mrs. Raven asked, "Now what was it you wanted to know, Trish?"

All Trish could think about were how tasty these pancakes were, "Why aren't you eating any pancakes?" she asked.

"Not enough for everyone and you two are my guests."

Cindy added, "Scarf them up." Then she turned to her mother and twitched a bit before blurting out, "I need to find him, Mom. I left him there."

Mrs. Raven said, "Hush, child."

"But mother! I love him!"

Trish wrinkled her nose, "Who do you love, Cindy?"

Cindy tried to hold it in; something compelled her to say it, though, "Matthew Gillard, of course!"

Mrs. Raven froze in her place, glaring at her daughter in anger.

George and Trish asked as one, "Who's Matthew Gillard?"

Mrs. Raven let out a sigh. Even with that twinkle in her smile, she couldn't keep from crying.

George got introspective, "Why are you crying, Mrs. Raven? Do you want some of my pancakes?"

Mrs. Raven patted his hand, "No dear, it's not that. You eat your fill."

"Why are you crying, then?"

Mrs. Raven didn't respond. She just clasped a picture of her son to her chest.

The Ravens were as good as their word, delivering food, water and shelter to the people of Wheelbarrow Creek. The death toll was catastrophic. People were claiming some mysterious disease had struck, causing madness and cannibalism. The terms creeper, spooks, and zombies were thrown about.

As the weeks passed the shouts of loss and mourning over horrific deaths dissipated altogether. Only a few remembered the zombies, namely those who had their own food to eat and drank water from their own wells. The rest, receiving aid from the Ravens, thought of those few as a bunch of crazies. The local library recorded the truth of course, stating nothing about creepers. August second was forever known as the night the levees broke, causing the worst flood Wheelbarrow Creek had ever endured.

Clipped Wings

by
Amanda White

Hunter placed his glass of tea on the mantel and watched beads of water trail downward. He heard his father slam down the phone in the background. The room became silent, magnifying a dull ringing inside his ears. He watched his father's reflection in the closed glass doors of the fireplace.

Darrus sat at a wide mahogany desk, hands grasping his forehead. Hunter took another sip of his tea and marveled at how well the housekeeper balanced the sugar and mint. He remained still and observant. His father began to sway from side to side and then plummeted to the floor.

"Finally." Hunter loosened his tie and walked across the study. Rolling his father over to check his pulse, he said, "No need to get up, Dad. Coop and I can take care of everything." Hunter smiled and clapped his Dad across his cheek, then straightened the older man's head into a more natural position.

The sound of footsteps ascending stairs behind the study's back wall broke the silence. They stopped abruptly and Hunter said, "Come on in."

A portion of the wall swung open to make a doorway.

A young man strode into the study, carrying a stretcher and blanket. "Please tell me you didn't kill him."

Hunter silenced him with a glare and motioned for the stretcher. "Just like we practiced, let's move."

The two men rolled the large, well-dressed man onto the stretcher and met each other's gaze as they lifted him from the floor. Hunter lit a small flashlight and placed it on his father's chest. His arms screamed at the dead weight as they descended the dark stairwell. He and his cousin, Cooper, had practiced this day many times after his father had retired for the evening. Once they had even loaded the stretcher with cinderblocks to add realism.

Cooper stumbled on the last step and cursed, "Stop— I'm tripping on something." Hunter braced himself against a wall, irritated at his younger cousin. "Oh," Cooper laughed, "just my ear bud cords."

"Let's go." Hunter couldn't understand how his cousin could be a veritable computer genius and, at the same time, be so unrefined and clumsy.

The passageway door at the bottom of the stairs opened. Hot, humid air greeted them, adding to their discomfort. They remained silent despite their struggle crossing the large backyard. Moonlight shone through the tall pine trees, gently lighting the stone path leading to the gazebo. Hunter turned the stretcher so that he took the stairs first.

"This is so crazy," Cooper said as they rolled his uncle onto the gazebo floor.

"What? This activity is breaking news to you?" Hunter picked up the stretcher and glanced around, "Are you reconsidering?"

Cooper stiffened, "No. I just feel bad leaving him out here all night."

Hunter began walking back toward the house and withdrew a black bottle from his pocket. He began spraying a light mist across the stone path where they had walked. Glancing back he stated, "He's safer in this backyard than most people are locked in their homes. You know this, maybe even better than me. You said it was the best security system you've designed."

"Maybe," Cooper said. "Don't forget to cover the stairs…your sister."

"What?" Hunter stopped spraying and, for the first time, looked unnerved.

"Katy and I used to play all sorts of games in that stairwell. She might think to look back there." Cooper rubbed his mouse-brown hair and Hunter could see the guilt playing on his facial features.

"I had forgotten about that," Hunter shrugged, "I was planning on covering our tracks there anyway. I guess it doesn't increase our risk. She spends so little time here."

Hunter tossed his suit coat onto the hood of his black BMW parked in the family's drive and resumed spraying the mist up to the passageway door. He smiled as the scent of patchouli wafted through his nostrils. When creating this mixture, he had decided to treat himself to his favorite scent.

"Stay by the car; I'll be back once I'm through with the study. I think we are running late; the last thing we need right now is to tick off Astrous."

The study was as they had left it. His father lived alone, save for the family's ancient housekeeper. He gulped down his tea and removed a silver device about the size of a pocket knife from his pocket. Hunter tossed the device into the air and, catching it, slammed it to the ground. It sprang to life, bathing the room in a sharp, white light. Footprints surrounding the indention from the stretcher became visible. Hunter sprayed these areas and the surface of the desk, smiling as the mist erased all signs of their trail. The bumbling police officers who would eventually be called to the house would find no clues about what had happened to his father. Most importantly, neither would his family.

"Damn." He glanced down at the empty glass in his hand and decided the safest action was to place it in the dishwasher, which Nila would run in the morning. He descended the stairs quickly by taking two of the marble steps at a time. The kitchen still smelled of his father's cologne, his uneaten plate of food now cold in the microwave. Hunter placed the glass in the dishwasher and then stood for a moment looking out of the window into the backyard. Moonlight illuminated the large gazebo. He felt a sudden pang of doubt in his abilities and wondered if he would be able to succeed.

A tapping sound jolted him out of his reverie. With a laugh, he realized it was his own nervous movement. His Raven family ring was knocking against the steel sink. Hunter's confidence renewed itself as he looked at the jewel-encrusted ring. Even in the dim light, he could make out the family's crest: a black raven with outspread wings under the large blue center stone. This ring belonged to him, as well as should this house, his family's business and all the things he had created over the years. He was tired of waiting. Waiting would only result in his inheriting the family's stagnant wealth and power. It was time for something new.

Hunter watched his father's mansion in the rearview mirror as he drove away. His success or failure over the next few hours would ensure he would not only inherit this home, but also enable him to buy more like it. Glancing over at Cooper, he hoped his cousin wouldn't hurt his chances of winning over the most powerful Shade in Shreveport.

Hunter smiled at the guard as he entered Shreveport's most affluent neighborhood. They approached the plantation-style mansion, and Hunter pulled into the driveway once the gates opened to admit them. He passed under broad oak tree limbs as he drove the short distance to the house on the brick-paved driveway. Parking behind a yellow convertible, he eyed two large animals walking the perimeter.

Most Shades took to renting out large houses broken into apartments to remain less conspicuous. Not Astrous. He had purchased the largest home in the neighborhood and had surrounded it with a black wrought-iron fence. Hunter felt the familiar stab of fear in his chest that occurred when he was about to deal with a Shade.

Cooper jerked away from the window. Two piercing green eyes, unnaturally illuminated by the streetlights, peered into the car. They could hear a low growl in cadence with the vision of sharp, white teeth. "I don't know why you bring me here with you!"

"The dogs serve a purpose, Cooper. He'll call them off." Hunter straightened his tie and ran his fingers across his short, black hair. Glancing in his visor mirror, he couldn't help but think of his twin sister when he looked into his own shining blue eyes. No other feature gave away their genetic bond more. It would be difficult to keep his meetings with Astrous a secret from her.

"Peach and Ginger! Away with you." A slim, well-dressed man appeared on the porch.

"I can't believe those are the names he chose for those animals." Cooper laughed despite himself and placed his golf hat on his head.

"You- don't say a word," Hunter said through clenched teeth before exiting the car. "Astrous, it's good to see you."

"Likewise, Hunter. I see you have brought Cooper with you. How convenient-- my web service has just gone down, and I'm in the middle of cooking a new dish. The recipe has now vanished from the screen." Astrous wrapped a bony arm around Cooper's shoulders. Although he stood almost a foot taller than Astrous, it was obvious that he was terrified.

"Sure, Mr. Astrous, whatever you need," Cooper said as he escaped the man's touch by walking ahead of him.

"I was beginning to think you were standing me up, Hunter," Astrous said as he shut the large front door behind them. The sound echoed in the large foyer.

"Never." Hunter straightened his posture and held his arms still at his sides. "We were a bit delayed by a task from my father." Hunter and Cooper exchanged quick glances as they each experienced the brief nausea that humans encountered when entering the house of a Shade.

Astrous's mood appeared to improve, and he led the two men into the kitchen. Two other Shades sat on stools at the kitchen's marble bar. The female, in a business suit, ignored their entrance. The male, however, stood and walked to Astrous's side.

"Thomas, I'd like you to meet Hunter and Cooper Raven."

The man's light brown eyes deepened to black, and his jaw bone became animated under his skin. "Raven," he stated, "I have suffered much as a result of your creations."

Although the larger man intimidated him, Hunter knew not to show vulnerability with a Shade. "That is regrettable. However, it is not personal; it is our family business."

"Thomas, let's not bring up the past, but look toward the future. Hunter has much to share with us." Astrous placed his hand on Thomas's shoulder and gave him a light push away from the Ravens. "Now, Emily and Thomas, I'd like you to join Hunter and myself downstairs. Cooper, I'd be delighted if you could have that recipe available to me when we are finished."

Hunter nodded to Cooper as he moved to follow the three Shades into a large office. The walls of the room were adorned with a hodgepodge of weapons, from both the present and the past. AK-47 rifles hung near samurai swords, and automatic handguns were placed next to muzzle loaders. If Hunter hadn't been so distracted by the importance of this meeting, he would've enjoyed this room immensely. Weapons were his passion.

"Please, everyone, have a seat." Astrous sat behind a

large, white desk and motioned to the various chairs placed throughout the room. Thomas did not sit, but stood behind Emily's chair. Emily stared at Hunter as if he were mud on her designer stilettos.

"Hunter, do share your proposal to Emily and Thomas. They are my armory directors, if you will. They are most interested in your unexpected…how do you humans say… that, 'change of heart.'"

Hunter unbuttoned his suit coat and moved to the edge of his chair, meeting Thomas's protesting eyes; he was clearly the one to convince. "As you know, my family dabbles in weapon creation. Historically, we have assisted the Illumin with their military needs. We may now be of service to your kind."

"What do the Illumin have to say about this?" Emily said.

"I don't consider this any of their concern. We have no contract. My family works to provide goods to customers, both human and non-human. It's that simple."

"What if they find out? How do we know you won't share information about our 'goods' to them?" Thomas placed his hand on Emily's shoulder and glanced at Astrous.

"Once you use the new weaponry, they will know you have found a new source. They may suspect me. This will be inconsequential, as they will be unable to prove anything. Even your kind will not be privy to how or where these weapons are made," Hunter said.

"I don't trust him." Thomas spoke to Astrous, "Just because our primary Shade supplier has become obsolete doesn't mean we have to trust a human for such an important matter—maybe the most important matter. You know that I am searching for another Shade source."

Hunter sat motionless as he watched Thomas speak. He recalled hearing Thomas's name spoken among the Illumin. Although they saw Shades as a lower life form, they appeared to hold Thomas in higher esteem. Hunter wondered at his intelligence; his eyes suggested a bright mind to match his physical strength.

"Yes, that was unfortunate." Looking to Hunter, Astrous stated, "Ill-fated accident with an invisibility stone; instead of making his head invisible, he deleted it. Such a loss." Astrous stood and walked to the window seat where a broadsword rested. "Thomas, surely you realize that Hunter is no fool. He knows that we are not playing games. We are no gentle Illumin." Astrous took a sip of brandy as he stroked the sword and smiled. "And Thomas, you may continue your search for other providers, but I think Hunter may be able to help us in a new way."

"I should like to hear of your ideas. If they are not impressive, I expect never to see you again." Emily's face showed a clear emotion for the first time.

"Come now, Emily. We both know this decision is not yours to make," Astrous said. "Besides, new weapons may help satisfy your desire to damage that detective, D'Nas."

Emily's face changed from a ghostly white to a near-crimson, and her eyes reddened in a dotted fashion as if someone had poked her eyes with tiny needles. Hunter felt his stomach turn, and his ear drums throbbed painfully as they often did when he spent too much time with the Shades. The female Shade's anger permeated the room and somehow worsened the negative energy.

Eager to complete his business and leave, Hunter said, "I acknowledge that I may seem an unlikely source to provide you with weaponry as it is no secret we also deal with the Illumin. However, it makes sense when you consider how it benefits you because I know more than anyone the weaknesses of this armor. I am the one who created it." Hunter stood and moved away from Emily as the pain in his ears became distracting. "In turn, I gain another customer and a rewarding opportunity to expand my skills."

Thomas's eyes brightened at this declaration. A chocolate color replaced the black, and he took several steps toward Hunter. Hunter continued, "I have an idea in mind that I think you may want to consider. The Illumin's most loved weapon is what I called 'The Distracter.' As you are likely aware, they use this weapon to confuse a Shade if attacked. Your kind temporarily forgets who they are and loses their focus, rendering them helpless in a fight. It also tends to have the side effect of one losing his bowels." Hunter coughed at the irritated looks he received, "Quite unintentional, I assure you."

"I have designed a weapon that will reverse the effects of 'The Distracter' onto its user." Hunter worked to suppress a look of pleasure. The room seemed only moderately impressed.

"I have heard of this weapon, but have never seen one. If you say it is their 'favorite,' why haven't I been exposed to it? Fighting is what I do," Thomas stated.

"It is very expensive and time-consuming for me to make; therefore, only the highest-ranking Illumin possess them," Hunter admitted.

"If your business is so small that you cannot supply all of them with this weapon, what is your strategy to meet our needs?"

"I have arranged for that already. I am currently training two apprentices, and they both show incredible promise. I will employ them in my simpler duties, and take on all Shade business personally." Hunter continued, "You must understand, making weapons is… what I do."

A hint of amusement played behind Thomas's eyes. "Do you have more ideas for us? Because I have some of my own."

"I do. Let's plan to discuss your ideas. That is, if we have a business agreement."h

Cooper breathed a sigh of relief as they drove out of the driveway. "I'm glad not to see those dogs, or whatever they are. That black one has it in for me." Hunter just smiled and turned up the air conditioner. His ears were already starting to feel better. He had just made the deal of his life.

"I don't know if 'Ginger' or 'Peach' is the black one, but you may be right; these are Shade pets, after all." Hunter removed his tie and relaxed. So much accomplished in one day. No wonder he had graduated magna cum laude with his mechanical engineering degree from Louisiana State University.

"I wonder when the family will find Uncle Darrus." Cooper removed his golf hat and ran his fingers through his hair.

"I expect Nila will find him at some point. Or maybe Katy will try to reach him and come looking for him."

Cooper nodded and seemed unconcerned, which pleased Hunter. Astrous seemed to like Cooper, so he always brought him to his home. Despite the fact that he could be unrefined and wasn't someone he took to formal social functions, Cooper was bright. "Man, Katy would be so pissed if she knew what we did today."

"Who cares? She has basically forfeited her say in anything the family does."

"Lucky for you," Cooper said.

"And lucky for you." Hunter had promised Cooper a cut in the Shades' weapon money for helping him remove his father from his position. Hunter ran his hand along his shirt's pocket. Excitement rose in his chest as he felt the key to the Shade's safety deposit box. He knew he was born for this work, not merely to manage the family's finances and community outreach under the careful watch of his father. He had already created the perfect piece for the Shades. They would soon be relying on him more than they could imagine.

Katy woke to the sound of her dog's nails clicking across the wooden floor. She didn't need an alarm clock. Her little red dachshund, Oscar, always woke her at exactly 7:00 am, giving her plenty of time to get ready for work. She rolled over and looked down at him, an action that had become a ritual over the last two years. He looked up at her with his dark eyes and wagged his bony tail. The coffee pot sounded its readiness and Oscar whined, waiting for her to feed him. As she pushed back the sheets, she caught a whiff of the lavender linen spray she used on her sheets each night. This was her favorite time of day. In the midst of her morning ritual, she could pretend that her world was normal.

After feeding Oscar and drinking her coffee, Katy picked out her outfit for the day. She had recently purchased a yellow sundress that brought out the blue of her eyes. She wove her long, black hair into a single braid down her back. During mirror inspection, she realized this was not a practical outfit for inventory day. Halfway through her sulking walk back to the closet, a sudden joy seized her. She didn't have to wear practical clothes. As of last week, she was the owner of The Spicy Perk and could do whatever she damn well pleased.

The drive to the shop was pleasant with the Louisiana summer at its peak, the sky as blue as the Caribbean Sea. Although most people hated this time of year, she loved it. It would easily reach 100 degrees today, and she decided that after work she would head to her father's house to swim. She smiled as she passed under arching oak tree limbs and beside beautiful, old homes. Her shop was nestled among a handful of other stores in the center of Shreveport's historical district. It was only a few miles away from her home, and Katy relished being able to spend much of her time in this beautiful part of town.

Miranda, her second-in-command, had opened the shop and was straightening magazines and pillows upon Katy's arrival. The smell of fresh coffee and cinnamon scones hit her as she walked in.

"Good inventory morning!" Katy said as she almost tripped over the shop's feline resident, Nina.

"Good morning." Miranda smiled, "I made the lemon bars early. I figured it would be good for morale."

"Yum. I could eat one now." Katy lifted Nina from the floor and buried her face in her black fur.

"I hate to bring you down, but…"Miranda blew a piece of loose hair out of her face, "I realized when I woke up this morning that we scheduled Lea Brannon's book signing today."

"No…no, we didn't!" Katy ran to the shop's computer and pulled up the schedule. Sure enough, on the same day they had to inventory the store, one of the city's most eccentric authors would be signing her new book. "I can't believe I didn't catch that!"

"Maybe we were all in denial," Miranda said as she walked to the kitchen in the back of the shop.

Lea Brannon wrote about paranormal happenings in the state, mostly in their area. During her book signing, Lea's fans often brought pictures or videos of what they perceived to be paranormal events in hopes she would review them. Katy hated hosting her book signings, but her father was a big supporter of their community's local arts culture, and insisted.

The morning flew by as Lea's fans entered in anticipation to the signing. They filled the couches near the table set out for her, waiting with books in their laps. Two men and a woman huddled together and discussed her newest release, The Hidden Forces of North Louisiana. The woman leaned toward the men and stated, "I believe the story about the spirit at the Hooka Palooka. My husband used to practically live at that bar. One night I went looking for him there and found him playing pool with his brother and some strange man."

The woman smoothed back her frizzy gray hair and glanced around, "Now, my husband Stewart was an even-tempered man. I can recall only a handful of times in our marriage that he raised his voice to me. When I walked in the bar, Stewart's face was red, and he was shaking his fist at the stranger. He accused him of cheating and told him to return his money, or they were going to sort it out in the street. The stranger glanced over at me and winked. Stewart was distracted for just long enough for that man to flip him over the pool table and jump through the ceiling."

The woman readjusted her skirt, moved to the edge of the couch, and lowered her voice, "Practically every man in that bar rushed to the second floor. But, they never... found... him. The only sign that he'd been there was an open window, like he'd just flown out of it."

Katy felt her stomach knot. The two men contemplated the woman's story, although they were the type willing to believe anything with supernatural suggestion. Katy knew stories like these and more. The difference for her was that she knew they were real. She watched the trio while arranging the table for the author. She envied them. They had the luxury of speculation, while she had the burden of knowledge. Shades were no ghosts. The city's inhabitants had no idea what dangers surrounded them.

Lea Brannon made her usual dramatic entry by wearing bright colors and a long, flowing skirt. She wore her hair in a cropped pixie style, trendy for a woman in her seventies. "Katy, darling, you are looking lovely. How is your father, is he well? And by that I mean, is he still available?"

"Yes, ma'am. He's well, and by that I mean he is attached." Katy projected a look of innocence as Lea frowned at her, "Congratulations on your new book." Katy gestured to the table, "Everything is ready." Walking to her table as if moving across the red carpet, Lea eventually took her seat and picked up a pen. Her fans sat at attention and shifted in their places. One thin man wearing glasses shot out of his stool and took giant steps toward the table.

"Now, now," Lea stated with a wave of her hands. "We have plenty of time for everyone's book to get signed."

Just when it felt like the store couldn't hold any more bodies, the door swung open and Suriel entered. Katy inwardly groaned at the sight of the enormous blond man. At least that's what the people in the store saw. Her employee, Lisa, pushed her way through the crowd to reach him. He smiled down at her, then, placing his hands around her waist, raised her to his face. The couple gazed at each other, unaware of any spectators.

"I warned you, I told you," Miranda danced up to Katy's side, waving her arms to an invisible beat. "I said, 'You don't want to make this bet, Katy. There is no way Lisa can make it a full day without seeing her giant.' Too bad for you that you never take my advice."

"Well, a girl can always hope."

"So, you really going to let me off next Saturday?" Miranda asked.

"Of course. It's the risk I took, I suppose." Katy smiled as Miranda danced around in the small space behind the counter. Once danced out, Miranda took in Katy's expression and asked, "So, why do you hate him so much?"

"What makes you think I hate him?"

"Well, for one thing, your whole mood heads south when he comes in. Last weekend when he was here, you ground beans for a solid hour. Remember? We all had to take some home."

"Oh. Well, I guess I just feel like Lisa gets distracted when he's here. I am the one paying the salaries now." Katy winked to soften her words as Miranda grimaced. It's probably weird having your best friend as a boss.

"Well, whatever you say. It just seems like something more to me. Like, maybe you dated him once?" Miranda teased.

"You know everyone I've ever dated." Katy shivered at the thought of dating an Illumin. They weren't like regular men. If they wanted to, they could convince you to believe anything or do anything. Luckily for the unsuspecting population of regular folks, they had sworn an oath never to use their powers to manipulate. Katy did not believe it. Oaths could be broken.

Suriel looked over at Katy as if he could sense her

distaste. She held his gaze until he looked away. She felt pleased, as she knew he didn't likely look away from simple humans often. The din of the crowd became quiet, and all eyes turned to Suriel. Lea was staring at him, holding a copy of her book in the air. She seemed almost in a trance. Katy watched as Suriel became more and more uncomfortable. Lisa looked at Katy for an explanation, but she was already jogging to the table.

"Mrs. Brannon, are you okay?" Katy stood between the Illumin and the table.

"Yes, dear," she whispered and looked at Katy with clouded eyes. "He's not one of us, you know?"

Katy could not believe what she was hearing and her heart began pounding in her chest. She shot Suriel a look-- he didn't need a second urging to leave the shop. "I think you need a break, Mrs. Brannon. Let me get you some tea and you can rest in the back for a little while." Mrs. Brannon stared at Katy then began blinking her eyes. Katy watched as her eyes cleared and regained their focus.

"Goodness, child, do move out of the way or we will be here into the night." Lea pushed her aside with her book.

Katy stepped away and rolled her eyes as the fans regained their excitement. They relished unordinary behavior from Lea. It was rumored among them that she had some sort of psychic gift. Over the last year, Katy had entertained suspicions that Lea Brannon was starting to see the Illumin. Today's behavior confirmed her fears. Either Lea had completely stopped using the town's water, or she was becoming immune to the potion her family spiked into the supply. She hoped her father would be at home when she drove over to swim. Even though Lea would be low on his list of priorities, he needed to be told.

A few hours later, the crowd began to dwindle. Katy watched the street fill with cars during rush hour. As the owner, she could leave early and entrust the store to Miranda. She rested her forehead against the shop's glass and thought of her newfound freedom, picturing herself taking the first dive into the swimming pool and drinking Nila's mint tea. A pang of regret struck in her chest as she realized she had avoided her father's house all summer. Once she told him about Lea's awakening, he may feel disappointed that the visit wasn't just because she missed him.

Katy drove to her family's home and idled at the main entrance. The Raven's family crest loomed down at her from the top of the black iron gate. A sense of dread filled her as she punched in the security code. Fearful thoughts had filled her mind since Lea's declaration. It was the first time any human outside of Katy's family had spoken to her about the Illumin. Was something wrong with the potion? Was it only Lea because she did have psychic ability? Or was all of Shreveport about to awaken to the realization that their lives were intertwined with beings they had thought imagined? Katy envisioned an elderly lady dropping dead of a heart attack when her pharmacist morphs from a kindly middle-aged man to a vision of horror with black eyes and unnaturally colored flesh.

Katy parked behind her father's car in the garage then tossed her towel across the pool fence. "Dad, I'm here!" she shouted as she raced up the stairs to her old bedroom. "I'm going to change, then I need to talk to you." She shut the door and leaned against it, taking a few seconds to stare into the room. Its familiar smell jerked her out of the present. The room remained unchanged; the walls still the fluorescent green color she had chosen during high school. She walked to a window and looked out over the sun-soaked front yard. Childhood memories flooded back to her as she surveyed the small pond adjacent to her family's property. Her weather-worn paddle boat remained tied to the dock. While growing up, riding to the center of the pond had provided her welcome reprieve. She would read her books or spend time staring into the woods pretending she was from a normal family, trying to imagine what her life would be like if her mother was still around.

Her father's office was empty, but his cell phone was lying on his desk. She called to him while walking through one of Shreveport's largest and oldest homes. Despite having spent most of her life here, Katy still felt spellbound by the beauty of the marble stairs, the height of the ceilings and the many fireplaces. She ran her hand down the cool railing while taking care to descend the stairs in her flip flops. A pink glow enveloped the kitchen as the summer sun began its westward decline. She closed the refrigerator and sighed in frustration. She had yet to find her father, and Nila hadn't made any fresh tea. Maybe he was trying to enjoy his time with the girlfriend he didn't think she knew about.

She glanced out the window and scanned the backyard. With a start, she realized that the dogs had not greeted her at the car. Leaning over the sink and squinting to see farther, she looked into the gazebo. One of the family's Dobermans was lying next to something and staring in her direction. For a moment, stunned disbelief held her fixed in the kitchen, gripping the edge of the sink. Reality forced its way in as she recognized the bottom of a shoe.

Pure fear gripped her body as she raced to the gazebo. "Daddy!" she screamed, tripping up the steps and landing on her father's legs. He was lying motionless in a suit and tie, soaked with sweat. The Doberman whined as she searched her father over. He was still breathing and his pulse didn't appear to be too high or low. She placed her hand over his chest and called his name in an effort to wake him. After an agonizing moment of indecision, she decided to call her uncle who often worked as the family's physician. Her father had warned her not to utilize the public authorities unless there was no other choice.

Her uncle promised to come over immediately, and the wait for him to arrive was brutal. Every sound across the yard, even the pool's compressor turning on, spooked her. She half-expected a gang of Shades to encircle the gazebo. Although the Raven mansion was protected from Shade entrance, her brother, Hunter, had begun to show an interest in them. He had even tried to convince her father to engage in a business deal.

A strong breeze ruffled the trees bordering the property. In the midst of the swaying branches, a winged creature appeared to jump from one tree top to another. Katy shut and then opened her eyes. The object was gone, but despite the heat of the day, fear chilled her body. Seeking to comfort herself, she gazed down at the purple tattoo encircling her wrist. Tapping it gently, she watched it writhe and begin to form into a solid shape. She observed as her hand disappeared, then her arm. If she allowed it, her body too would be invisible soon—to both non-humans and humans alike. Hearing a car screech into the driveway, Katy shook her arm, returning it to normal.

An hour later, Katy paced the floor beside her father's bed. Her uncle had declared her father stable, but could not identify the source of his unconsciousness. Her brother glared at her from across the room. "Katy, sit down!" he ordered.

She returned his stare and continued pacing. She hadn't spoken to her twin brother in months. Their contrasting ideas about the family's role in Shreveport had divided them in recent years. She missed the closeness they used to share.

Benjamin Raven adjusted the medical equipment and turned to Katy and Hunter. "Hunter, we will need to call the family together—tonight. With Nila being on leave for several days, I'm sure when this happened. There is no doubt he has been poisoned, and not by any human-crafted poison. I've found nothing traceable in his system." He crossed his arms and waited for each of them to meet his eyes. "It's time for the two of you to put aside differences. We need to work together now—you can go back to your childish fighting when your father is well again."

Katy could see Hunter bristle from across the room. He angered rapidly when he felt disrespected. She waited for him to rebuke their uncle or send a stinging remark her way, but he surprised her by nodding his head in agreement. He walked over to her and put his arm across her shoulders, "I am sorry I snapped at you. I'm sure you were scared when you found him. We are so lucky they were gone when you arrived."

Katy regarded him with suspicion. They had spoken few words to each other since Christmas. "What are we going to do now?"

"I will handle Dad's affairs; you need to run The Perk." He smiled down at her, and she looked into the blue eyes that mirrored hers. "Look, if you want to skip out on the family meeting, I'll make an excuse for you."

She felt both relief and anger. Hunter knew how much she wished to be released of her family's responsibilities. However, leaving him to lead the family meeting alone would mean allowing him to push his own agenda.

"Thanks, but I think I'll manage to make it through this one."

"Whatever you want," he stated and shrugged his shoulders. He began to walk out of the room, nodding to Cooper, who had been standing in the doorway.

"Wait, I have to tell you something," Katy said. "It's the reason I came over today."

"You didn't come to swim?" Hunter raised an eyebrow as he gestured toward her swimsuit cover up.

"Obviously, I was planning to swim." Katy took a deep breath. They could easily lapse into an argument. "Lea

Brannon was at The Perk today for a book signing. She recognized Suriel, Lisa's Illumin boyfriend."

"What do you mean, 'She recognized him'?"

"I mean she saw him for what he is—at least for a moment anyway. Her eyes glazed over, and she announced to me and at least a couple of others that 'he's not one of us.' Suriel saw it, too, and left." Katy watched Cooper and Hunter exchange glances.

"Maybe it was a fluke, probably nothing to worry about." Hunter stared past her to their incapacitated father. "I'd say we have bigger concerns at the moment."

"Don't you remember? I talked to you and Dad about it at Christmas. I've seen her looking at them. It's like her vision is clearing."

"At least no one will take her seriously." Cooper smiled. "If she starts telling people that there are 'giants' or 'monsters' walking among us, she may sell more books, but it will be from a mental institution."

"I'm so glad that I've brought this problem to your attention. Glad to know I can count on the two of you to fix things," Katy quipped.

Hunter smiled at her on his way out the door, "As long as it's just Lea, we have little to worry about."

Katy watched Cooper follow Hunter around like a puppy. She thought it was so odd that the two of them had formed a pair. Cooper liked to enjoy life and play golf. Hunter, on the other hand, was born to be serious. Even as a young child, Hunter had often asked their father if he could attend family business meetings.

Katy walked over to her father's bed. "Daddy," she

whispered, "If you don't wake up soon, I don't know that I can stop him. Please wake up." Her father continued to lie motionless. All Katy could do was sob.

Hunter held a glass of Brandy in front of Katy's face, "Something to help you sleep in the old house tonight?"

"I'm sure I can manage it sober." She walked into the living room where the family had started to gather.

Hunter lifted the glass to his face and inhaled. He set the glass on an end table and relished the thought of the celebratory drink he would have later. His chest tightened with nervous tension as he entered the home's largest common area. The room was dimly illuminated by lamplight. A span of ages from young to elderly sat tensely in their seats. Even his Aunt Tebe, senile and asleep, was brought for the emergency gathering. Only his Uncle Daniel was missing, but that was typical.

"If I can have everyone's attention, please. I now call this meeting to order," Uncle Benjamin said. He nodded at Hunter and relayed to the family his brother's condition. "The short of it is this—Darrus has been poisoned and it's supernatural. I will do everything I can to bring him back around, but until then, we could all be at risk."

"As you know," Hunter stated, "I have become increasingly concerned about safety. Since I've taken over our weapons business, our dealings with the Illumin have doubled. This is great for our finances, but I believe doing business with the Illumin and not with the Shades takes out our neutrality. It's only a matter of time until the Shades see us as a threat."

"I'm so sick and tired of this theory," Katy stood up from the piano bench and glared at him. "This family needs less interaction with these beasts-not more!"

"Katy, this family has a living to earn. It's what we do." Hunter glared at her. He had hoped her father's condition would sober his outspoken sister.

"'Earning a living, please! It's all about greed with you. This family has long ago had plenty of money. I know that making weapons is your sole reason for living, but you don't have to put us in harm's way. You could make just as much money selling them to the other city holds overseas."

Benjamin moved between the two of them, looked at Katy and said, "We are in too deep to start dreaming that we can back out now. As much as we'd like to, we will never be simple humans again."

"Hunter," she pleaded, "It is illogical to think that dealing with the Shades will make things safer."

"No, it is illogical to think that we can bury our heads in the sand and pretend we are the same as the ignorant mass." Hunter walked to the center of the room and met her eyes. "You can go back to your coffee shop and let the rest of us deal with protecting this family."

He could see in her eyes that his words had struck true. Her eyes darted to the one remaining family picture that included their mother.

"So, what is your earth-shattering plan?" Hunter's cousin, Sarah, looked over her cell phone mid-text. She pushed back her multi-colored hair and feigned interest.

"First, I plan to find out what I can do to get my Dad back," he snapped. "In the meantime, each one of you needs to be on alert. Remember, we don't know for sure this was Shade doing."

Everyone in the room began protesting at once.

"What? Who else could it be but a Shade?"

"You heard what Benjamin said; this was a supernatural attack."

"Oh, come on!"

Hunter held his hands in the air, "Yes, people, I know it seems unlikely. But, we know the Illumin have their own agenda. Just because they don't look scary doesn't mean we should assume them innocent."

"That, young man, is a preposterous idea," Aunt Tebe interjected, rejoining the present. "The Illumin are true to their word, always have been. The Ravens have sided with them for decades. We aren't about to turncoat now."

"Nice… 'turncoat.'" Sarah laughed and began typing on her phone.

"What reason would an Illumin have to attack our Dad?" Katy had returned to the piano bench and sat sulking while running her hand over a candle flame.

"Simple. They know we will assume it was a Shade. Although Cooper is excellent at securing our information, we are all aware of how much the Illumin know," Hunter said.

"You've let it slip, then, that you are considering dealing

to Shades?" Katy frowned, "I can't believe you. Dad said no about that, remember?"

"Dealing with the Shades?" Aunt Tebe attempted to pull herself to standing with her walker. "Boy, we will not deal with the Shades! It will be the end of us."

Hunter focused on his aunt, "I hardly think it will be the end of us, Aunt Tebe. I just think we need to improve our leverage. We increase our safety by becoming necessary to both sides."

"We are already necessary. They need our water potion to keep this city blind. You haven't gone and let that formula slip, have you?" Aunt Tebe glared at Hunter.

"No, ma'am, I have not." He paused and held her gaze. "Look, everyone is tired. I will keep you apprised of Dad's health, and I'm going to request that y'all check in with Cooper through the secure webcams each day. No cell phones." Hunter snatched Sarah's phone from her. "I will call another meeting once we have more information, or if Dad's condition changes."

"That will be all for tonight. Thank you all for coming." Uncle Benjamin helped Aunt Tebe to her feet. He nodded to his wife, who took over and ushered their aging aunt out of the room.

"So, we are concluded?" Benjamin placed his hand over Hunter's shoulder and whispered, "Please tell me you won't sell weapons to the Shades until you are certain they weren't responsible. I don't know when-or if-I can get your father well again."

"Let's keep that part about Dad between us, Uncle Ben. Besides, one benefit of dealing with the Shades: if they aren't responsible for poisoning him, maybe they can help. We both know there are more than Illumin and Shades lurking around this city." Hunter gave his uncle a quick hug. Benjamin had been Hunter's favored uncle since he announced he wanted nothing to do with the family's business, effectively paving the way for his rise.

"Maybe, but let's not get panicky and risk everything we have." Benjamin walked out of the room, calling back, "I'm going to check on him now, and I'll be back in the a.m."

As Benjamin walked away, Hunter motioned for his cousin Trent to approach. "How are things going with the problem in Wheelbarrow Creek?"

Trent frowned and watched the family file out of the room, "Things are fine, but you wouldn't believe the mess left behind. I went by the lake cabin on my way here. Your guest was sound asleep when I left."

"So you managed to slip him the sedative?"

"He was so thirsty; I think he would've swallowed dirt to get to that water."

Hunter smiled up at his cousin. Trent was his best asset. Being stocky in build and aggressive by nature, he was a menacing character. Even the Shades took note of his presence.

Hunter smiled and clapped Trent on the back, "How about a drink? Let's plan to head over there tomorrow. He should come around by then."

"We don't want him getting lonely, do we?" Trent's dark eyes gleamed with amusement.

Katy sat beside the pool, not bothering to wipe the tears from her face. Her father had remained unmoving during the night. She had watched him for hours, searching for any sign of awakening. Several times he had moaned as if having a bad dream, but nothing she tried stirred him. Her last memory of the lonely night was of dawn beginning to break. The stars had melted away as the sky brightened beyond the tall pine trees. Hours later, she had awakened on the floor with sunlight glaring at her.

In an effort to comfort her, Nila had placed a bowl of fruit beside her. She took a bite of a strawberry and felt her heart dip in sadness. The taste reminded her of swimming with her mother in the pool. Her mother liked to float the strawberries around in a plastic bag. When she wanted one, she would ask Katy to 'swim the fruit' to her. On most days, Katy could no longer remember what she looked like or the sound of her voice. After her disappearance, Katy spent hours in her mother's closet, pleading to God to preserve her scent. Finally, one day, the familiar smells were gone, and with them her memories began to fade.

Katy glanced over at the diving board and dropped her strawberry with a scream. Her mother was standing on it looking at her. She walked to the edge of the diving board and with a grace only she could carry, dove into the water. Overcome, Katy rushed to the side of the pool, but saw only the pool's mosaic depiction of a raven staring up at her. The warm air around her stirred, and despite her quickening heartbeat, she felt her muscles relax. With a disappointed slap to the face, she realized the experience had been a long forgotten memory. An Illumin was nearby.

Katy heard footsteps approach the pool gate. She felt no need to turn around, "May I help you?"

The gate opened and someone approached. "Good afternoon. I'm Detective D'Nas, and this is my partner, Gabriella."

"What do you want?" Katy asked. She had little patience for Illumin on a good day, let alone one wrought with strife.

"I'm sorry if we've caught you at a bad time, but we understand that Mr. Raven has fallen ill."

Katy whirled around, "Really? And why would that knowledge bring y'all to my home?"

D'Nas stood unmoving, looking down to meet her gaze. The male Illumin were huge, and to Katy, colossal wastes of space. He removed his sunglasses and sighed. Nila stood behind him, shifting her weight from one foot to another.

"I'm sorry, Katy. Your father tells me to let them in." Nila said.

"It's fine. Go on back inside, Nila." Katy managed to send her a smile before turning her back to the pair and seating herself on the lounge chair.

"We are concerned for his well-being, ma'am. My understanding is that he has been poisoned," D'Nas said. His partner moved closer to Katy and sat in a pool chair as if they were old friends.

Ignoring Gabriella, Katy said, "That is also my understanding. You will need to talk to my Uncle Ben about his condition. I have no information for you, Detective." Katy placed her straw hat across her face. Through the weave, she could see he was unfazed by her cool attitude. She became aware of anger boiling at the base of her throat, then she remembered that they could sense her emotions.

"Miss Raven, I need to see your father," D'Nas said.

"You must be joking." Katy removed her hat and frowned at him, "My brother is taking care of this matter. You will need to contact him for permission."

"I need no one's permission." The detective replaced his sunglasses and walked in the direction of the house, motioning for Gabriella to follow him.

"Hey! You are not welcome in my house." Katy rushed to follow him, slamming into his back when he stopped at the pool gate. She found herself inches from him as he turned and glared at her. Her breath caught in her throat as she craned her neck to look into his face. She felt silly for arguing with him. He was going to do whatever he pleased.

"You and I both know that your family is an exception to the rules. We have the authority to enter your house." He smiled and lifted his sunglasses once more to make eye contact. Katy was startled by his appearance. She expected the azure eyes typical of all Illumin, but not the cropped style of his hair or the stud piercings adorning the length of his ears. A tattoo in his language ran the length of his neck. Male Illumin were handsome, but always bland; this one was unique.

"You don't belong here," Katy filled the loaded statement with as much venom as possible and shoved past him. She figured she would at least beat them to the door, maintaining some semblance of control.

As she ascended the stairs, she glanced back. D'Nas and his partner stayed several steps behind her and looked at the surroundings. She felt invaded. Hunter described their family as free, but they were nothing more than indentured servants. The detective met her eyes and she saw him sense her resentment. As she reached the top step, she glanced down and saw a vision of her brother as a teenager staring though them. Katy said, "I would think reigning in your mental projections would be the least you could do."

"If you would calm down, it would be easier for me to control," he stated.

Her father was lying on the bed in the same position. His hands remained still at his sides. Sunlight warmed the room and held a silence that made their entrance all the more intrusive to her. Gabriella hovered by the door, examining the room. Katy shot her a nasty look which, to her surprise, was returned.

The detective approached the bed and placed his hand on her father's forehead. He leaned near his face and spoke unintelligible words. Against her will, his language calmed her body and cleared her thoughts. She walked closer to the bed to see her father's face. The detective wore black boots with thick, cleated soles, and his pants were the cargo style typical of law enforcement. A gun was strapped to his side. He was not part of the community's police force, but a member of the Illumin's elite team.

"He's in deep. This isn't something I've seen before. His body is sleeping, but I sense no dreaming, no thoughts," D'Nas said.

"Detective, I'm sure my uncle can help him. You needn't be concerned."

"Please call me D'Nas. Miss Raven, I'm a friend to your family. We all are."

"D'Nas," she said through clenched teeth, "I'm afraid you are speaking to the wrong Raven. We are not friends."

"Has an Illumin wronged you in some way? If so, please give me an opportunity to set it right." He stood and crossed his arms. Gabriella moved to stand behind him and crossed her arms, "Yes, Miss. Raven, please enlighten us so that we can better understand your nasty attitude."

D'Nas shot Gabriella a reproachful look and raised a hand to silence her.

"My father is in this bed because of your kind. My family was ripped apart because we deal with you. If you want to set things right, then stay away from us! Make your own weapons." Katy struggled to contain years of wrath.

"I'm sorry, but it isn't up to me who makes our weapons. And, I'm sorry about your mother. I didn't know her, but I understand she was loved by many." The fight seemed to drain out of him and he sat back on the bed. He touched her father's arm with the tip of his finger. Katy felt helpless as she watched his finger turn bright red. He placed a small amount of her father's skin into a vial, then placed his palm over the wound. When he removed his hand, the wound had healed.

"I will have our lab analyze this sample." He moved to

the door, "We will let your family know of our findings."

"Oh, Detective, any word on finding my mother?" Katy asked.

"What?" He frowned in her direction.

"Right. Just wanted to clarify why I won't be holding my breath for 'your findings.' You all were just so helpful before."

Katy watched a flash of emotion cross his face. He nodded his head and descended the stairs, Gabriella on his heels. Katy held her stare until they were out of sight. As soon as the front door slammed, she lost the last shred of control. Grabbing a vase, she threw it with force down the marble stairs. It broke into a million pieces and brought Nila running into the foyer. Katy screamed and threw herself at her father's bookshelf. She tossed book after book across the room then fell to the floor sobbing.

She hated them. All of them. He could make her mother appear alive again, but could offer no real help. She was tired of pretending they didn't exist. As much as she hated it, she was going to have to start fighting back. At the rate her family was dissipating, it was time for a change. She was the only one with the wisdom to see what needed to be done.

Hunter swallowed a pain pill with the anti-nausea medication then glanced in the mirror. His face was pale, and he could still see the pink marks under his eyes where his blood vessels had burst from vomiting. After tonight, he was going to have to take a break from the Shades; the side effects were beginning to take a toll.

He shut the door to his car and smiled as he glanced back to look at it. The black exterior gleamed in the sun. Not many men in their late twenties were able to afford such luxuries. The best part was he could easily afford three of these cars. Patience was one of his better virtues. He would soon have enough money to retire—if he wanted to.

He knocked on Thomas's front door and waited. He found himself grateful for each moment he could stay on the porch. The bitter smell often sent him reeling once inside one of the monster's homes. He could hear Thomas's steps approach the door, giving him just enough time to dread the encounter. The door opened and the large Shade stared down at him. Hunter was relieved to see that his eyes were russet and not the black color they became when he was angry. The pain in his ears was always so much worse when they were angry.

"You don't look so good. Are you going to be able to manage?" Thomas looked at him with pity, which Hunter found maddening.

"Of course. It's just as hot as Hades out here." Hunter stepped into the home and headed straight for the weapons room.

"Maybe if you didn't wear a suit in the summer." Thomas gestured to his own clothing; even when he was in baggy jeans and a polo style shirt, his black hair and dark eyes were foreboding.

"I wouldn't if I didn't have to attend all these board meetings for my father. The old goats still think it's the '50s. They believe you show up dressed for work or you don't show up at all."

"Aren't you the boss now?"

"Yes, but I'm more persuasive to them if I look respectable." Hunter smiled at the thought. The older men were becoming putty in his hands. Many of them should have retired years ago.

They entered Thomas's arsenal room. It was not like Astrous's weapon room. Thomas rented a townhouse and had a landlord to worry about. In what Hunter thought was an ingenious idea, Thomas had purchased several antique storage pieces and hid weapons under sliding compartments. On top of the false bottoms he placed blankets, books and magazines. Even more impressive was Thomas's knack for weapon design. He had many ideas formed, but he needed someone with the ability to build to carry them out.

"I'm disappointed; I thought you were going to bring me something today. You look empty handed," Thomas said as he sat in one of two chairs in the room.

"Then I have achieved my goal of being inconspicuous." Hunter laughed and drew a small stuffed rabbit out from his interior coat pocket.

Thomas's eyes darkened when he saw the toy. "What do you think I am, some sort of fool?"

Hunter waved his hand and said, "Please, calm down. You are killing my ears." He held the rabbit out to the Shade. "This quarter pound toy can mask the scent of a Shade for two days—even if the scent was on a human. It is a weapon of deception. You should recognize this idea; it was yours."

Thomas laughed and ran his hands through his hair. "I apologize. I forgot for a moment you are as passionate about weapons as I am."

Hunter returned the smile. "Yes, it's a shame we are just now learning this about each other. We have no time to waste."

"All right, I am going to need your help understanding why you made this a toy." Thomas leaned back in his chair and laughed again. "You have got to let me take that to Astrous! I can only imagine the look on his face when I tell him that this is a product of our meetings."

"As a token of our new friendship, this is yours; you can do what you want. Please just make sure I am nowhere near when you mess with Astrous about this. I'd puke all over his newly tiled floor." Hunter removed his tie and jacket and sat across from Thomas. He held the rabbit up for him to see. "I used the rabbit as a prototype. My little cousin dropped it behind our couch. I can create this weapon with anything that has a fabric casing. "

Thomas smiled, "So how is this going to be useful in a war?"

"Easy-- anyone could carry this and it can be placed anywhere. The protective radius is over 1000 feet." Hunter smiled, pleased with himself.

Thomas turned serious and leaned toward Hunter. "This better not be a trick. I'm having a hard time understanding why you are helping us now."

"It's simply good business. Making weapons is my passion. Shades and Illumin alike know this." Hunter cringed as his stomach roiled.

"Your family has agreed to this, then?" Thomas took the rabbit from Hunter and smelled it, wincing at the sweet scents inside.

"They know I'm thinking in this direction. The weapons are much more my area anyway. My most adamant opponent has already forgotten that she denied me the right to deal with your kind."

"You injured someone in your own family to shut them up?" Thomas smiled.

"No, she's senile." Hunter leaned back in his chair. "The rest of the family is busy with their own day jobs, vacationing… even my sister is occupied with running the coffee shop."

"I remember your sister. She is beautiful. Single?" Thomas asked.

Hunter cringed at the thought of the Shade being interested in his sister.

"She's single, but sorry; she's not an option for you. She hates Shades almost as much as she hates the Illumin."

Thomas rolled his head back and laughed at this admission. "She hates the Illumin? Well, she and I would be fast friends. Introduce us?"

Katy stood behind the counter staring at the espresso machine. After spending several restless nights in her father's house, her cousin had agreed to relieve her so she could sleep in her own bed. Her exhaustion had made casualties of at least two customers, a carrot cake and a coffee mug.

"Katy, your brother is coming down the street," Miranda announced as she walked to the door to switch off the open sign. "He is with some hot guy."

"Well, if he's a friend of Hunter's, you should probably go hide in the back." Katy crossed her arms to hide her clenched fist.

Miranda shot her a look of disbelief, then smoothed her hair and hid the dirty dishes behind the counter rather than hauling them to the kitchen. "Wow, who is he?" she asked as Hunter strode through The Spicy Perk's front door as if he were walking into his own home.

In her fog of fury, Katy realized that she had not returned her brother's greeting. She was too busy staring at the tall, dark-haired Shade accompanying him. Miranda was seeing a handsome man, but Katy saw the blackness surrounding him, the gray circles around his eyes, and felt the air take on a dense feeling. Her glare met her brother's amused eyes.

"Katy, this is Thomas—Thomas, this is my twin sister,

Katy. Oh, and this is Miranda."

"It's nice to meet you, Katy." Thomas nodded to Miranda and moved closer to the counter. "I can see the resemblance, but you win the beauty ribbon." The Shade winked at her.

"Can I get the two of you anything?" Katy asked as she swallowed hard to fight sudden queasiness. She frowned at Thomas. It had been a long time since she had been this close to a Shade. She had forgotten how their presence causes humans to become nauseated.

Hunter said, "Sure, just give me a coffee of the day with maybe a shade of caramel syrup in it."

Thomas laughed once and shook his head. Miranda shot Katy a questioning look.

"Miranda, take these dishes to the back, please." Miranda shot her an injured look before picking up the dishes. Once her friend was out of sight, she whispered, "Hunter, you seem to have mistaken me for one of your doormat friends. The two of you get your drinks and get out of here."

"You don't have to be so rude, Katy," Hunter said.

"It's okay. You told me she didn't like Shades." Thomas held his hands in a surrendering fashion, "I'm sorry you feel that way; it's such a nice change being around a human woman that actually sees me."

Katy met his eyes and felt a chill down her back. She loathed being this close to him, Shades were unpredictable. "Should I give you a few muffins for the road, Hunter? Not looking so well. I take it you guys have been hanging out."

It was her turn to see him uncomfortable. "Thanks, but it's just the loss of sleep. I worry about our father too, you know."

"We can discuss that later." She glared at Thomas and slid the coffee cups across the counter, "Then again, maybe you could just ask your friend for the antidote, and we could both sleep better."

Thomas made an effort to look wounded, but he couldn't keep his eyes from darkening. "I didn't harm your father, and I would know if it was one of us."

"I'm touched." Katy waved her brother's money away, hoping it would speed their exit. "Do I look like a sucker to you?"

"No. It would be foolish, however, to continue believing a Shade harmed your father. You should be looking elsewhere." Thomas picked up his cup and smiled at her. "I'm willing to help your family root out this...problem. Your brother and I have a lot in common, you know; we both work in defense."

"Well, isn't that just precious?" She smiled at them when Miranda re-entered the room, throwing her purse across her shoulder. "You guys have a good night."

"Who's that?" Miranda asked and pointed to the front door. To Katy's horror, the Illumin detective was standing at the entrance. At the sight of the Shade, his face darkened.

"Miranda, why don't you go on home, it's getting late. I'll lock up." Katy could already feel her stomach roil as the two beings stared at each other. Thomas had placed his coffee down and moved his hand to his back, reaching for a hidden weapon.

Miranda didn't argue and walked to the door, "Wow, my head is really hurting. Good night."

As soon as the door closed, Katy jumped between the

two beings. "Both of you get out of my shop. If you are going to fight, it's not going to be in here." Hunter grabbed her arm with an iron grip and pulled her out of the way. "This is my shop, my life, Hunter! I may have to tolerate them out there, but Shades and Illumin are not welcome here."

Thomas glanced back with a surprised look on his face. "That's all right, Katy. Hunter and I were just leaving." He picked up his coffee and stalked out the front door. Katy thought she heard a low hiss when he passed the detective.

"Calm down. You are acting ridiculous." Hunter loosed her arm and pushed her away from him. "That was a dumb move. Stop thinking your anger makes you invincible." Katy rubbed her arm and was stunned at the pain she felt. Looking into his face, she saw his eyes were blood shot. Even during heated fights, Hunter had never been aggressive with her. This was new.

"Mr. Raven, it's convenient that you are here. I am D'Nas; I have been working on your father's case."

"It's not 'convenient' for me, particularly considering you and my associate cannot be in the same room together. He is my ride…you will have to excuse me," Hunter said. He turned on his way out of the shop, "Besides, as I've informed your chief, my family is not requesting Illumin services. We are handling this matter on our own."

"Your family's wishes in this matter are of no importance to me. I'll let you know if I discover anything." D'Nas stood straight with his hands relaxed by his sides, but his eyes glowered at Hunter.

Katy shot Hunter a meaningful look. She knew Hunter remembered their arguments over their lack of freedom from the supernatural creatures. D'Nas had just settled that in her favor.

Hunter walked toward the Illumin, stopping less than a foot from him, "What did you say your name was?"

"D'Nas."

"We shall see what your chief thinks of your attitude. You don't rule my family; you don't rule me." The muscles in Hunter's jawline twitched as he stared into D'Nas's face, "Katy, don't tell him anything."

She nodded and watched him walk out of the store and meet up with Thomas. The two men seemed to consider coming back into the store, then changed their minds.

"I think you and I can talk later, Detective. I'm really tired." She surprised herself with the resignation in her voice. Although she had felt D'Nas's calming presence before, in contrast to Thomas's pain-inducing temper, it was a welcome change.

"I won't stay long. I came to give you information rather than illicit it." He sat on one of the couches and rubbed his eyes.

Katy didn't respond, but instead checked to make sure the machines were shut down and wiped the condiment table. After shutting off all lights except one lamp, she sat on a stool opposite the Illumin.

He had waited for her, watching her as she worked. She wondered if he had sensed her need for re-centering. It had been this way for her after her mother's disappearance. When the Illumin couldn't find her, she began to hate them as much as she hated Shades. Maybe even more.

Katy remained silent, but met his eyes. "I got the results

back from the lab. They did find a contaminant in his system. It's not one we have seen before. The most likely creator of this poison," he paused and sat forward on the couch, "is a human."

"How could you possibly know that?" Katy asked.

"We sense Shades from miles away. It would be impossible for us to miss something they created. This is not by their hands."

Katy stood and walked closer to him. Leaning down and looking into his eyes, she said, "What about an Illumin?"

"No." He returned her gaze. "That is impossible."

"You are wrong. Not only is it possible, but also I believe plausible if you are right that this wasn't Shade doing after all."

"Has an Illumin ever hurt your family?"

"No," she resigned, "but they have not added any happiness either."

"It is dangerous for you to have such tunnel vision. Would you at least consider that a human may have done this?" He stood and paced across the shop. "Your father is well-known. Surely he has enemies."

"I don't need you to tell me about what is dangerous." She walked over to the lamp and turned it off, leaving them in near darkness. She looked at D'Nas and caught her breath. She could just make out his figure in the dim light from a street lamp. His eyes appeared to radiate light of their own. She was stunned by his beauty and started when she realized he had been speaking to her.

"Miss Raven, are you okay?" He took a few steps in her direction.

"Yes," she replied, "Detective, I'm tired, I need to go home now."

"Of course, I'll be in touch." She rolled her eyes at his determination to interfere.

"Please consider our theory. You and your family could be in danger. You must at least raise your suspicions of those around you."

"Detective...."she sighed. She had no fight left. "Whatever you say."

She ushered him outside and locked the shop. As he stood behind her, the Illumin's scent drifted to her. She instantly had memories of relaxing in her father's study with his closest Illumin friends pulling her onto their laps when she was a girl. That was before her mother's disappearance. Even her father seemed to lose love for them after she was gone.

"Miss Raven..."

"Please, just Katy. My mother is Mrs. Raven." She breathed in his scent and decided that if she was going to have to deal with him, she might as well benefit from his calming abilities. She hoped it would help her get some much-needed sleep.

"Katy, can I share something with you in confidence?" he asked.

She chuckled, "D'Nas, who am I going to tell... anything?" She turned to face him directly, "I am alone, sir, I am alone."

"I tell you this hoping to make you more cautious. There have been some unusual events happening. It's more than just Shades and Illumin causing a stir, I'm afraid."

She winced and impulsively grabbed his hand, "Please, do not tell me! I want to know less, not more." Her eyes filled with tears, "Please, just...." She walked backward, away from him, holding her fingers to her lips.

He nodded and allowed her to retreat.

Hunter watched his cousin tense as they neared the family's lake cabin. A full moon brightened the night sky. The white light reflected off the water and illuminated the cypress trees growing in the water. Moss hung from the branches and swayed in the humid breeze. Trent turned his truck onto the cabin's driveway, the muscles in his forearms tensing as he gripped the steering wheel.

"What's got you so worried?" Hunter shifted the air conditioning vent toward his cousin.

"He just doesn't look right, man. I threw him into the wall when he wouldn't move away from the door, and he just laughed at me. " Trent frowned in Hunter's direction.

"I'm not sure what to expect from him," Hunter admitted. "Either way, he's mortal; you or I could easily take him down. Lucky for us the amulet activated on such a small person. Now, if he was your size, that would be a bigger problem."

Trent smiled and nodded. He appeared to relax and ran his hand across his bare head. Trent pulled his truck under the car cover and gestured to Hunter to move back while he reached into the glove compartment. "Just in case."

Hunter placed his hand on Trent's arm, "I'll hold the gun. He won't do us any good if you take him out for looking at you wrong."

"Fine, but it will be worse if he escapes from the cabin alive, man. Pull the trigger if you have to. We can make money another way." Trent jumped out of the high truck and paused on the cabin's steps to wait for Hunter.

Hunter snatched some bags of food from the truck's bed and surveyed the cabin and surrounding property. Even at night the oppressive heat was causing him to sweat, despite his wearing shorts and a t-shirt. The cabin was isolated with its nearest neighbor being over a mile away. The Ravens had owned this property for many generations. Satisfied that there was nothing to be concerned about, he handed the food supplies to Trent and entered the cabin.

"Aww, Hunter, he freakin' smells!" Trent covered his mouth and nose with his shirt.

"The man has been running with zombies, as in the living dead. Of course he smells." Hunter tried to laugh but had to suppress a gag. Setting the food items on the kitchen table, Hunter walked slowly toward the back room. He pulled out his identity card and ran it through the sensor. The door unlocked with a near silent click. The sliver of light illuminated a slight figure crouched in the corner of the room.

"Matt, you hungry?" Hunter held the gun behind his back as he slowly opened the door.

The figure glanced up at him. Hunter could see the

reflection of drool across his chin. "We brought you some food. Do you want any?" He was a young man, caught in that frustrating age between being old enough to fight in a war, but too young to drink. He was dirty, and his face was obscured by smears of filth.

Trent stood behind Hunter, holding a bag of hamburgers and fries, shifting his weight as the prisoner rose to his feet. He watched the men standing in the doorway and took a few steps in their direction. "Whoa, you go sit on the bed. I'll put the food over here."

Matt did as he was told and sat gingerly on the bed. Hunter wondered if he would be able to hold his food to his mouth. He looked weaker than when he had first found him. Hunter could hardly believe his luck; he had been searching for that amulet since he was a boy. His father warned him its existence was only a myth, but he knew better. Its powers were thought to be the strongest ever possessed by his family.

Trent and Hunter watched Matt pick at the food for the first few bites, then struggle not to choke as hunger drove him to shove the food in his mouth. Once he began slowing, Hunter stated, "We are here to help you, Matt, but you need to cooperate. No more trying to fight us- we will win. Do you understand?"

Matt wiped his face with a napkin and glared at Trent. In a low, stuttering form, Matt spoke, "Him…that big one. Tell him not to kill me." Matt looked down at his hands, tears rolling down his cheeks.

"No one is going to kill you, as long as you do what we say. Don't you want to get that thing off of you?" Hunter gestured to the amulet. It was faintly glowing silver as the skin around it turned black.

"I don't think…you can really help…me." Matt's eyes shone like he had a high fever. He laughed and held his hair away from his forehead with both hands. He continued laughing and looked out the room's small window. Trent had placed bars to keep Matt in, and anyone else out, for Hunter didn't have the heart to lock someone away with no view of the outside world. The fact that Matt would never leave the room alive had elicited unusual feelings of guilt from Hunter. It was clear the amulet would take his life whether he was wearing it or not.

Matt calmed himself and lay back onto the bed. "What now?" Trent asked.

"Let the meds take effect. Once he's asleep, we will make certain this is the amulet. I don't want to start bargaining with Thomas only to realize I had made an error."

"I hope we are doing the right thing." Trent watched the boy on the four poster bed start to twitch. "I hope you are right that the amulet will only work on one of us, or he may try and take it."

"He won't; I'm sure he's heard of the legend. We did, despite them trying to hide it, right?" Trent nodded and Hunter said, "This guy must have been a product of either someone's affair or a hidden pregnancy somewhere in our heritage. We just have to keep him alive long enough to use it."

"Well, I'm not wearing that thing…ever, man," Trent shuddered at the huddled figure on the bed.

"If we can harness it correctly, maybe no one will have to wear it again." Hunter patted Trent's back, "This is going to make us rich and forever seal a pact with the Shades. No more worrying at night or glancing in the rearview mirror waiting for one of them to take us out."

Trent opened the refrigerator door and closed it again. "I hope you are right that the Illumin won't seek revenge. We would be screwed."

"The Illumin will be paying rent to the Shades by the time we are finished. They will need my weapons more than ever." Hunter removed a bottle from a wine stand and as he twisted the corkscrew, smiled and stated, "Besides, they owe our family. The risk is mainly on me, as they will likely believe the rest of the family is loyal. The fact is, most of them are loyal. Just not the siblings whose mother they lost."

Katy filled a chilled decanter and thought about how there was nothing better than a summer night by the pool with a glass of wine. The heat felt like a gentle blanket on her bare skin. Crickets chirped in the woods surrounding the pool. The roses were in full bloom and left the air smelling of their perfume mixed with that of chlorine. She placed her feet in the pool and took a drink of her Chardonnay, enjoying the relaxing environment.

The pool gate swung open with a creak and Miranda's flip flops slapped the concrete as she walked toward Katy. "Hey, I couldn't find any paper plates, so I brought these out." She held up two plates of china.

"Yeah, that'll do." Katy laughed. It would be just like her friend to select the priciest dishes in the house for picnicking use.

The two girls sat in silence eating vegetable pizza and sipping wine. "Man, I love the summer. It's the one thing that remains constant, no matter how far the years take me from my childhood; I just have to come sit by the pool and it all returns. Ya know?" Katy said.

"Yeah, I was just thinking about senior skip day. Remember? We all went down to Valentine Lake. We drank that boy's cheap beer, then sat out on the end of the dock and watched the sun go down." Miranda smiled in her direction.

"That was a fun day."

"And your brother showed up. We made fun of those two preppy girls because they kept following him around. They had no shame." Miranda shook her head at the memory.

"Well, as weird as this may sound coming from me, compared to most of the guys, Hunter was pretty buff. He knew it, too; that's why he never bothered with a shirt." Katy took a sip of her wine and gazed at the back of her father's house. It had been almost a week; still he had not stirred, and her uncle was no closer to healing him. She and Nila worked to rotate him every few hours to prevent bed sores and keep his blood flowing. His heartbeat and low breathing were the only signs he was alive.

"Do you remember when Hunter and your cousin found that vine? The one they used to swing across the creek?" Miranda asked.

"Oh, wow. Yeah." Katy gave Miranda's hand a squeeze.

"I used to love how they would toss us back and forth over the water."

"That was very trusting of us."

"I wouldn't do that now if you paid me," Katy said.

Miranda laughed, "I doubt the vine would hold us now."

"No, I wouldn't trust either one to catch me." Katy shook her head and wiped pizza sauce from her leg.

Miranda was silent for a moment, then leaned across the table to meet her eyes. "Will you please tell me what happened?"

Katy stared at the ground for several seconds. She and Miranda had held countless conversations through the years, but Katy had never been able to tell her the full truth. She stalled by draining her wine glass and offering Miranda some more.

"Please?" Miranda took the decanter from Katy, forcing her to meet her eyes.

"Hunter and I don't agree on how to handle some of our businesses." Katy shrugged.

"You know, I understand you may not be able to tell me everything, but don't lie to me. It's embarrassing to both of us." Miranda stood and walked over to the pool. She gathered her curly, dark hair in her hands and stared into the water.

"I guess it's just complicated," Katy stated. "Hunter wants to… engage, I guess you could say, riskier business partners, and my dad and I think it's a bad idea. Hunter is too passionate about the business."

"There could be a down side, I suppose. But, there could be a payoff with him being so ambitious," Miranda said.

"He loves money more than he loves our family. I can't

find an upside, Miranda. No matter how I look at it." Katy stood and walked to the diving board. Looking back over her shoulder, she said, "He's not the same boy who used to swing us across the creek."

Miranda eased herself into the pool and looked up at Katy as she stared down at the water. They had set the pool light to alternate colors each minute. She watched as the water turned from blue to red, matching her mood. "He's not the same," she repeated.

"He didn't look good when he came to the shop. Why?"

"Well, you know the saying, 'birds of a feather,' right?" Katy held her arms out to feel the soothing caress of the hot air. "That guy he had with him, he's no good."

"I thought you were just meeting him, how could you know that?"

Katy hesitated for a second then said, "I can just feel it." She met Miranda's questioning glare. "Are you telling me you couldn't feel how negative that guy was?"

"Sorry, I thought he was hot. Maybe it was just your brother bringing you down?" Miranda smiled, wanting to lighten Katy's mood. "Or maybe….you could've just been super attracted to his new friend, but were so mad at Hunter, you projected your negative feelings onto him."

"Whatever! Sounds like someone is starting to listen to her psychology teacher." Katy ran to the front of the diving board and bounced high, yelling, "Don't quit your day job!" before hitting the water.

Katy allowed herself to sink to the bottom of the pool, feeling the glass mosaic tiles of the raven under her feet. She hovered on the bottom of the pool then swam gently to the side. As she floated toward the surface, she glimpsed a distorted view of the stars through the top of the water. As she was emerging, a large figure suddenly loomed over her.

"I was beginning to think you would never come up!" the figure laughed, and, to her shock, Katy found herself dragged from the pool by her arms and placed on her feet.

"Whew! You aren't as light as you used to be."

"Yeah, well, I didn't ask to be yanked out of the pool, jerk! I'm a person, not a parcel, ya know?" Katy glared at the large man in front of her. The pool's green light reflected off the surface of his shaved head.

"Sorry! Damn, had no idea you were such a princess these days." Trent stared down at her, hurt radiating from his face.

"Well, you freakin' startled me. Jeez." Katy tried to soften her tone.

"Hey, Trent! We have some pizza over there if you're hungry." Miranda exited the pool and walked to him, directing him to the food. She glanced over her shoulder and, out of his view, mouthed the words, "Chill out."

Katy gritted her teeth. Trent had stopped being family to her long ago. She knew he loved her, but his dark side made him untrustworthy. She wanted to relax tonight, just have one night not to be on guard. She watched as Miranda chatted easily with her cousin. She touched his shoulder and giggled at something he said. Miranda had difficulty resisting handsome men, and Trent was very much her type. Tall and muscular, he worked as a personal trainer by day and a bouncer at night. No one wanted to be on his bad side.

"Katy, is there any beer in the house?" Trent asked

through a mouthful of pizza.

"I don't know; Dad drinks brandy. Go check if you want." Katy wrapped a towel around herself, irritated that her evening had likely come to an end.

"I'll go check; does anybody want anything else?" Miranda offered.

Katy and Trent sat in uncomfortable silence for a minute, then Trent offered, "So what exactly did you tell her had happened to your Dad? She's not that oblivious." Katy faced him and was startled by his appearance. His eyes were dark around the edges, and anger radiated from his body.

"I told her that his heart had been acting up and Uncle Ben sedated him so he could sleep."

"That worked?" He asked.

"For now. Why are you here?" Katy wrung out her wet hair and watched the water fall to the ground.

"Hunter is busy. Asked me to come check on your Dad…and you."

"Why me?" Katy asked and glared in Trent's direction.

"He told me that Illumin detective has been hanging around you a lot. Don't forget what he is, Katy. Don't be talking to him about our business."

"Talking to him about what, exactly?" Katy could feel her anger toward her brother resurfacing. "If Hunter is so concerned about what I might say to D'Nas, then maybe he should've stayed at the coffee shop and dealt with him instead of leaving with his freaky Shade friend."

Trent stiffened and glared at her, "First name basis?"

"Like Hunter told you, he's been coming around." Katy crossed her arms and leaned in Trent's direction. "You'd rather I spend time with an Illumin than a Shade, right?"

Katy heard Miranda's feet padding from the house to the pool. Trent lowered his voice and spoke, "I just know you don't need to be talking to that detective. You need to keep your mouth shut."

Katy's jaw slackened in surprise at her cousin's tone. As Miranda approached, she left the table and returned to the pool to hide the tension. Katy's heart pounded as she swam laps. She had long known her cousin had a temper, but he'd never spoken to her with such disrespect.

The diving board bounced as Trent cannon-balled into the water. Not wanting to share the pool with him, Katy swam to the ladder, but he caught her feet and dragged her beneath the water. He pulled her into the deep end and shoved her hard to the floor of the pool. Horrified, she kicked with all of her strength. Her lungs burned with the need for air. He moved to hold her knees together with one arm and used his other arm to grip her hair and force her head backward. She began to see spots in the water, now yellow from the oscillating pool light. Just as she was sure he had no intention of freeing her, he released her legs. Miranda had jumped in and was clawing at his face. With the last of her energy, Katy kicked his face as hard as she could, feeling her toe come into contact with his nostrils.

Katy and Miranda swam to the top, blood streaming from Trent's face into the water. "Get out, quick!" Miranda pulled her by the arm as she crawled out of the pool.

Trent surfaced, shouting, "What the hell?!"

"Run, Miranda! Inside!" Katy was breathless, and her knees felt bruised from his iron grip.

The two girls ran into the home and Katy instinctively rushed to the most secure room in the house, her father's bedroom.

"In here!" Katy pushed Miranda into the room and, using all of her strength, slammed the door behind her. She bolted several locks and walked Miranda away from the door, both breathless as they waited.

"He's big enough to knock that door down, Katy!" Miranda's eyes filled with tears as she stood shaking and dripping onto the woven rug.

"No, it just looks like wood. It's reinforced steel."

"Thank goodness," she shuddered. Snapping her head back at Katy, she asked, "Why is the door reinforced steel?"

Katy felt a stab of fear in her chest and trying to think quickly said, "Lucky for us, Dad got paranoid after Mom disappeared."

A muffled hammering could be heard as Trent banged heavily on the door.

Katy wrapped her arms around Miranda's shoulders and the two stared at each other. Katy picked up the phone in her father's room and dialed "9" so Trent couldn't take another phone off the hook, leaving them with no communication.

The two women stood wet and shivering in the cold air-conditioned room. They could see the shadows of Trent's feet under the door. After what seemed a lifetime, the shadows disappeared. Katy released Miranda and went to the window. She heard a vehicle start, then watched Trent's large black truck exit through the gate.

Despite trying to restrain the terror, sobs began to rack Katy's body. She was empty of strength and slid to the floor, curling up against the window. "I thought….he was going to kill me."

"So did I. Katy, you guys were down there for so long." Miranda sat on the floor next to her and held her hand. "Please, I'm begging you, come clean with me. What is going on? Why didn't you call the police?"

"I know this will sound crazy, but I can't tell you." Katy looked in her father's direction. "Thank you so much for what you did tonight."

"Katy, we've known each other since we were in first grade. You can tell me anything." Miranda stood and helped Katy to rise. "Besides, there is less to hide from me than you think."

"What do you mean?" Katy asked.

"The first time Lisa brought Suriel into the shop, your whole demeanor changed. Under your breath, you whispered something. After your Mom disappeared, do you remember how I practically lived here with you?"

Katy nodded and felt her hands grow even colder. "You were so distressed," Miranda continued. "Every night, you talked in your sleep. There was one word you repeated every night, the same word you called Suriel: 'Illumin.'"

Katy stared at Miranda. She snapped her jaw shut and placed her hands over her face. Silent tears dripped through her fingers. She no longer had the desire or strength to lie to her best friend. Lowering her hands to her lap, Katy met Miranda's concerned gaze. "I need to know if you can keep a secret."

"You know that I can." Miranda gently pushed a string of wet hair from Katy's face.

"Miranda," Katy said, "This will be unlike any secret you've had to keep. It's more than who is cheating on whom or how much weight someone has gained. It's going to change what you understand about our world."

"You can trust me. Katy, I know your family is different. With each passing year, I've asked myself so many questions, and I've never shared my concerns. Not with anyone."

Katy hugged her friend then released her and took a deep breath. Her heart fluttered as she told her story aloud for the first time.

The words seemed to spill out as Katy told Miranda about the existence of the Shades and Illumin and her family's role in their world. Miranda sat on her father's Persian rug and remained silent and unmoving.

"Where do they come from? The Shades and Illumin?" Miranda asked.

"I'm not sure about the Illumin's source, but I know they are protectors of some sort. When I was a little girl, before my mother disappeared, their kind was in our house as regularly as any of my parents' human friends. There was one in particular that I loved. He had white hair that he wore in a long ponytail, and he looked as old as my father, which is unusual for Illumin. Most of them are young looking."

Katy pointed to a picture on her father's desk. "Pick up that black and silver picture frame."

Miranda's eyes grew large when she recognized the Illumin from Katy's description. Katy walked to Miranda's side and traced the outline of her father's face through the glass. Sams and her father were so proud of the trophy they had won that day at the fishing tournament. It was one of her father's favorite memories.

"I didn't know your father fished." Miranda shook her head.

"He spent his free time with Sams. Dad always seemed to be happy when he was around." Tears sprang unbidden as long forgotten memories resurfaced, "So was I."

Katy continued, "I must have asked Sams a hundred times about where his kind was from and why they were here. He was always patient, but his answer never changed. 'We are here to make sure people continue to have free reign of their world. Your freedom and safety is my top priority.'"

Katy opened her father's closet and removed two small blankets, offering one to Miranda. "Sams also told me to keep away from the Shades. Regarding their origin, I do know they are here by human doing. My father told me that the Aztecs used to worship the Shades—or as they called them—the Gods of Stone. They performed a ritual that resulted in putting a Shade spirit into a jewel, which then could be transferred to a human body."

"The Shades were unwilling participants. Unfortunately for them, the ritual opened some kind of portal in the universe. The Illumin call it the 'Shifting Plains.' Anyway, they were sucked into our world and have been unable to return."

"That's really hard to believe, Katy." Miranda sank onto her father's leather couch, wrapping her blanket around her, "For starters, they look just like us."

"To you they do. I can see a darkness in them, even smell a difference. They completely change the feel in a room. Their anger has painful consequences to humans: nausea, headaches, ear pain, disorientation," Katy said. "Our family enhances the Shreveport water supply with additives that shield you from most of these effects."

"So, my head started hurting at the shop that night because of Thomas? Because he is a Shade?"

"Right," Katy nodded and, with a hint of a smile, said, "That's why I was so certain he would be a poor dating choice."

"Are you actually finding a way to joke about this?" Miranda's eyes filled with tears.

"I'm sorry. I've never talked about this with anyone outside the family. All of this is normal to me."

Katy stood at the edge of the park, watching the crowd inside. She placed her hand on the fence railing and slipped off her sandal, running her foot across the rich, St. Augustine grass.

"You know, a dog probably peed there." Miranda smiled and put her lollipop back in her mouth.

Katy grimaced and stuck her foot back in her shoe. She glanced over at her friend as she stared toward the crowd, twirling her pop in her mouth. Her brown hair was extra wavy in the humidity, and stray curls bounced in the hot breeze. Nothing in her demeanor showed how much her world had changed in the last few days.

Miranda put her arm around Katy's shoulder and,

speaking around her candy, said, "The earlier we do this, the sooner we can be sitting on your porch with a glass of Riesling and some strawberry pie."

"Maybe we should go do that now. Lord knows, crawfish and burgers are not motivation enough to make this fun." Katy smiled as Miranda took her hand. "I am kind of proud of the community though; lots showed up. I hope it makes things better for those people in Wheelbarrow Creek."

Miranda pulled Katy down the sidewalk in the direction of the melee. Several hundred people had gathered and were sitting at concrete picnic tables, standing in line for food or dancing to a live Cajun band. "Your family always could throw a party. Who better than the Ravens to help people spend their money?" Miranda let go of her hand and eyed her with an expression of wonder, "Then again, your family influences people in ways they can't imagine."

Katy shot her a guilty look, and fear turned in her stomach. If Miranda ever broke her word on keeping her secrets, she was going to get in royal trouble.

As the pair approached the crowd, a large man walked over to them and said, "This is awesome, Katster!"

Katy groaned inwardly as she recognized one of her former classmates. Ted had been a star in high school, but his glory days had passed. "Hi, Ted. How are you?" Katy forced a smile.

Ted gestured with his beer and swayed as if riding in a boat. "I'm great. The food is fantastic. I love how you guys have the best of both worlds—crawfish and barbecue. Watch out for the corn though, my lips are steaming!"

"We'll be sure and do that." Miranda smiled and pushed

Katy toward the crowd.

Once they were out of earshot, Miranda said, "Please tell me there are better men somewhere in this town."

"There's your boyfriend!" Katy said and gestured to a scruffy, middle-aged man who couldn't hold his alcohol and was upchucking into a trash can.

"You suck!" Miranda laughed and punched Katy's shoulder. She shook her head and whispered "Ew!" as the man heaved once more.

Miranda's smiled faded as she spotted someone behind Katy. "Trent's here." She wrapped her hair into her fist and said, "I don't know Katy, I really don't want to talk to him."

"I know; we won't." She pulled Miranda toward the food line. "Let's go eat."

Katy filled a plastic tray with boiled crawfish, corn and potatoes. The aroma lifted her mood, reminding her of pleasant memories from summers passed.

Katy felt a tap on her shoulder, "Hey, Hunter wants you." Her youngest cousin Sarah stood staring up at her with an annoyed look on her face. Katy returned the look and frowned at the newest colors in her hair. Sarah shifted her weight, "Well?"

"I'm hungry, I'll find him after I finish eating," Katy said. "Where is he anyway?"

Sarah rolled her eyes, "Do you need to borrow my GPS? At the front table with the rest of the family, hello."

As Sarah walked away, Miranda snorted and said, "What a big attitude for someone so small. It's amazing she can still hold her head up with all that eyeliner she's wearing."

"She's been like that since she hit puberty. At least that's her mother's theory." Katy rolled her eyes and went back to creating her special dipping concoction of vinegar with chili powder and cayenne. She felt pleased that the ingredients had been made available; that was her Uncle Ben's doing for certain.

"What's your theory?" Miranda asked as she bit into a hot potato while balancing her tray in one hand.

"She's a typical Raven, living the good life and not worrying about anyone else's needs."

"That doesn't describe all the Ravens I know," Miranda smiled and started walking toward her family's table.

Katy chose their seats at the far end of the bench, next to the elder members of the family. It was the easiest way to avoid Trent and Hunter. She had not told her brother about the incident with Trent and knew deep down that he might not do anything to defend her. That would hurt even more than Trent's attack.

A warm wind gusted across the table, scattering napkins in the air. The band transitioned to a slower tempo, and some of her aunts and uncles left the table to dance the Two-Step. The family had spared no expense on this fundraiser, and the band was no exception. The group had traveled from the Atchafalaya area in the southern part of the state. Nearly all their songs were in Cajun French, which no one in Shreveport could understand, but Katy preferred it that way. It reminded her of Louisiana's thick cultural heritage.

Katy watched Miranda try to conspicuously pull bits of corn from between her teeth. "That's why I cut my kernels off with a knife," Katy laughed.

Miranda grabbed a large crawfish and animated it with

a pitiful South Louisiana accent, "An' you look silly doin' that, cher."

"I can't bring you anywhere," Katy said and snatched the crawfish from her. Katy looked around the crowd and smiled when she saw the diversity of people.

Her Aunt Beatrice approached the table and sat across from Katy. "I cannot believe how hot it is out here; these had better be tasty." She smiled and daintily draped a napkin across the neck of her pink business suit.

"Maybe if you would've gone home and changed after your meeting, Aunt Bea," Miranda smiled.

"My sundress wearing days are long past, Miss Smarty Pants, and you know it," Aunt Beatrice said as she ripped a crawfish in half with her jewelry clad hands. "Katy, would you be a dear and get me a glass of Chardonnay?"

Katy poured herself and her aunt a glass of wine and was heading back to the table when Hunter stepped in front of her. "I sent Sarah to get you."

"She did; I was going to eat first," Katy said and took several sips of her wine.

"I wanted to thank you for taking such good care of Dad. I'm sorry I haven't helped...things have been hectic with the Board." Hunter looked down at her with tired eyes.

"It's not so easy to fill his shoes, huh?" Katy watched an indiscernible emotion cross his face. His white polo hung loosely on his body, and his cheekbones protruded more than usual.

He leaned toward her, "Would it be such an inconvenience to dance with your twin brother?"

Katy drank several gulps of her wine. After a second,

she said, "Sure, let me take this to Aunt Bea."

When the band started a new song, Hunter pulled her onto the dance floor. The wine had relaxed her, and worries were receding. She found herself smiling at Hunter as he whirled her around the small platform. She had not danced this way in years; it felt familiar and good.

"You and I should spend more time together, you know." Hunter said. "We are the upcoming strength of the family."

Katy sighed and said, "If you feel that way, why don't you spend more time with me and less with the Shades? It would certainly be healthier for you."

Hunter squeezed her hand a little too hard. "Must you be so close- minded? Thomas has been a good friend to me. I think our partnership will move us forward, get us out of stagnation."

Katy stopped dancing and stared at him. "I can't believe you!" She lowered her voice as people stared, "Why? Why do you trust him? You know that he will turn his back on you. It's only a matter of time."

"You don't know that. I'm beginning to think the stories the Illumin told us when we were little weren't for our protection, but their own." Hunter grabbed her waist and pushed her into dancing again. "Besides, why is it okay for you to have a change of heart, but not me?"

"What do you mean?" she asked.

"You used to loathe the Illumin. Now you seem to be warming up to that detective. It disturbs me a little, actually."

"I'll be fine. You know as well as I do the Illumin aren't the dangerous ones. Hunter, you've changed, you don't look good. And Trent…." She broke off, conflicted about sharing the story.

"What about Trent?" he asked.

Katy met her brother's eyes and was shocked to see real concern. His face reflected the brother she had missed over the last year and she found herself burying her face in his chest, relating the terrible ordeal. "And that's why…" she stammered, "I know being around the Shades is bad for you. Trent's basically losing his mind."

He wrapped his arms around her and squeezed. "I will deal with Trent," he said through clenched teeth. He walked off the dance floor and moved them away from the crowd.

"Katy, I don't think you and I will agree on the supernaturals anytime soon," Hunter whispered as he gently swept her long hair away from her tear-soaked face. "I just need you to know that I work for the good of this family. I may do things you don't understand or agree with, but I promise you, this family is my main concern."

Katy stared up at him, her mind blank for words. After a few moments of silence, she said, "I think I want to go home. Miranda and I are going to sit on the porch swing and eat strawberry pie."

"Of course," he said. Katy felt her face redden in response to his tone. The Hunter she preferred had hidden away again, and the stern brother, the one who was frustrated by her lack of strength, lack of involvement in the family, was gazing at her.

Katy walked back to the table and sat next to Miranda. "Are you okay?" she whispered.

"Yes, it's time to go. We've made our contribution; let's go eat some more at my house." Katy forced a laugh.

"We've got to go to the bathroom first and wash your face. You are going to get a "What's the matter?" from a dozen people before we get out of the park."

Miranda waited outside, occupying one of Katy's relatives so she could wash her face unnoticed. Two women exited the bathroom, leaving her alone. She stared into the heat-warped mirror and fresh grief waved inside her chest as she recognized her brother's eyes in her own. A shuffling noise outside startled her, and she looked in the direction of an open window, placed high in the corner of the bathroom.

"What the hell happened between you and my sister?"

"I don't know, man; I didn't mean to hurt her."

Katy's mouth dropped open. She couldn't believe Hunter was confronting Trent in public. She could tell they were behind the small concrete building, hidden from the bulk of the crowd, but it wasn't like Hunter to risk a scene.

"Is that what really happened to your face the other day?" Hunter demanded.

Trent flew through the details of that night. "Look man, it's what I've been trying to tell you. I can't be spending so much time in the cabin. That amulet is affecting me." Trent's voice was hoarse with fear. "I don't know what came over me. When I heard her call the Illumin detective by his first name, my blood boiled. It makes me fume just thinking about it."

Katy's hands began to shake; her brother had the amulet in his possession.

"You see this?" Hunter said.

"Come on, man. I said I was sorry." Trent whimpered.

"If you so much as frown at my sister again, this barrel

will be the last thing you see. And another thing, I've waited for years for a deal like this. If you want to be rid of the amulet, then straighten up! If Thomas gets suspicious, he will kill us both."

Katy removed her sandals and ran to Miranda. Relieved that Miranda was alone and occupied with her phone, Katy whispered and grabbed her arm, "Don't say a word, let's go now."

Katy squeezed her cell phone, trying to decide who to call and to ignore the hot tears streaming down her face. Miranda had cut her a piece of pie and, placing it in front of her, said, "Desserts always make me feel better."

Katy looked up and smiled at her. She forced herself to take a bite and nodded, "This is good. Thanks." Katy really needed a minute alone to think. "Hey, would you mind walking Oscar for me? Just a few blocks, that's all he needs."

"Sure. I'd love to hang with my little stretched pal," Miranda laughed and dangled the leash.

Katy watched them walk out the door then stared at her pie. Her brother had the amulet. When they were children, she and Hunter had discovered a strange symbol of a skull with large eye-balls on one of their ancestor's gravestones. Both of them had worked to convince Aunt Tebe to explain its meaning. She said it was the symbol of death for the Aztec people. Later, their father had tried to debunk the story and say that it was an ancient tale and no longer relevant to her family. Katy had believed him, until the last day she saw her mother.

Katy had repeated that day in her memory many times since her mother's disappearance. The sound of her mother's voice was gone to her, but she could remember the exact events and conversation from that morning. Katy was nine years old and had taken a comb from one of the Illumin's pockets. It was unusual for her to steal, but the comb was unlike anything she had for her hair. It was a translucent, deep blue with a texture similar to stone and had a clear jewel encrusted on the handle. The comb contained a single strand of the Illumin's golden hair. Katy had wound it around her fingers, feeling the power emanate around her hands.

Katy had placed the hair in her jewelry box and noticed that her entire body tingled even after she walked away. Thinking of pleasing her father with something the family could sell, she had created her first weapon. She felt the urge to mold something with her hands while they tingled. Picking up the comb, she found that it gave shape to her every whim. Slowly, she had created a sharp edge and, with a twisting motion, created a base. She held the knife to the sunlight pouring through her window and through it saw her mother peering at her, mouth hanging open.

Her mother had watched her, unmoving, as she explained her newfound talent. "I think it's time you and I have a grown up discussion," she said as she closed the bedroom door. Her mother leaned in and said, "I have been watching you. So have the Illumin. You seem to have inherited the Touch, the same as your great, great grandfather." Placing her hands on Katy's shoulders, her mother explained, "He was the family's first weapon maker. He is also the one who made it possible for the Shades and Illumin to exist in this city without being seen." She then handed her a leather-bound journal and told her to read it, then lock it in her safe and tell no one of its existence. That day had remained Katy's blackest day, until now.

Katy opened her purse and removed a business card. She stared at the name and felt her stomach turn. In order to stop her brother's madness, she would have to engage in some of her own.

She could not tell who was actually more stunned that she had contacted him—her or Detective D'Nas. The Illumin's smooth voice instantly calmed her, and she wondered why she had been so fearful. Immediately after hanging up, the calm induced by his power faded and distress crept its way back into her chest. She shook her head and resolved that she had had no other choice. It was either this or risk her family's entire existence, and possibly the safety of the city.

An hour later, Katy watched D'Nas walk from his car to her porch. His dimly glowing eyes watched her as he stepped onto the porch. Oscar stood up on her lap and wagged his tail, creating loud thumps against the suspended swing. She could not hold back a smile; like people, Oscar could not resist the positive presence.

The atmosphere on the porch changed so drastically

that Katy had to grip the journal and think of her mother to return her emotions to their sour state. She was glad that Miranda had agreed to go home, despite her desire to look at the detective again with her fresh knowledge.

"Thanks for coming." She forced a smile, "Please, let's go inside."

The scent of her vanilla incense calmed her as they walked through the house to the kitchen. Tears sprang to her eyes when she passed family photos from her childhood. In one of her favorites, Hunter was pushing her on a tire swing. The picture captured her in mid-air, laughing toward the sky. She could have never suspected that her most trusted companion would lead her down such a lonely road.

"Would you like some coffee, a drink?" Katy placed her hands on the counter to hide their shaking.

"No, thanks." D'Nas seated himself on a bar stool and peered at her. "On the phone, you stated this matter was urgent."

A wave of guilt flashed over Katy; it felt like she was about to betray herself. "My brother has captured a man wearing an amulet that was given to my great grandfather many years ago. Holding up the aging book she said, "My mother gave this to me the day she disappeared. According to this journal, my great grandfather was able to see your kind as well as the Shades. Once the amulet was in his possession, dormant gifts were awakened inside of him and these gifts have since passed down through the generations."

"What does this amulet do?"

"I'm not sure. It seemed to give him extraordinary abilities. He created the water potion that we continue to use today and made the first weapons sold to your kind."

"May I see the journal?" Seeing her back away, he stated, "I will not take it from you." He smiled down at her, and his blue eyes took on an amused glow, "You should probably start trusting me now, don't you think?" This Illumin was such a dichotomy. His neck tattoo and ears lined with hoops and studs were dissonant against his gentle nature.

Katy relented and handed him the manual, "It was given to him by your kind, the Illumin."

D'Nas began thumbing through the manual, and it opened to the place she had marked with a dried rose. He began reading aloud, "I have begun to make friends with the fair creatures, the ones who call themselves Illumin. They have entrusted me with a valuable but volatile amulet and I fear that I may regret accepting this responsibility."

"I am working hard to avoid the dangerous ones and have discovered the ability to create weapons that I believe will be most effective deterrents of these evil creations. At night I cannot sleep and now have an array of weaponry. I cannot tell if the power of these weapons is coming from my physical contact with the Illumin, from the amulet, or both. I just know I cannot wait to be rid of it. The aching memory of my old life taunts me each morning. May I one day return to it."

"It later explains that he was told by the Illumin to pass the amulet on to the heir of his choice. He was to instruct the heir only to touch the amulet once and never to put it on. The journal was not to leave the wearer's hands, but, somewhere along the way, the amulet left our family. The journal remained behind. No one in our family knew of its presence until now."

D'Nas looked up from the journal, "It has been found then?"

Katy avoided his stare by lifting Oscar into her arms and burying her face in his neck of red fur. "My brother has found it and is keeping it at our family's cabin by the lake. Hunter…plans to collaborate with the Shades." Her voice cracked. "I cannot let him do this, but I will need help."

"Of course. You have my help and that of any Illumin." He set the journal down and walked toward her and pet Oscar on the head. "How do you know this?"

"I overheard him talking to my cousin Trent tonight at the Wheelbarrow Creek fundraiser." Katy put the dog down and walked across the kitchen to place distance between herself and the Illumin, then relayed her evening as quickly as possible.

"Thomas is known to us. He is a minion of Astrous, one of the two most powerful Shades. Astrous and a Shade called Zyne battle each other over this territory." D'Nas leaned down and scooped Oscar up with one hand. "Astrous is delusional though; Zyne and his forces are much stronger. Your brother's friend Thomas, did you know that he is a weapon maker?"

"Yes." Katy shuddered with the realization that the Illumin would now be aware of her brother's intentions to expand his business. They had become targets of the Raven weapons themselves.

"The other night, in your coffee shop, you asked me not to tell you about things happening in the supernatural spectrum. I think, despite your discomfort, you need to be more aware." He walked over to her and, taking her by the arm, placed her in a seat at her dining room table. Warmth spread upward from her arm to her neck and face. She felt grateful for his presence and, for the first time since her mother's disappearance, wondered if she had been wrong about them.

When she did not protest, he continued, "About a week ago, in Wheelbarrow Creek, there was an uprising of what you would call…zombies. Your brother was in charge of handling it, which he did with great precision. The flood was not an accident."

"Please tell me you are joking," Katy said and shook her head. "I don't know what I believe less, that zombies actually walked or that my brother is that powerful."

"It's true. This just confirms for me that he found the source of this event. The Aztec amulet must have started the whole thing," D'Nas said. "I should have known."

"Well, either way, that amulet belongs in my family. It belongs to no one else—not a Shade or an Illumin. I don't want my brother harmed, but I cannot ignore this danger. Who knows what could happen."

"It's not going to be easy. I have worried that buying weapons from your brother was dangerous. How do we know that he can't somehow nullify their powers?"

"No, he can't do that. I am certain. However, the Shades will side with him, and it is likely he has weapons prepared for them." D'Nas walked to a window and put his back to her.

She watched him as he stared into her backyard, his retracted wings moving slightly as he breathed. Coming to a decision, she told him, "You have less to worry about than you think." She rose from the table and motioned for him to follow her. "Lucky for us, my brother has considered me incapable of the Touch for years."

She led D'Nas into a guest bedroom and, pushing aside a small bureau, opened a hidden door. They walked down a short corridor, and she opened a pocket door on the side. Katy smiled in satisfaction as he emitted a low whistle behind her. Weapons lined the small, secret space. Silver light blanketed them as the power in the weapons responded to D'Nas's presence. In the center a small blue knife hung facing downward.

Hunter stood on the cabin's porch, watching the sun come up. He sipped his iced coffee and tried to shake off his fears. His career-or lack of one-would be determined by this morning's meeting with Thomas.

He thought about his fight with his cousin at the fundraiser and gritted his teeth as he recalled the incident. Trent had said the amulet made him feel sick, and he thought back to how Trent's behavior had changed over the last few days. More than once he had found him in the cabin's bathroom sitting on the floor in a stupor. He had put it out of his mind; there was so much riding on this deal.

Hunter tried to replace his negative emotions with

calmness when he heard Thomas's car start up the gravel drive. He took a sip of his coffee then waved to the Shade as he parked and walked to the porch.

The two shook hands, then Hunter smiled at Thomas and said, "I have something for you. You are the only one I know who can truly appreciate this."

When they entered the room, Matt lay sedated and bound to the bed's frame. He was shirtless, and the amulet remained embedded deep within his chest, only the top being visible. His lungs whined as he struggled to breathe. Despite being provided with ample food and water, his skin was sallow, and his ribs protruded so that the skin sunk between them.

Thomas leaned over the dying man, "Hunter, is that the remaining Aztec amulet? The one that contains our last Original?

"The very one." Hunter watched the Shade, trying to discern his reaction. Despite the need to control his emotions, Hunter felt himself unable to contain his bitter feelings. "I have looked for this amulet my entire life. My family tried to convince me that it was only an Aztec myth, but they shouldn't have tried so hard. They gave themselves away."

"The Amulet is more powerful than you understand, Hunter. This boy is going through a transformation. I don't think you want to be present once it is complete."

"From what I've learned, we can harness its strength for our own."

"What you learned is false. All you have harnessed here is death. The Original Shades were gods once, gods from stones set free in willing souls. As the years pass, we find fewer and fewer of the Stone-Born. Thomas shook his head and placed his hand on Hunter's shoulder. "The longer their imprisonment, the stronger they become. This human is becoming one of our Originals."

Hunter stared at Thomas, then began pacing across the small room, running his fingers through his hair, "What I learned is this: only one member of my family can wield it at a time. For each possessor, a different power manifests. With this man, Matt, the amulet brings to life his dreams. That's why we keep him heavily sedated; we don't want another zombie problem."

"I'm failing to see how he can be of use then." Thomas crossed his arms and faced Hunter.

"This is where you come in. When I was a boy, I used to eavesdrop on my father's business meetings. One day, I overheard an Illumin say that although you cannot bring about memories like they can, your kind can manipulate our dreams while we sleep. I'm hoping fervently that this is true."

"Indeed," Thomas's eyes brightened as a slow smile crept onto his face. "I can keep his transformation in check and manipulate what he dreams. What is the plan after he dies?"

Hunter crossed his arms as he felt the Shade's emotions shift. Hunter could see movement under his shirt as the bony wings flexed. "I don't know what power it will give me, but I'm betting it will capitalize on my existing strengths." Hunter smiled, "I hope that my skills in weapon creation will be magnified, leaving me in high demand not only to the Shades in this city, but also to those living throughout the world."

Thomas raised an eyebrow and asked, "Compensating for something?"

Hunter rolled his eyes, "I plan to establish myself in this field no matter the costs, but the amulet would help me get there much faster."

"Why should I help you become more powerful?" Thomas asked.

Hunter winced as a sudden queasiness gripped him, "If you help me wield this amulet, I promise only to use its power to help your kind and my family."

The door opened and slammed against the wall. Astrous stood in the doorway with his pets growling by his side. Hunter opened his mouth to speak but couldn't. His body flew across the room and struck the wall. When he hit the floor, he rolled onto his stomach and gasped to regain his breath. His eyes were blurred from the impact, and he looked at the floor to try to regain focus. An immense, black paw became clear directly under his nose. He could feel the beast's hot breath on his neck.

"Hunter, it's so unlike you to greet guests indisposed." Astrous stood behind his large beast, a grave expression on his face.

"Astrous, I didn't know Thomas was bringing a friend." Hunter struggled to get up but felt glued to the floor by his own weight.

"Neither did he." Astrous pointed to the door, and the dog-beast gave Hunter a snort and moved to lie at the threshold. "I see the two of you boys have been busy." Astrous placed the end of his walking cane under Hunter's chin and lifted his face upward. He wore a suit of burnt orange, and his black hair hung loosely around his face. The irises of his eyes were blood red.

"Astrous, I fully planned to include you. Thomas just learned of this himself. I had to make certain this was indeed the last known Aztec amulet."

"That's convenient." Astrous walked over to Matt. "Why don't we pry this off and see if the legends are true?" In a seamless motion, Astrous lifted Hunter to his feet. Hunter's arm felt as if it was being burned by a hot iron.

Trembling, Hunter said, "I feel certain if we take it off of him, he will die. He can still be useful to us."

"To us," Astrous said, "What would be of interest to us?"

Feeling his anger rise, Hunter replied, "My plans are simple: the amulet will only respond to one person in my family at a time; a Shade can manipulate his dreams, which will get us all what we want."

Astrous stood so closely that Hunter could feel his breath brush his eyelashes, "What common goal could we have? Our enemy is your meal ticket." Thomas moved to stand over the pair, suspicions darkening his eyes.

"Our goal is one and the same." Hunter staggered under the pain in his ears. He could hear his own ragged breathing. "I desire business with you to accomplish two objectives: gain the power and financial backing to lead my family… and rid Shreveport of the Illumin."

"I don't trust it." Astrous backed Hunter into the wall. He could feel blood begin to pour out of his nose. "You know, I've had your sister followed. She's your twin, I believe."

"She is no threat—to either of us. Her fiercest desire is

to live away from…." he gestured toward Astrous, "scenes like this. She hates the supernaturals."

"She spends a lot of time with the Illumin's detective to have disdain for 'supernaturals,'" Astrous stated.

"No, you've got her wrong. She hates them…" Hunter began to gasp as his vision darkened. Astrous was beginning a slow kill. Astrous swiped off his human cloak, allowing his Shade form to manifest. The guant, gray face with red pits for eyes smiled down at him. "Katy would not help the Illumin." Hunter struggled to focus.

"And why not?" Astrous asked.

"For the same reason I plan to provide Shades with the means to exterminate them," Hunter said. He caught a glimpse of restraint roll across Astrous, and stated, "They are the reason my mother is gone. For all of our disagreements, Katy and I agree on this one belief."

Astrous and Thomas exchanged glances. Matt rasped on the table and began to convulse. "If we are going to use him, we can't stop playing around." Hunter's hopes begin to fade as Matt lived his last moments.

"How can I be assured, if this plan works and you possess the amulet, that you will not abuse its power and interfere with our affairs?"

"I will be busy using the one Illumin I plan on keeping alive to help me discover what happened to my mother. D'Nas will either lead me to answers or lose his wings feather by feather."

Hunter felt a fleeting gratification over the dread that appeared in the Shades' faces. They knew about the torture of wing mutilation.

"Very well, but if you fail us, your family will disappear one by one. First to vanish will be your sister." Astrous rapped his cane on the floor three quick times and removed his jacket. He smiled at Hunter and patted Thomas on the back, "So glad we can be friends again. Would've been such a shame to have wasted the two of you." The cabin's front door swung open, and a group of armed Shades entered the home.

Hours later, Hunter was shaking with frustration. "You must make up your mind, Astrous!" he said. The Shades had spent the day arguing over whether they trusted him enough to use the amulet. Matt's breathing was slow and ragged. Astrous bent over him with a wicked smile on his face. Hunter said, "You must give him the nightmare now."

Astrous leaned over Matt and placed a handkerchief over his face. "I am sorry, Hunter, but I believe he is beyond that use. His brain waves are fading; he will not support a dream." He looked at Matt with resignation, "I know you believe it, but I do not. Drawing a dream of the Illumin's death into his nightmares will, at best, have no result. At worst, we risk a backfire. We know how you turn weapons against us. I am not willing to risk wiping out my kind."

Hunter's eyes burned with anger. He tried to soothe himself, knowing that the amulet was still useful.

Clipped Wings

Astrous stood over Matt and laughed, throwing his head back. The walls seem to quake with the sound, "Hunter, you Ravens are more powerful than I had ever dreamed. Imagine, Thomas, they are able to wield the power of an Original."

The door slammed and a small Shade pushed her way through her counterparts. Hunter was stunned by her beauty. Her short blond hair curved around pixie-like features. With eyes glowing red, her hands were wrapped around one of his earlier weapons, a set of keys that transformed into an effective wing-ripper. She shouted to Astrous, "They are coming! They will be here in minutes!" Glancing at Hunter, she continued, "His sister. She comes with the detective and a legion of them. We've been set up!" She glared at Hunter.

Hunter shook his head. "Well, Katy may be with him, but she isn't leading an 'attack' on anyone. She hates the Illumin!"

Astrous flattened Hunter with his cane. "You told me your sister was of no threat."

Hunter knew as soon as he hit the floor that his elbow was damaged. Struggling to slide away from Astrous's cane, he reached with his good arm for something to help pull himself up. His hands wrapped around something furry. Frigid dread bathed his body. He looked up at Ginger, seeing her sharp teeth bearing down on him. In this proximity, he could see silver scales like those on a fish beneath her fur.

"Please, Astrous, you must believe me. I want to take the Illumin down, maybe even more than you."

"How did they find us?" Thomas's black eyes bore down on Hunter. Betrayal shadowed his face.

"I honestly don't know. I've told her nothing of this.

284

Nothing!" Hunter rolled his eyes. "You know that I'm telling the truth; I know you can sense it."

"We shall see." Astrous raised a hand to quiet the chaos of the Shades, then removed a small revolver hidden behind his suit coat. He smiled at Hunter as he held up the translucent red bullets that Cooper had delivered to Astrous the previous day.

Despite being dressed in a tight, straight skirt, Emily leapt onto the kitchen table. Her eyes had taken on the spotted fashion that Hunter had seen in Astrous's house upon their first meeting. "D'Nas is mine! I will kill him slowly."

"Emily, come down from the table." Astrous smiled up at her and handed her the revolver. "You are my best shooter; get on the roof and kill the first Illumin you see; the result will tell us of Hunter's loyalty."

"Please, don't kill D'Nas! I need him…kill the rest of the bastards, I don't care." Hunter managed to get to his feet.

Emily hopped off the table and took the gun from Astrous. She took two steps toward Hunter, then spat in his face. "I'll kill the first one I see, Astrous," she said as she marched out the door.

"What about your sister?" Thomas put his hand on Hunter's shoulder and surprised him by the look of pity on his face.

"Let me deal with her," Hunter managed through dry heaves. There were at least ten angry Shades in the cabin, and their anger was taking a toll on him. His nose and ears had begun to bleed, creating a small pool of blood on the floor. Through the agony, he was filled with anger and fear for his sister. How could she have known they were here?

Why was she helping the Illumin?

"Thomas, please, don't let them kill her," Hunter pleaded as he watched the Shade open weapon containers brought in from his car. The table and floor in the kitchen were overflowing with weapons of all sorts. Thomas extracted something that resembled a bow from a box. Under the false bottom there were thin projectiles, clearly built for speed and quick death. Likely dipped in poison, the ends of the rods did not hold a triangular blade like an arrow but were razor sharp points.

"Do you know how to use a weapon like this?" Thomas offered.

Hunter answered, "I can't wield the weapons I make for your kind, Thomas."

"That's why the amulet was so important to you. You can use that yourself." Thomas strapped a holster across his chest and slid a broadsword across his back.

Thomas nodded and looked up, seeing that the Shades were ready for battle. They were all staring at him, wondering at his loyalty. A few of them seemed to be contemplating disposing of him. Thomas stepped in front of him, "Leave him be. Like Astrous said, the success of his weapons will decide his fate."

An otherworldly sound pierced the air, somewhere between a loud growl and a screech. Emily screamed, "Q'uikaaa!!" Thumping resounded off the roof as Illumin dropped from the sky. A shot fired out, and an Illumin toppled from the roof and dropped past the kitchen window. Hunter and Thomas scrambled to see the victim.

The Illumin writhed on the ground as Hunter's poisonous

bullet took effect. The beautiful being transformed in front of their eyes. Pale, youthful skin withered and blackened as the mortality drained from the creature. The Illumin locked eyes with Hunter until they popped out of his head, one by one. Then, he lay motionless on the ground.

"Well done." Thomas patted his back. Hunter shuddered inwardly, feeling both pride and disgust. Thomas grabbed his weapon, and with one last glance at Hunter, left him alone in the cabin with Matt.

Hunter stumbled to Matt's bedside, nursing his arm. He watched as Matt's breaths came further and further apart. Hunter held his hand over the amulet, agonizing over the choice he must make.

Hunter could hear shuffling sounds on the roof as the beings battled. A screech pierced the air, startling Hunter into decision. As he reached for the amulet, a cold blade was flattened against his chin. Its wielder said in a breathless voice, "Oh, I think he's beyond even our aid."

Hunter leaned into the creature so that he could turn and see his face. "Is my sister with you?" he asked.

"She's outside. Katy's been quite helpful to us." D'Nas threw Hunter to the floor, causing him to scream out when the force struck his injured elbow.

Regaining his composure, Hunter glared up at the detective, "Don't you dare call her Katy; you are not worthy even to look at her."

D'Nas ignored him and leaned over Matt, placing his hand on his forehead. Matt opened his eyes for the first time in days and, seeing D'Nas, begged, "Please, end this."

D'Nas wrapped his hands around the amulet, shouting

in his language as he worked it free from Matt's chest. Hunter smelled singed flesh, and D'Nas's retracted wings quaked as the amulet's power resisted him. There was a loud crunch, and Matt emitted a gurgled scream as blood coursed out of his mouth.

D'Nas fell to the floor, the amulet glowing red in his hand. He dropped the amulet on the floor and looked at his singed flesh. The amulet dimmed within seconds, and D'Nas placed it in a blue velvet bag, tying its strings around his belt.

The silence was so thick in the room it was as if time had stopped. Matt lay unmoving on the bed, staring blankly into the ceiling. D'Nas and Hunter sat on the floor staring at one another.

They both started as the window's outer protective bars were wrenched away. A gloved fist shattered the glass, and a Shade invaded the room. The white curtains became stained with blue Illumin blood that dripped from his black wings and double bladed sword. Hunter backed away in fear when he observed that Astrous was uninjured. Only a truly powerful Shade could slaughter that many Illumin and remain unscathed.

Astrous's face contorted and his fangs grew as he twirled his sword in preparation to kill D'Nas. His muscles jerked under pale white skin, and he laughed a sound so grotesque that Hunter writhed on the ground in anguish.

D'Nas's skin turned bright blue, warming the room and providing comfort to Hunter. D'Nas jumped to his feet, drawing a small blue dagger from his waist.

Astrous spoke in a gravelly voice, "You insult me. Put that toy away and kneel before me so that I can lop your head off."

D'Nas spoke in the language of the Illumin and laughed. Despite the pain, Hunter remained still.

Astrous rushed at D'Nas with his blade held high. D'Nas ducked below him and, in a blur of movement, jumped to the ceiling and hung upside down. "Is that all you have, Shade?" he asked and opened his wings to their full capacity. As his wings opened, Hunter heard what sounded like the tinkling of a hundred bells.

Astrous growled and rushed at him, but D'Nas wrapped his wings tightly around him, and retracted them, spraying the Shade's black blood into the room. Hunter ignored the splatter on his face as he watched D'Nas's wings rake away Astrous's skin with tiny razors. He wondered who had given him such a weapon and inwardly cursed himself for not having thought of that first.

The two beings slammed into each other once more. Astrous forced D'Nas into the corner of the room and dodged a slash to his face from the blue dagger. D'Nas tried to slash him again, but Astrous knocked the dagger from his hands.

Bringing his sword around, Astrous shouted, "Say goodbye to your head, old foe," and slashed sideways with his weapon. In what seemed like a futile attempt at defense, D'Nas held up an arm covered with a leather shield. The sword struck the shield and flew across the room. Astrous screamed and grabbed his hand--steam rose from bubbling flesh. He bounded after his sword, but the weapon wrenched itself from his hands and flew away from him again.

D'Nas glanced down at Hunter for a brief second then took the opportunity to make his escape. Astrous saw him leave, but did nothing to stop him, just stared down at his sword. A Shade stuck his head in the window, "Shall I call Him, my Lord? We are losing."

Hunter had to find Katy, get her to safety somehow. He rushed onto the porch and held onto the porch railing, its familiarity returning his focus. Winged creatures flew between trees and fought in the air. Most had rid themselves of the uniforms of the natural world and were in full battle gear. The Shades' language defiled the air and caused the trees to wave dangerously in different directions.

He spotted a female form dressed in tight jeans and tank top. She had a long black ponytail and wingless back. In his relief, he ran toward the woman then stopped short, realizing she had a sword strapped to her back. He began to retreat when she turned to him, blue eyes blazing.

"You," she said. She made for him, tears flowing down her face. "How could you?" She drew her sword; a beautiful melody sang from it. Hunter stumbled backward.

"Katy, that is an Illumin weapon. How….?"

"This is not an Illumin sword; it's mine," Katy said. Hunter's mind raced to understand how his docile sister had created a supernatural weapon.

Katy forced him to the ground with the point of her sword. It radiated coldness, cutting through the August morning, reminding him of how it felt to put his face in front of an air conditioning vent.

"I've never wanted this fight. I hate the life of a Raven, but I will not let you destroy our family," she said. Hunter started to rise, but she touched his throat with the tip. "You will not destroy the Illumin with your weapons."

"But you hate them! Don't you see? If we have the Shades on our side, we have leverage. We can find out what happened to Mama." She slapped him across the face, and he could feel his nose resume its bleeding.

"Your words mean nothing to me. You and Trent are nothing but Shades to me now. Maybe after spending some time away from them, when I can see color return to your face and you start eating again, then, we can talk about Mama."

Loud screams pierced the air, causing Hunter and Katy to look upward. Astrous was in the air with the remainder of the living Shades, shouting curses at Illumin on the ground below.

D'Nas aimed a Trapper at the hovering beasts and fired. Astrous and Thomas dodged in time, but the other two straps found their mark, wrapping the Shades' feet and dragging them to the ground.

In the confusion, Hunter kicked Katy in the back, sending her reeling. He stomped on her fist, trying to pry the sword from her. She screamed in pain and released the weapon. As he grabbed the hilt, he was stabbed in the stomach from behind. Falling to his knees, he looked back to see Cooper holding a bloody steak knife. He stared up at his cousin in confusion. "Cooper," he rasped, "Traitor."

"I'm sorry man, but I can't let you hurt Katy." He backed away from Hunter, wrapping his arms around Katy protectively, even as she raised her sword. "You said we were just going to make weapons for them. You never said anything about taking the Shades' side!" He furrowed his brow, anger rising, "Never once mentioned that you found the amulet. That belongs to the family!"

Hunter could feel blood in his mouth and knew he was going to die if one of the Shades or Illumin didn't rush to his aid. Behind Cooper, Hunter spotted Thomas in the air watching their group. He felt a spark of hope that he would not be left to die after all. Maybe he had not failed yet.

"Katy, we must go!" D'Nas retracted his wings; the soft blue glow surrounding his body began to fade. "In his desperation, Astrous has beckoned Zyne's army; even with your weapons we cannot match them." D'Nas grabbed her arm.

"What about Hunter?" she struggled as he pulled her away.

"He is on his own." He lifted her off the ground and raced with the remaining Illumin to the cars, Cooper trailing behind. He felt her resist and said, "Thomas will help him."

"The Amulet?" Katy struggled to hold onto her sword as he tossed her into an SUV. D'Nas looked grim and removed the ornament from a bag. It was surrounded by festering flesh. She stared at it as he handed it to her, feeling her stomach surge with nausea at the grotesqueness of it all.

Cooper got in the vehicle beside her, placed his head between his knees and sobbed. As they sped down the road, Katy reached around the back seat and touched D'Nas's arm.

She smiled through her tears as the soothing effect of his touch warmed her body and stilled the quaking. "Thank you, D'Nas," she said.

He only nodded as he turned onto the highway and increased speed. An Illumin, unknown to Katy, was in the passenger seat. He turned to her smiling, "Thank you, ma'am! I always expect that we will win, but we've never won like that before." He leaned his head back and laughed, punching D'Nas on the shoulder. Katy couldn't help but smile. The Illumin wore a cowboy hat over a long blond ponytail. He seemed relaxed, as if he had just come from seeing a movie. The only sign that belied he had been in a battle was the black patch of Shade blood beginning to dry on his t-shirt.

"Did they have the effect I wanted?" she asked. She saw Cooper turn his head toward her. He had stopped sobbing, but he had remained in the bent-over position, head in his lap.

"Yes!" the cowboy Illumin said. He held up one of Katy's daggers. "Would you believe it affected his ability to dodge? It was like your knife held him captive, like a magnet."

D'Nas chuckled, "You did well, Katy." He looked in the rearview mirror and met her gaze. She felt herself smile as his blue eyes met hers. One of his ears was bleeding from a torn piercing; otherwise, he looked unharmed. D'Nas continued, "If it hadn't been for the arm shield you gave me, I wouldn't be driving this car right now. Not only did it repel Astrous's sword, but he was unable to use it. It saved my life."

Katy shook her head in wonder. "I'm glad," was all she could say without giving her emotions away. Tears stung her eyes as she thought of her brother and wondered when she would see him again.

For so long she had wanted nothing to do with the supernaturals. She shook her head, thinking of the irony. She had hated them all for so long. Now, she had stepped into Hunter's place, in the center of things.

Cooper touched Katy's arm. "I need to give you something. But, please promise me, no matter how mad you get, don't let them kill me." He looked at the Illumin warily, and his hands began to shake.

"Cooper, you saved my butt back there. That was really stupid of me to turn my back on Hunter, him being injured or not." Katy shook her head.

She watched as Cooper took something out of his pocket. He held up a small bottle with a blue liquid in it. As he handed it to her, his chin quivered and fresh tears streamed down his face. "I have no excuse for going along with him the way I did. But, Katy I swear to you, I didn't mean for it to go this far." He sobbed a few times then said, "I really thought he had the family's interests in mind."

Katy turned the bottle in her hand. "Cooper, what is this?"

He choked back a sob then forced himself to meet her eyes. "The antidote to Hunter's Sleeping Beauty potion."

"What?" Katy slapped him hard in the face. "You and Hunter poisoned my father?!"

"I'm so sorry, Katy. He told me we would give him the antidote as soon as he fixed the deal with the Shades. He was sure if he had proof of success-and money-that your father would come around." Cooper held his hand to his face, tears running through his fingers.

"Oh, like Daddy would just forgive him for knocking him into a veritable coma for two weeks?" Katy felt the relief take over the anger as she realized she was about to get her father back.

"Well, Katy, we weren't planning to tell him that." Cooper could not hide the hint of amusement behind his eyes.

She rolled her eyes and, despite herself, laughed and enjoyed the release of tension from her body. If the Illumin had not been in the car she would have been feeling something entirely different. "I'm still mad at you," she said while glaring at Cooper. "You will be watched like a hawk and will no longer work as our security consultant. Even if I have to hire from outside the family, I will find a way."

Cooper nodded, "I know. I do still have my day job."

Katy bounced with anticipation as D'Nas pulled up to the black gate. Holding the bottle to Cooper, she said, "I'm going to ask D'Nas's friend here to hang out with you in the car. If anything bad happens to Daddy after I give him this, you will be in serious trouble." She placed her face within two inches of his, "Is there anything you need to say before I go?"

"No, Katy, I love Uncle Darrus. I promise, Hunter said this would wake him up. He'll just think he was asleep." Cooper said.

Katy stepped out of the SUV. Handing the amulet to D'Nas's Illumin friend for safekeeping, she followed D'Nas into the house. "Hey, what happened to the person whose skin is all over that thing?" Katy asked.

"He's gone." D'Nas shrugged.

"Oh, so my brother managed to actually kill a family member after all."

"No, I mean he's gone—he somehow got out of the cabin during the fight. I thought he was dead, so I ripped it off him, burning my hand in the process," he lifted his hand, the tips of his fingers burned. "I guess it's up to you now to decide what to do with it."

She stopped at her father's bedroom doorway and peered in. He lay unmoving on his side; her Uncle Benjamin was sitting on the side of the bed with his head in his hands. He looked up at Katy with a quizzical look, and she held up the bottle. She handed it to him as he approached. "Try this Uncle Ben; you'll just have to trust me." He nodded, and she could see a faint glimmer of hope touch his face.

Once her uncle returned to her father's bedside, Katy looked up at D'Nas. She had felt his eyes on her since they entered the house. "You know things will be different for you now. I have to ensure your protection until this issue with your brother is resolved."

Katy smiled, "I'm actually okay with that. I can't do this alone anymore." She reached out and held his hand. "Besides, what good is it being a weapon maker if I have no one to create them for?"

"You were right; combining Illumin and Shade powers was ingenious. I don't know how you did it successfully, but we will be able to protect this city so much more with you on our side."

"Can we keep that secret between us? I'd rather not be that much of a hot commodity. I'll make the weapons, but

I need you to make sure I have some amount of freedom."

He leaned over and whispered to her in his language. Her knees weakened and she heard herself actually giggle. He wrapped his arms around her and kissed her cheek. She leaned into his warm body and looked into his eyes. Unable to stop herself, she placed her hands on the sides of his face and rose on her tiptoes to kiss him.

"Well, now! This is not something I ever expected to see! I don't know what's more shocking: finding myself in bed when I was just sitting at my desk, or seeing Katy in the arms of an Illumin." Katy's father stood in the center of the room. His bare arms were outstretched as her uncle removed his IV tube.

Katy raced to him and hugged him so hard he nearly fell over. "I love you, Daddy!" He wrapped his arms around her and laughed. Katy laughed with him then sobbed, tears pouring down her cheeks. Outside the open window, she could see the pond with the paddle boat in the distance. For the first time, she realized she did not want to be anyone else. She was born a Raven, and it was time she started acting like one.

About the Authors

Jason Craft

Born and raised in northwest Louisiana, Jason did very little to escape the area outside of writing about fantastical worlds. He is a legitimate nerd who enjoys PC gaming, arguing about time paradoxes, and the indomitable table-top game, Warhammer 40K. One day he plans to have his entire Tau Empire army fully painted. He currently resides in Shreveport, Louisiana and is employed as a full-time computer programmer to support his writing and nerd habits. You can catch him on the interwebs by his super-awesome handle, VigRoco. Challenge him to a StarCraft II match, and he will gracefully lose to you.

Blog: http://VigRoco.com
Facebook: http://facebook.com/VigRoco
Twitter: http://twitter.com/VigRoco

B.L. White

Brian Lee White lives as a bachelor in the American heartlands of Shreveport Louisiana; he is seen there, teaching piano and playing in his local Baptist church. He loves book reading and writing, trail bike riding, movie watching, and video game playing. Long walks on the beach are out of the question.

Blog: http://DeepWellBridge.wordpress.com

Amanda White

Amanda has lived in various Louisiana cities and has grown to know and love the state's rich culture. She works in the field of Psychology and enjoys using her knowledge to enrich her characters. When not working or writing, she enjoys biking, running, reading, and spending time with her friends and family.

Facebook: http://facebook.com/amanda.white.54772

www.ingramcontent.com/pod-product-compliance
Lightning Source LLC
Chambersburg PA
CBHW021945170626
46808CB00001B/31